STARBOUND

Ace Books by Joe Haldeman

WORLDS APART

DEALING IN FUTURES

FOREVER PEACE

FOREVER FREE

THE COMING

GUARDIAN

CAMOUFLAGE

OLD TWENTIETH

A SEPARATE WAR AND OTHER STORIES

THE ACCIDENTAL TIME MACHINE

MARSBOUND

STARBOUND

Ace Books edited by Joe Haldeman

BODY ARMOR: 2000

NEBULA AWARDS STORIES SEVENTEEN

SPACE FIGHTERS

Ace Books by Joe Haldeman and Jack C. Haldeman II

THERE IS NO DARKNESS

STARBOUND

JOE HALDEMAN

ACE BOOKS, NEW YORK

THE BERKLEY PUBLISHING GROUP
Published by the Penguin Group
Penguin Group (USA) Inc.
375 Hudson Street, New York, New York 10014, USA
Penguin Group (Canada), 90 Eglinton Avenue East, Suite 700, Toronto, Ontario M4P 2Y3, Canada
(a division of Pearson Penguin Canada Inc.)
Penguin Books Ltd., 80 Strand, London WC2R 0RL, England
Penguin Group Ireland, 25 St. Stephen's Green, Dublin 2, Ireland (a division of Penguin Books Ltd.)
Penguin Group (Australia), 250 Camberwell Road, Camberwell, Victoria 3124, Australia
(a division of Pearson Australia Group Pty. Ltd.)
Penguin Books India Pvt. Ltd., 11 Community Centre, Panchsheel Park, New Delhi—110 017, India
Penguin Group (NZ), 67 Apollo Drive, Rosedale, North Shore 0632, New Zealand
(a division of Pearson New Zealand Ltd.)
Penguin Books (South Africa) (Pty.) Ltd., 24 Sturdee Avenue, Rosebank, Johannesburg 2196,
South Africa

Penguin Books Ltd., Registered Offices: 80 Strand, London WC2R 0RL, England

This is an original publication of The Berkley Publishing Group.

This is a work of fiction. Names, characters, places, and incidents either are the product of the author's imagination or are used fictitiously, and any resemblance to actual persons, living or dead, business establishments, events, or locales is entirely coincidental. The publisher does not have any control over and does not assume any responsibility for author or third-party websites or their content.

FIRST EDITION: January 2010

Library of Congress Cataloging-in-Publication Data

Haldeman, Joe W.
  Starbound / Joe Haldeman.
    p. cm.
  ISBN 978-0-441-01817-8
  1. Married people—Fiction.   2. Human-alien encounters—Fiction.   3. Interplanetary voyages—
Fiction.   I. Title.
  PS3558.A353S73 2010
  813'.54—dc22

                                                                        2009040932

PRINTED IN THE UNITED STATES OF AMERICA

10 9 8 7 6 5 4 3 2 1

For Gay, Judith, and Susan: Muses, Graces

STARBOUND

PART 1

THE SEED

I

NATIVITY SCENE

An hour after my children were born, we went up to the new lounge to have a drink.

You couldn't have done any of that on the Mars I first knew, eleven years ago. No drink, no lounge, no children—least of all, children born with the aid of a mother machine, imported from Earth. All of it courtesy of free energy, borrowed energy, whatever they wind up calling it. The mysterious stuff that makes the Martians' machines work.

(And is, incidentally, wrecking Earth's economies. Which had to be wrecked, anyhow, and rebuilt, to deal with the Others.)

But right now I had two gorgeous new babies, born on Christmas Day.

"You could call the girl Christina," Oz suggested helpfully, "and the boy Jesús." Oz is sort of my godfather, the first friend I made in Mars, and sometimes it's hard to tell when he's joking.

"I was thinking Judas and Jezebel myself," Paul said. Husband and father.

"Would you two shut up and let me bask in the glow of motherhood?" The glow of the setting sun, actually, in this new transparent dome, looking out over the chaos of construction to the familiar ochre desert that was more like home now than anyplace on Earth.

It wasn't much like conventional motherhood, since it didn't hurt, and I couldn't pick up or even touch the little ones yet. On their "birth" day, they were separated from the machine's umbilicals and began to ease into real life. As close to real life as they would be allowed to experience for a while.

Josie, Oz's love, broke the uncomfortable silence. "Try to be serious, Oswald." She gave Paul a look, too.

A bell dinged, and our drinks appeared on a sideboard. Paul brought them over, and I raised mine in toast. "Here's to what's-her-name and what's-his-name. We do have another week." Actually, there was no law or custom about it yet. These were the first, numbers one and two in a batch of six, the only twins.

Children born naturally in Mars hadn't done well. They all got the lung crap, Martian pulmonary cysts, and if they were born too weak, they died, which happened almost half the time. When it was linked to an immune system response in the womb, in the third trimester, they put a temporary moratorium on natural births and had the mother machine sent up from Earth.

Paul and I had won the gamete lottery, along with four other couples. For all of us, the sperm and ova came from frozen samples we'd left on Earth, away from the radiation bath of Mars.

I felt a curious and unpleasant lightness in my breasts, which were now officially just ornaments. None of the new children would be breast-fed. None of them would suffer birth trauma, either, at least in the sense of being rammed through a wet tunnel smaller than a baby's head. There might be some trauma in suddenly having to breathe for oneself, but so far none of them had cried. That was a little eerie.

They wouldn't have a mother; I wouldn't *be* a mother, in any traditional sense. Only genetically. They'd be raised by the colony, one big extended family, though most of the individual attention they got would be from Alphonzo Jefferson and Barbara Manchester, trained to run the "creche," about to more than double in population.

My wine was too warm and too strong, made with wine concentrate, alcohol, and water. "They look okay. But I can't help feeling cheated."

Josie snorted. "Don't. It's like passing a loaf of hard bread."

"Not so much the birth itself, as being pregnant. Is that weird?"

"Sounds weird to me," Paul said. "Sick all the time, carrying all that extra weight."

"I liked it," Josie said. "The sickness is just part of the routine. I never felt more alive." She was already 50 percent more alive than a normal person, a lean, large athlete. "But that was on Earth," she conceded.

"Oh, hell." I slid my drink over to Paul. "I have to take a walk."

Nobody said anything. I went down to the dressing room and stripped, put on a skinsuit, then clamped on the Mars suit piece by piece, my mind a blank as I went through the rote safety procedure. When I was tight, I started the air and clomped up to Air Lock One. I hesitated with my thumb on the button.

This was how it all began.

2

HISTORY LESSON

Carmen Dula never set out to become the first human ambassador to an alien race. Nor did she aspire to become one of the most hated people on Earth—or off Earth, technically—but which of us has control over our destiny?

Most of us do have more control. It was Carmen's impulsiveness that brought her both distinctions.

Her parents dragged her off to Mars when she was eighteen, along with her younger brother Card. The small outpost there, which some called a colony, had decided to invite a shipload of families.

A shitload of trouble, some people said. None of the kids were under ten, though, and most of the seventy-five people living there, in inflated bubbles under the Martian surface, enjoyed the infusion of new blood, of young blood.

On the way over from Earth, about halfway through the eight-month voyage, Carmen had a brief affair with the pilot, Paul Collins. It was brief because the powers-that-be on Mars found out about it immediately, and suggested that at thirty-two, Paul shouldn't be dallying with an impressionable teenaged girl. Carmen was insulted, feeling that at nineteen she was not a "girl" and was the only one in charge of her body.

The first day they were on Mars, before they even settled into their cramped quarters, Carmen found out that the "powers"-that-be were one single dour power, administrator Dargo Solingen. She obviously resented Carmen on various levels and proceeded to make the Earth girl her little project.

It came to a head when Dargo discovered Carmen swimming, skinny-dipping, after midnight in a new water tank. She was the oldest of the six naked swimmers, and so took the brunt of the punishment. Among other things, she was forbidden to visit the surface, which was their main recreation and escape, for two months.

She rankled under this, and rebelled in an obvious way: when everyone was asleep, she suited up and went outside alone, which broke the First Commandment of life on Mars, at the time: Never go outside without a buddy.

She'd planned to go straight out a few kilometers, and straight back, and slip back into her bunk before anyone knew she was gone. It was not to be.

She fell through a thin shell of crust, which had never happened before, plummeted a couple of dozen meters, and broke an ankle and a rib. She was doomed. Out of radio contact, running out of air, and about to freeze solid.

But she was rescued by a Martian.

3

GERM THEORY

Humans call me Fly-in-Amber, and I am the "Martian" best qualified to tell the story of how we made contact with humans.

I will put Martian in quotation marks only once. We know we are not from Mars, though we live here. Some of the humans who live here also call themselves Martians, which is confusing and ludicrous.

We had observed human robot probes landing on Mars, or orbiting it, for decades before they started to build their outpost, uncomfortably close to where we live, attracted by the same subterranean (or subarean) source of water as those who placed us here, the Others.

With more than a century to prepare for the inevitable meeting, we had time to plan various responses. Violence was discussed and discarded. We had no experience with it other than in observation of human activities on radio, television, and cube. You would kick our asses, if we had them, but we are four-legged and excrete mainly through hundreds of pores in our feet.

The only actual plan was to feign ignorance. Not admit (at first) that we understood many human languages. You would eventually find out we were listening to you, of course, but you would understand our need for caution.

We are not good at planning, since our lives used to be safe and predictable, but in any case we could not have planned on Carmen Dula. She walked over the top of a lava bubble that had been worn thin, and fell through.

She was obviously injured and in grave danger. Our choices were to contact the colony and tell them what had happened or rescue her ourselves. The former course had too many variables—explaining who we were and what we knew and all; she would probably run out of air long before they could find her. So our leader flew out to retrieve her.

(We have one absolute leader at a time; when he/she/it dies, another is born. More intelligent, larger, stronger, and faster than the rest of us, and usually long-lived. Unless humans interfere, it turns out.)

The leader, whom Carmen christened Red, took a floater out and picked up Carmen and her idiot robot companion, called a dog, and brought them back to us. Our medicine cured her broken bones and frostbite.

We are not sure why it worked on her, but we don't know how it works on us, either. It always has.

We agreed not to speak to her, for the time being. We only spoke our native languages, which the human vocal apparatus can't reproduce. Humans can't even hear the high-pitched part.

So Red took her back to the colony the next night, taking advantage of a sandstorm to remain hidden. Left her at the air-lock door, with no explanation.

It was very amusing to monitor what happened afterward—we do listen to all communications traffic between Earth and Mars. Nobody wanted to believe her fantastic story, since Martians do not and could not exist, but no one could explain how she had survived so long. They even found evidence of the broken bones we healed but assumed they were old injuries she had forgotten about, or was lying about.

We could have had years of entertainment, following their tortuous logic, but illness forced our hand.

All of us Martians go through a phase, roughly corresponding to the transition between infancy and childhood, when for a short period our bodies clean themselves out and start over. It isn't pleasant, but neither is it frightening, since it happens to everybody at the same time of life.

Somehow, Carmen "caught" it from us, which is medically impossible. Our biologies aren't remotely related; we don't even have DNA. Nevertheless, she did have the transition "sickness," and we brought her back to our home and treated her the way we would a Martian child, having her breathe an unpleasant mixture of smoldering herbs. She expelled everything, especially the two large cysts that had grown in her lungs. She was fine the next day, though, and went home—which was when the real trouble started.

She had apparently infected all the other youngsters in the colony—everyone under the age of twenty or so.

It was all sorted out eventually. Our leader Red and a healer Martian went over to the human colony and treated all the children the way they had Carmen, not pleasant but not dangerous. Unfortunately, no one could explain how the "disease" could have been transmitted from us to Carmen and from Carmen to the children. Human scientists were mystified, and, of course, we don't have scientists as such.

The children seemed to be all right. But people were afraid that something worse might happen, and so the humans on Earth put all of Mars under quarantine, where it remains to this day, although there have been no other incidents. People who come to Mars do so in the knowledge that they may never see Earth again.

There is still no shortage of volunteers, which makes me think that Earth must be a very unpleasant place.

4

NO ORDINARY HERO

I had to name the boy Red, after my friend who gave his life to save us all. Paul and I tried on various names for our daughter, and settled on Nadia, Russian for "hope." Which we need now. (They both had the middle name Mayfly, sort of a joke between me and the memory of Red.)

There were probably a good number of human boys and girls named after that particular Martian. You couldn't say the name *in* Martian, a series of clacks and creaks and whistles that means "Twenty-one Leader Leader Lifter Leader." He saved me from dying of exposure, or stupidity, and a few years later, he saved the world by putting himself on the other side of the Moon when he realized he'd become a planet-destroying time bomb. Not something that happens to ordinary heroes.

The Martians had told us about the "Others" early on—the other alien race that supposedly had brought the Martians to Mars, tens of thousands of years ago. At first we wondered whether they were myth, or metaphor, but the memory family (those who always wore yellow, like Fly-in-Amber) insisted that the Others were actual history, though from so far ago the memory was all but lost.

They were as real as dirt, as real as death.

The memory family didn't know that they had another function, besides using their eidetic memories to keep track of things. They also retained a coded message, generation after generation, that would be transmitted to humans when the time was right.

The decoded message seemed innocuous. By means of a checkerboard digital picture, a "Drake diagram," we learned that the Others were a silicon-nitrogen form of life; they evidently lived immersed in the liquid nitrogen seas of Triton, Neptune's largest moon.

Various mysteries began to come together after the Others revealed their existence, like the paradoxical combination of high technology and scientific ignorance in the Martian city. (They apparently lived only in one huge underground complex, about the size of a large city on Earth, but with more than half of it covered with creepy fungoid agriculture.) The Others had built the city and populated it with thousands of bioengineered Martians, evidently for the purpose of keeping an eye on Earth, an eye on humanity.

The city had no obvious power source, but they had apparently limitless power from somewhere. Human scientists eventually figured it out, which gave us unlimited power as well, evidently bled off from some "adjacent" universe. I wonder what we'll do if they show up with a bill.

The Other that lived on Triton—many other Others were light-years away—gave us ample demonstration of what unlimited power can do.

It nearly destroyed the satellite Triton in one tremendous explosion. An instant before the explosion, it escaped, or something did, in a spaceship that screamed away at more than twenty gravities' acceleration. Its apparent destination was a small star called Wolf 25, about twenty-four light-years away.

Before the Other made its spectacular exit, it prepared an equally spectacular exit for the human race. The head Martian, my friend Red, was unknowingly a direct conduit to the otherworldly source of energy that powered the Martian civilization, and when he died, that connection would open up, with world-destroying intensity.

The world it destroyed would not be Mars. The Other had contrived to send Red to Earth before the time bomb was triggered.

Red knew he didn't have long. He asked my husband Paul, who is a pilot, to take him to the other side of the Moon to die. There was no way of knowing exactly how large the explosion was going to be, but presumably the Moon had enough mass to block it.

It did. Red's funeral pyre was bright enough to be seen light-years away, but only a few gamma rays leaked through.

Would the Others see the flare and assume that their little problem—the existence of the human race—had been solved?

That was not likely. We had to go to them.

5

LOGICS

Magic trumps science for most people, and wishful thinking drives a lot of decision-making. So a large and vocal fraction of the human race thought the best way to deal with the Others would be to lie low.

If we didn't try to contact them and didn't broadcast any signals into space—who needs to, since everybody has cable?—then the Others would think that their plan had worked, and so would leave us alone.

Of course there's no cable between Earth and Mars, but the idea of abandoning Mars actually sounded pretty attractive to some, since without Mars none of this would have happened.

Then there was also the problem that we didn't think to turn off all the transmitters right after the big explosion on the other side of the Moon, so it would be like closing the barn door long after the horse had trotted off to Wolf 25.

A different kind of logic asserted that we had better start building a defense against the Others *right now*. Assuming that the ship that left

Triton couldn't go faster than the speed of light, it would be more than twenty-four years before they got back home and found out Earth had survived, and a similar time before they came back.

A half century can be a long time in the evolution of weapons. Fifty years before Hiroshima, soldiers were still killing each other with bayonets and single-shot bolt-action rifles.

With unlimited energy, we could make our own planet-buster. And a starship to take it to them.

A lot of humans (and all Martians) thought that was a really bad idea. There was no reason to assume that what they did on Triton and the Moon represented the pinnacle of the Others' ability to do damage. If we got them angry, they might flip a switch and blow up the Sun. They might send us all off to wherever the energy was coming from. Or some other place from which there would be no returning.

Meanwhile, the Earth's various economic and political systems were trying to deal with the mixed blessing of free energy. It wasn't quite literally free, since someone had to pay for the manufacture of an outlet. But there were dozens of factories, then hundreds, then one on every block, popping them out for pocket change. A black box with a knob and a place to plug in, for alternating current, or a couple of terminals, for DC. There were other ways to access different kinds of power—like the direct matter-to-energy inferno that would power *ad Astra*.

The consortium that had built the Space Elevator, which put things in orbit cheaply and made endeavors like the Martian colony possible, had grown into an enterprise that had an annual cash flow greater than all but the two wealthiest countries. It had a lot of influence on matters like whether or not to build a fleet of starships and go kick some alien butt. It could have made the largest profit in the history of commerce if it had decided to encourage that, but a version of sanity prevailed: it would only make a *small* fleet of warships, and leave it here in the solar system. And before it did anything aggressive, it would send a peace-seeking delegation to Wolf 25. Sacrificial lambs, some said, and of course its best-known public representative, "The Mars Girl" Carmen Dula, would be one of them. She was not thrilled by the idea.

6

EARTH AND MARS AND IN BETWEEN

None of us who had set foot in Mars was allowed to return to Earth. The logic was clear: until we knew why everyone of my generation and younger simultaneously came down with the Martian lung crap, there was no telling what other strange bugs we might harbor. So we're all Typhoid Marys, until proven otherwise.

We could live in Earth orbit, though, inside a quarantined satellite, Little Mars. I commuted back and forth, Little Mars to Mars, on the one-gee shuttle, which (without spending months in free fall) took between two and five days. I was happier in Mars, and would have settled down there if the Corporation would have left me alone. See my kids often enough for them to remember my face.

In Little Mars, I could don a virtual-reality avatar and electronically walk around on Earth without infecting anyone. Usually my avatar looked like a twelve-year-old girl in shiny white tights who staggered a lot and ran into things, with my face and voice, kind of. When I visited Starhope, though, the spaceship factory, for some reason they gave me a male avatar. Six feet tall, broad-shouldered, glossy black. Still clumsy and a little dangerous to be around.

It was even more clumsy than the girlish avatar I was used to, because everything I did and said went through a censoring delay, in case I inadvertently said, "Hey, how are those warships coming along? The ones we're going to use against the Others?"

It was a ribbon-cutting ceremony for the mostly symbolic completion of *ad Astra*, the ship we were eventually going to take to Wolf 25. All that was really complete, though, was the habitat, the living and working quarters for the crew of seven humans and two Martians. The ship itself was being built out in space, attached to the huge iceball that would provide enough reaction mass to go twenty-some light-years and back.

A miniature version of it was already well past the Oort Cloud, the theoretical edge of the solar system. It had more spartan quarters and the modest goal of going a hundredth of a light-year and back without exploding or otherwise wasting its test pilot.

Our ship would be reasonably comfortable, bigger than the *John Carter*, which had taken twenty-seven of us on an eight-month journey to Mars. We'd been weightless then, though; on our trip to the presumed home of the Others, we would be traveling at one-gee acceleration, once the ship got up to speed. Then turn around at the midway point and decelerate at the same rate.

Scattered among the merely real humans at the ceremony were eight avatars identical to mine, I guess standard issue at Starhope. One of them was Paul and two would be Moonboy and Meryl, the other two xenologists who were going with us. Maybe three of the others were the Corporation/UN team, who couldn't be in Little Mars—no place to hide—but might have been in orbit somewhere. Or just in the next room, for that matter, their identities hidden.

(We'd never met face-to-face, but we had exchanged letters. Nice enough people, but a married threesome, two men and a woman, seemed odd to me. One man is hard enough to handle.)

I missed some of the oratory. It's easy to fall into a drowse when you're standing motionless in VR. If I missed something important, I could trivo it back.

Our mission was so vague I would be hard-pressed to write a speech about it more than a minute or two long—or shorter than a book. Go to the planet we think the Other went to, just to demonstrate that we could. Then react to whatever they do. If "whatever they do" includes vaporizing us, which doesn't seem unlikely, then the fact that we didn't try to harm them first will have been our default mission. Aren't you sorry you killed us?

As soon as the ceremony was over, they started taking the habitat apart. It broke down into modules small enough to be lifted by the Space Elevator.

Once the habitat was delivered, Starhope would settle down into what would be its regular business for the next forty years: building warships.

It was a really stupid idea, since the Others had already demonstrated how easy it would be for them to destroy the Earth. Why aggravate them?

Of course, the warship fleet's actual function was more about keeping the peace on Earth than carrying war into space. It gave the illusion that something was being done; we weren't just a passive target. It also provided employment for a large fraction of the Earth's population, who might otherwise be fighting each other.

The fleet was never mentioned in any broadcast medium; people used euphemisms like "space industrialization" to keep the armament project secret from the Others. I supposed it could work if the Others weren't listening too hard or were abysmally stupid.

It was good to get out of VR and shower and change. When I was finished, there was a message from Paul saying he was down in the galley with fresh coffee and news.

The coffee was a new batch from Jamaica. He let me take one sip and gave me the news: the Earth triad was coming up to get to know us, ahead of schedule.

"No idea why," he said. "Maybe Earth is too exciting."

"Probably just scheduling. Once they start shipping up the pieces of *ad Astra*, it's going to be hard to find a seat on the Elevator." But it was odd.

7

INTRODUCTIONS

I had thought about this moment for some time, often with dread. Now that the moment had come, I just felt resignation, with an overlay of hope. On the other side of this air-lock door was exile from humanity, perhaps for the rest of our lives. Until the Mars quarantine was lifted.

I looked at my mates, Elza and Dustin. "I feel as if someone should make a speech. Or something."

"How about this?" Dustin said. "'What the fuck was I thinking?'"

"My words exactly," Elza said. "Or approximately."

We were floating in a sterile white anteroom, the hub of Little Mars. There were two elevator doors, facing one another, slowly rotating around us: EARTH SIDE and MARS SIDE. People could come and go from the Earth side. The Mars side was one-way.

I pushed the button. The door, which was the elevator's ceiling, slid open. We clambered and somersaulted so that our feet were touching the nominal floor. I said "close," and the ceiling did slide shut, though it might have been automatic rather than obedient.

As it moved "down" toward the rim of the torus, the slight perception of artificial gravity increased until it was Mars-normal, very light to us. An air-lock hatch opened in our floor, and we climbed down a ladder. The hatch closed above us with a loud final-sounding clunk. A door opened into the supposed contamination of Little Mars.

I'd expected the typical spaceship smell, too many people living in too small a volume, but there was a lot more air here than they needed. It smelled neutral, with a faint whiff of mushroom, probably the Martians' agriculture.

I recognized the woman standing there, of course, one of the most famous faces in the world, or off the world. "Carmen Dula." I offered my hand.

She took it and inclined her head slightly. "General Zahari."

"Just Namir, please." I introduced my mates, Elza Guadalupe and Dustin Beckner, ignoring rank. They were both colonels in American intelligence, nominally the Space Force. Israeli for me, but we spooks all inhabit the same haunted house.

She introduced her husband, Paul Collins, even more famous, who would be piloting the huge ship, and the other two xenologists, Moonboy and Meryl. We would meet the Martians later.

We followed them down to the galley. Walking was strange, both for the lightness and a momentary dizziness if you turned your head or nodded too quickly—Coriolis force acting on the inner ear, which I remembered from military space stations. It doesn't bother you after a few minutes.

Dustin stumbled over a floor seam as we went into the galley, and Carmen caught him by the arm and smiled. "You'll get used to it in a couple of days. Myself, I've come to prefer it. Sort of dreading going back to one gee."

The *ad Astra* would accelerate all the way at one gee. "How long have you lived with Martian gravity?"

"Since April '73," she said. "Zero gee there and back, of course, in those days. I've been back and forth a couple of times on the one-gee shuttle. I didn't like it much."

"We'll get used to it fast," Paul said. "I split my time between Earth and Mars in the old days, and it wasn't a big problem."

"You were an athlete back then," she said, with a little friendly mocking in her voice. "Flyboy."

Terms change. For most of my life *the old days* meant before Gehenna. Now it means before Triton. And a flyboy used to fly airplanes.

"Nice place," Dustin said. Comfortable padded chairs and a wooden table, holos of serious paintings on the walls, some unfamiliar and strange. Rich coffee smell. They had a pressure-brewer that I saw did tea as well.

"Pity we can't take it with us," Paul said. "Best not get too used to Jamaican coffee."

There was room around the table for all of us. We all got coffee or water or juice and sat down.

"We wondered why you came early," Moonboy said. "If you don't mind my being direct." He had a pleasant, unlined face in a halo of unruly gray hair.

"Of course not, never," I said, and, as often happens, when I paused Elza leaped in to complete my thought.

"It's about the possibility that we, or one of us, might find the prospect impossible," she said. "They want us to think this is all cast in stone, and they're sure from psychological profiles that we'll all get along fine—and at any rate, we have no choice; there's only one flight, and we have to be on it."

Moonboy nodded. "And that's not true?"

"It can't be, absolutely. What do you think would happen if one of us seven were to die? Would they cancel the mission?"

"I see your point . . ."

"I'm sure they have a contingency plan, a list of replacements. So what if the problem is not somebody's dying, but rather somebody's realizing that before the thirteen years is up, some one or two of the other people are going to drive him or her absolutely insane?"

"Don't forget the Martians," Meryl said. "If anybody here is going to drive me fucking insane, it will be Fly-in-Amber." The other three laughed, perhaps nervously.

"Walking through that air lock did trap you," Paul said. "There's no going back."

"Not to Earth, granted. But one could stay here, or go on to Mars," I said, looking at my wife. "You've never said anything about this."

"It just came into my head," she said, with an innocent look that I knew. Happy to have surprised me.

"It's a good point," Paul said. "A couple of days out, we're past the point of no return. Let's all have our nervous breakdowns before then."

It did cause me to reflect. Am I being too much of a soldier? Orders are orders?

Thirty-five years ago, in the basic training kibbutz, a sergeant would wake me up, his face inches from mine, screaming, *What is the first general rule?*

"I will not quit my post until properly relieved," I would mumble. Much more powerful than *I will obey orders.*

"What is the first general rule?" I asked her softly.

A furrow creased her brow. "What is the first what?"

Dustin cleared his throat. "I will not quit my post until properly relieved."

She smiled. "My soldier boys. We need a better first rule." She looked at Carmen and raised her eyebrows.

"How about 'Don't piss off the aliens'?"

"Except Fly-in-Amber?" I said to Meryl.

She gave a good-natured grimace. "He's no worse than the other ones in the yellow tribe. They're all kind of stuck-up and . . . distant? Even to the other Martians."

I'd seen that in our briefings. The yellow ones were the smallest group, about one in twenty, and with their eidetic memory they served as historians and record-keepers. They also had been a pipeline to the one Other we'd had contact with—a sort of prerecorded message that all the yellow ones had carried around for millennia, supposedly, hidden waiting for a triggering signal.

When the signal came, nine eventful years ago, Fly-in-Amber had been here, in Little Mars. He went into a coma and started spouting gibberish that was decoded pretty easily. The Other was announcing its existence and location and the fact that it had a silicon-nitrogen metabolism, and little else. It didn't mention the fact that it was about to try to destroy the world.

"I'm sort of like the soldier boys," Paul said. "I hadn't thought about there being an option."

Carmen laughed. "For you, forget it. You have to fly the boat." Actually, it was so automated and autonomous that it didn't need a pilot. Paul would oversee it and take over if something went wrong. But that was beyond problematic. Nobody'd ever flown an iceberg close to the speed of light before.

I could sense people sorting one another out socially. The three of us and Paul all had military service, and, in most mixed populations, that is a primary difference. A pseudospeciation—you have killed, at least theoretically, or been given permission to, and so you are irrevocably different.

We comprised one slight majority. The ones who'd lived on Mars comprised another, more basic. But I could see Paul being an instinctive ally in some situations.

Meryl got up and opened the refrigerator. "Anybody hungry?" A few assents, including my own. "Disgustingly healthy, of course." She took out a tray with white lumps on it, slid it into the cooker, and pressed a series of buttons, probably microwave and radiant heat together.

"Piloting this thing is a scary proposition." Paul looked down at the table and moved the salt and pepper shakers around. "No matter who does it—especially when we're light-months or light-years away from technical help."

Not that technical help would do much good if the Martian power source gave out. We might as well burn incense and pray.

"No use worrying about it till Test One gets back," Meryl said. She took the tray of buns out of the cooker and put them on the table.

"You check on him today?" Carmen asked Paul.

He nodded and took a notebook out of his pocket and thumbed it on. "He's about two and a half days from turnaround. Sixty-two hours." Test One was the miniature of *ad Astra* that was going out a hundredth of a light-year and back. "No problem."

The pastry was warm and slightly almond-flavored. I didn't want to speculate on where that came from. Not almonds.

"You haven't talked to him?"

"Not since yesterday. Don't want to nag." He looked at me. "I should be jealous. Another pilot in her life."

She laughed. "Yeah. I'll ask him whether he wants to come into quarantine for a big sloppy kiss."

"Test One isn't from Mars side?" I hadn't known that.

"No, they want to use it for local exploration. Don't want to give us lepers a monopoly on the solar system."

It made sense. The Moon was closed to people who'd been exposed to Mars, and it would probably be the same for the new outposts planned for Ceres and the satellites of the outer planets.

My heart stopped when a monster stepped through the door. Then restarted. Just a Martian.

"Hi, Snowbird," Moonboy said, and followed that with a string of nonhuman sounds. I didn't know you could whistle and belch at the same time.

"Good morning," it said in Moonboy's voice. "Your accent is improving. But no, thank you, I don't want to eat a skillet."

"Have to work on my vocabulary."

It turned to us. "Welcome to Little Mars, General. And Colonel and Colonel."

"Glad to be here," I said, and immediately felt foolish.

"I hope you're being polite and not insane. Happy to join an expedition that will probably result in your death? I hope not." It moved with a smooth rippling gait, four legs rolling, and put an arm around Meryl. Three arms left over.

I'd seen thousands of pictures of them, and studied them extensively, but that was nothing like being in the same room. They're only a little taller than us but seem huge and solid, like a horse. Slight smell of tuna. The head very much like an old potato, including eyes. Two large hands and two small, four fingers each, articulated in such a way that any could serve as thumb. Four legs.

This one was wearing a white smock, scuffed with gray. When she spoke she "faced" the person she was speaking to, though there was nothing like an actual face. Just a mouth, with fat black teeth. The potato eyes were really eyes, bundles of something like optical fiber. They looked in all directions at once and saw mostly in infrared.

"You're Snowbird?" my wife asked.

She faced her. "I am."

"So you'll be dying with us."

"I suppose. More than likely."

"How do you feel about that?"

A human might sit down or lean against something. Snowbird stood still, and was silent for a long moment. "Death is not the same for us.

Not as important. We die as completely, but will be replaced—as you are. But we're more closely replicated."

"A white dies and a white is born," I said.

"Yes, but more than that. The new one has a kind of memory of the old. Actual, not metaphorical."

"Even if you die twenty-four light-years away?" Meryl asked.

"We've talked about that, Fly-in-Amber and I. It will be an interesting experiment."

They don't reproduce at all like humans. It's sort of like a wrestling match, with several of them rolling around together, their sweat containing genetic material. The one who wins the match gets to be the mother, breaking out in pods over the next few days. One for each of the recent dead, so the population of each family remains approximately constant.

"You weren't on the Space Elevator roster," Carmen said, "and we didn't expect you until the message just before you got here. Is that a spook thing?"

All human eyes were on me, and probably a few Martian ones. "Yes, but not so much with Elza and Dustin. We all have ties to the intelligence community, but I'm the only one who's supposed to move in secret. Of course, when we're traveling together, they stay invisible, too."

"The secrecy," Snowbird said. "That's because you're an Israeli? A Jew?"

I nodded to her. Difficult to look someone in the eye when there are so many. "I was born in Israel," I said, as always trying to keep emotion out of my voice. "I have no religion."

That caused a predictable awkward silence, which Carmen eventually broke.

"A friend of mine's parents knew you in Israel, after Gehenna. Elspeth Feldman."

It took me a moment. "The Feldmans, yes, Americans. Life sciences. Max and . . . A-something."

"Akhila. You approved them for Israeli citizenship," she said.

"Them and a thousand others, mostly involved in the cleanup. The country had a real population shortage." I turned back to Snowbird. "You know about Gehenna."

"I know," she said. "Which is not the same as understanding. How did you survive it?"

"I was in New York all of 2060, a junior attaché at the UN. That's when the first part of the poison went into the water supply at Tel Aviv and Hefa."

"Anyone who drank it died," Carmen said.

"If they were in Tel Aviv or Hefa a year later," I said, "when car bombs released the second part of the poison. An aerosol.

"It wasn't immediately obvious, where I was. In an office full of foreigners. And it was a Jewish holiday, Passover.

"We had the news on, cube and radio—one of the car bombs had gone off two blocks away.

"Five or six people started having trouble breathing. All of them dead in a couple of minutes. They could breathe in, but couldn't exhale.

"We called 9-9-9 but of course got nothing. Went down to the street and . . ." Elza put her hand on my knee, under the table; I covered it with mine.

"Millions died all at once," Snowbird said.

"Within a few minutes. When we got outside, cars were still crashing. Alarms going off all over the city. Dead people everywhere, of course; a few still dying. Some had jumped or fallen from balconies and lay crushed on the street and sidewalks."

Snowbird spread all four hands. "I'm sorry. This causes you pain."

"It's been twenty years," I said. "Twenty-one. To tell the truth, sometimes it feels like it didn't happen to me at all. Like it happened to someone else, and he's told me the story over and over."

"It did happen to someone else," Elza said. "It happened to whoever you were before." Her fingers moved lightly.

"You probably know the numbers," I said to the Martian. "Almost 70 percent of the country dead in less than ten minutes."

"They still don't know who did it?" Snowbird said.

"No one ever claimed responsibility. More than twenty years of intense investigation haven't turned up one useful clue. They really covered their tracks."

"So it was done by someone like you," Moonboy said. "Not really *like* you."

"I know what you mean, yes. It wasn't some band of foaming-at-the-mouth anti-Semites. It was a country or corporation that had . . . people like us."

"Could you do it?" Paul said. "I don't mean morally. I mean could you manage the mechanics of it."

"No. You can't separate the mechanics from the morals. After twenty-one years, we still don't have one molecule of testimony. The people who drove the car bombs died, of course—and we don't think they knew they were going to die; they were all on their way to someplace, not parked at targets—but what happened to the dozens of other people who had to be involved? We think they were all murdered during or just after Gehenna. It wasn't a time when one dead body more or less was going to stick out. Every lead we've ever had ends that day."

Carmen was nodding slowly. "You don't hate them?"

I saw what she meant. "Not really. I fear what they represent, in terms of the human potential for evil. But the individuals, no. What would be the point?"

"I read what you wrote about it," she said, "in that journal overview."

"*International Affairs*, the Twentieth Anniversary issue. You've been thorough."

She smiled but looked directly at me. "I was curious, of course. We'll be together a long time."

"I read it, too," Paul said. "'Forgiving the Unforgivable.' Carmen showed it to me."

"Trying to understand why I was, why we were, selected?"

"Why military people were selected," she said. "The pressure for that was obvious, but frankly I was surprised they gave in to it. There's no way we can threaten the Others."

She was holding back resentment that I don't think was personal. "You'd rather have three more xenobiologists than three . . . political appointees? We're not really soldiers."

"You were, once."

"As a teenager, yes. Everyone in Israel was, at that time. But I've been a professional peacekeeper ever since."

"And a spook," Elza said. "If I were Carmen, that would bother me."

Carmen made a placating gesture. "We probably have enough xeno-biologists, and really can only guess what else might be useful. Your M.D. and clinical experience is as obviously useful to us, personally, as Namir's life as a diplomat is, to our mission. But we don't know. Dustin's doctorate in philosophy might turn out to be the most power-ful weapon in our arsenal.

"I won't pretend it didn't annoy me when I found out the Earth committee had chosen an all-military bunch—and then spooks on top of that! But of course I can see the logic. And it's reasonable in terms of social dynamic, a secure triad joining two secure pairs."

That dynamic is interesting in various ways. The committee wanted no more than three military people, so the civilians would outnumber us, but they didn't want to upset the social balance by sending up sin-gle, unattached people—so our family had a large natural advantage.

But how stable is it, really? Everybody's married, but Carmen and Dustin and Elza are all under thirty, and the rest of us are not exactly nuns and monks.

In the first hour all of us were together, I suppose there was a lot of automatic and unconscious evaluation and categorizing—who might bond to whom in the winepress of years that we faced? At fifty, I was old enough to be Carmen's father, but my initial feelings toward her were not at all paternal.

I could tell that the attraction was not mutual; she had me pigeon-holed, the older generation. But my wife was her age, actually a few months younger. She must have known that as a statistic.

Was I just rationalizing, being the pathetic middle-aged male? Assuming that a woman must be attracted to me just because I was instantly attracted to her?

And I was, though I wouldn't have predicted it, not "The Mars Girl." As a diplomat, I've dealt with far too many famous people. Carmen had none of the automatic assumption of importance that I find so tiresome. She was almost aggressively normal, this least ordinary of all women. Ambassador to another species, a fulcrum of history.

She was not physically the kind of woman I would normally find attractive, either; so slender as to be almost boyish, her features sharp, inquisitive. Her eyes were green, or hazel, which I had never noticed in photographs. Hair cut close for space, like all of us. There wouldn't be any need for that tradition on the long trail to Wolf 25.

Meryl was closer to my age and physically attractive, almost voluptuous. Olive skin and black hair, she looked like most of the girls and women I grew up with.

None of whom were still alive. I could not look at her without feeling that.

8

FAMILY MATTERS

I didn't expect to like Namir, but I did immediately. You might expect a professional diplomat to be likable, though in my "Mars Girl" experience that hasn't been the case. Of course, those meetings have always been public and strained, physical contact limited to rubber-glove virtual reality.

How odd-feeling and pleasant to actually shake someone's hand. Namir's constrained physical strength. His face was strong, too, chiseled but with warm laugh lines around his eyes.

Our three spooks were the first new people we'd met, physically, in years. So I was immediately aware of their physicality. Dustin and Elza were my age, Elza athletic and assertive but Dustin more a quiet scholarly type.

Namir had a barely contained charisma, an air of authority that had nothing to do with rank. Probably born with it, bossing around adults from the crib. I wondered whether Paul would have trouble with that.

I wondered whether I would. We hadn't planned on a hierarchy.

Paul would make the pilot decisions. If there were medical decisions, Elza would make them, and otherwise we'd just talk things out and go with the consensus. When we got to Wolf and met the Others, I saw myself as a spokesperson, but in fact we had no idea of what the situation would be—maybe they would only talk with the Martians, and Fly-in-Amber would be the logical choice. The rest of us just baggage, perhaps disposable.

That first meeting with the Earth people was cordial and reassuring. Moonboy, in his direct way, found out how they wound up a triune. Namir and Elza married in a conventional civil ceremony six years ago, in her last year of medical school. The American Space Force had paid her tuition, and she was commissioned as soon as she got her M.D. Namir pulled some strings, and she wound up working with him at the UN—which is where she met and fell in love with Dustin. At Namir's suggestion they expanded their union to include him, which was legal in New York and (I was surprised to learn) not particularly uncommon there nowadays.

I could only guess what their sleeping arrangements had been on Earth; on both Little Mars and *ad Astra*, each person had individual sleeping quarters. The bunks were large enough for two people to sleep together if they didn't mind touching. Unless they were both large. In our population, that would only be Namir and Paul, which I didn't see happening.

In *ad Astra* everything would be modular. They might choose to have one big bed in one big room. Hamster pile, as they say in college.

Of the three of them, only Namir had a little experience of living in space, but only a little. Of we other four, I had the least, but I'd been off Earth the past eleven years, which incidentally was close to the length of time we seven would be spending together, on the way to Wolf and hopefully back. About six and a half years there, and the same to return.

We would have to become a family of sorts if we were to survive. Tolstoi famously said, "Happy families are all alike; every unhappy family is unhappy in its own way." The old Russian didn't consider triune marriages, though, or families with two nonhuman members—we could presumably be unhappy in ways that he couldn't have begun to describe. At least none of us was likely to throw herself in front of a train.

For those of us used to life in the Martian colony or this satellite, the living space in *ad Astra* wouldn't be too confining. The combination of being isolated from the human race at large, while living in close contact with a few others, was not a novelty.

Our spooks were used to traveling around the world, constantly facing the challenge and attraction of new environments, new people. How well would they get along with this, a sardine tin that also had aspects of a goldfish bowl?

VR would help preserve our sanity, sometimes by providing alternatives to sanity. Both Moonboy and Meryl liked to go random places with the kaleidoscope filter, which provided a controlled degree of synesthesia, the data meant for one sense being interpreted as another. You could do it one sense at a time, or just spin the wheel and hang on. I might do more of it myself, with time on my hands. And on my eyes and nose and so forth.

But I liked the almost endless array of straightforward virtual travelogues, and often did them in tandem with Paul, as a way of getting away from the others. Usually nothing spectacular or culturally interesting, which of course made up most of the library. We'd just stroll down a country lane talking, or sit on a beach or in some woods. A pity we didn't have the complex porn interfaces, so we could do more than hold hands and talk, but that would be a little hard to get through the Corporation budget review.

Along those lines I had to admit a certain prurient curiosity about our new sister and brothers. If they did all hop into bed together, who did what to whom and with what? It could make for a crowded bed, though I supposed we could jury-rig something. Or just agree to stay out of the galley periodically and let them do it on the table.

I wasn't really drawn to either of the men in that way, although they were both likable and attractive. It was hard to believe that Namir was fifty. From the moment of our first meeting, I sensed a real physical attraction, though he may project the same kind of interest to any female not too young or old to make a sexual union possible. I know that degree of sexual indiscrimination passes for gallantry with some men in some cultures.

Actually, he didn't seem to project the same warmth toward Meryl, and she is prettier and sexier than me. Older, but still a decade younger than him.

Who knows? After a few years, we may be swapping partners like minks. Or not be speaking to one another.

Who will be the first to be thrown out of the air lock? Or leave voluntarily?

9

SECRETS

Carmen doesn't really know how completely she's being lied to—only by omission, but nevertheless lies. She really has no idea how bad things are on Earth right now, and what a nightmare we've been through.

We accept the necessity of total monitoring and censoring of all communication into space, since the Others can receive anything broadcast from Earth, assuming they're interested.

Maybe it's silly. A sufficiently weak signal would be so attenuated in twenty-four light-years' distance that no manner of superscience could separate it from cosmic background noise. But what is "sufficiently weak"? And how badly do you need the signal? If it were important to me as a spook, I could take any smallest signal—a man's heartbeat through a hotel window a mile away—and amplify and refine it, then pump it through a laser to another spook, or an Other spook, twenty-four light-years away.

So what could the Others do? Maybe they read all our mail. Maybe all our thoughts.

Whatever the reality, the controlling principle is that everything broadcast into space might be overheard by the Others, so everyone who lives in orbit or on Mars will have a systematically distorted view of life on Earth. Carmen was aware of that in regard to defense—she never mentioned the fleet and didn't expect any reports about it—but when we first talked, I realized that her image of life on Earth was no more realistic than a cube drama.

I caught her alone the second morning, by the sneaky expedient of checking the exercise schedule. At 0400 she was in VR, biking, so I took up the rowing machine and watched her pedal through the streets of a Paris that no longer existed.

We showered separately and met down at the mess for coffee. She brought up Paris, how she remembered it from the year she spent in Europe as a girl.

"I guess the VR crystal's pretty old," she said. "They hadn't started rebuilding the Eiffel Tower, but it was finished when I was there in '66."

"Still there," I said, "but it was damaged in the '81 riots, a piece of the base melted. They've left it that way, closed to the public."

"There were riots in '81?"

"Not just in Paris. Though hundreds died there, in the Champ du Mars."

"Hundreds." She sat absolutely still. "In the States, too?"

"All over. The States were . . . worse than most of Europe and the Middle East. Los Angeles and Chicago were especially bad."

"The East Coast?"

"New York and Washington were already under martial law when Paris exploded. There wasn't much loss of life."

"How long did it go on?"

"Well . . . technically . . ."

Her eyes got wide. "Still?"

I had an intense desire for a cigarette. I hadn't smoked since Gehenna. "In a way, it is still going on. Not martial law, but a kind of pervasive police state. Which doesn't call itself that."

"It's what they're calling internationalism?"

"Basically. One big happy police-state family."

She walked across the room and looked out at the image of the Earth. "Paul and I were talking about that the other day. The picture they project is too perfect; we've all known that. But a police state, all over the world?"

"Maybe I'm exaggerating. Many people do just see it as international solidarity against a common enemy. Everybody does have to sacrifice a certain amount of time, a certain amount of comfort. And freedom."

"For the future of humanity," she said in a broadcaster's voice. "Does everyone buy that?"

"Not at all. A significant fraction believes the business out at Triton and the explosion on the other side of the Moon were just pyrotechnics to make us believe the bullshit about the Others—the whole thing is an elaborate hoax to rob normal people of their rights and hand over their money to the rich.

"If you don't know anything about science, or about economics, a case can be made. But even then, you have to enlist the Martians in the conspiracy, or believe that they don't really exist."

"That's bizarre."

"Well, no one's allowed to go near one, unless they're part of the conspiracy themselves. Hollywood's been cooking up convincing aliens for more than a century, they say. Whoever's behind the conspiracy could afford a few dozen of the finest.

"If you start with that as a premise—everything about Mars is a hoax—then most of it falls into place. The Others? A perfect enemy, all-powerful, unreachable. You and Paul are part of the conspiracy, of course. The Girl from Mars married to the Man Who Saved the Earth? I wouldn't believe it myself if I didn't know it was true."

"But . . . who's supposed to benefit from all that?"

"The rich people. The white people. The Jews—speaking as an unofficial Jew myself, I know we're capable of anything. The military-industrial complex, to use an antique term. This gives them a black hole to throw money into for the next fifty years."

She slumped into the chair across from me and studied me. "This is where I say, 'Namir, you have learned too much. Now you have to die.'"

That actually gave me a little chill. "The more convincing explanation, I think, is that the Others are behind the whole thing. But they look just like humans and have infiltrated every aspect of government and industry."

She smiled. "It's like all the paranoiac explanations for Gehenna. Some people still believe it was a leftist takeover."

I snorted. "Which explains how liberal our government is now. If you call it a government. Maybe the Others took over Israel first, as an experiment."

She leaned forward, serious. "So . . . to what extent do ordinary people know what's going on—people who don't stalk the corridors of power, like you guys?"

"Most people do, people who can read. Newspapers have become a big industry again, print ones. Nobody reads the e-sheets for actual news. People who aren't literate have to make do with word of mouth or put up with the same version of reality the Others are being fed."

"The Others and *us*," she said, trying to control the anger in her voice. "Most of the people I know are on Mars, but I'm in touch with people on Earth all the time—"

"Who would risk the death penalty if they discussed reality. Everything's monitored." She was shaking her head, hard. "Look, even I assumed you were in on it. Self-censorship is so automatic. Nobody's going to call or write, and say 'They'll kill me for saying this, but—' "

"But it's so stupid! The Others aren't going to be *fooled*."

"There's no way to know. It might just take one slip."

"Maybe." The angry set of her mouth softened. "It never occurred to me to ask for a paper copy of a newspaper. I mean, who ever sees one?"

"Everybody, nowadays." Was some bureaucrat controlling the information they got, or was it an unintended consequence of draconian broadcast security? "You should ask for a Sunday *New York Times*— or I will. Say that I'm homesick. See whether they print up a special version with the news sanitized for us. I could tell."

I asked, and eventually the newspaper did appear—it takes a week for anything to come up. It did seem to be the same paper I read every week. Significantly, it had Jude Coulter's column, summarizing the past week's news that had been suppressed from the Others. And people in orbit or on Mars, incidentally.

The first two ships of the fleet are nearing completion; both are already crewed, awaiting weapons systems. They're somewhat bigger than the projected standard for the other 998, but cruder, rushed into construction in case the Other that left Triton five years ago left behind some belated surprise.

I think the fleet is a tactical travesty from inception to its present and future reality. Gnats attacking an elephant. If you want to protect the future of the human race from the Other menace, those resources should go toward moving breeding populations out far from Earth. Because Earth is unlikely to survive the first second of hostilities from the Others. A diffuse population hidden around the solar system might have a chance.

Or not.

10

NEW WORLD

Namir's newspaper reassured us a little bit. There wasn't a huge conspiracy trying to insulate us from reality. It was just a secondary effect
of the fanatic security effort. So now we were to get the *Times* and one
other newspaper every week. Delivered to your air-lock door.

Not a conspiracy, but certainly a pervasive bureaucratic mind-set.
You don't learn anything unless you have an official "need to know."

It was probably an empty gesture anyhow, presuming to fool the
Others with smoke and mirrors. Namir agreed. They had to know us
too well for that to work.

What might have worked, if there had been enough advance warning, would have been to shut Earth down electronically, completely, the
instant of the Moon explosion.

Even that would only have worked if the Others were just listening
to broadcast emissions and not spying on Earth any other way. And
it would have been impossible to build *ad Astra* and the fleet without
electronic communication.

The half of our satellite that's not under Martian quarantine, Little Earth or, to us, "earthside," serves as a conduit for communicating between the fleet and Earth. There's a lot of radio and image transmission that can be disguised as innocuous space industrialization—but the part that can't be disguised is written down or photographed and sent to Little Earth via "transfer pods," which guide themselves into a net and are sent down the Space Elevator to an Earth address. Messages that can't wait that long are de-orbited and dropped to Earth by parachute. I wonder how many of them actually make it to the final address.

It's a fragile house of cards, and we could collapse it just by a minute of frank broadband discussion. I talked with Paul about doing just that. What could they do, fire us?

"No," he said, "but we could have a tragic accident." We were talking in VR, walking and bicycling slowly down a country road in Cape Cod, Indian summer, cranberry bogs vivid red with floating berries and the smells of woodsmoke and autumn leaves powerful but relaxing. Squirrels scattered out of our way, and geese honked overhead, swifting south.

"You think they would go that far?"

"Well, I don't think we're indispensable," he said, braking the bike into a short downhill. "They could even manufacture avatar duplicates. They do it all the time with politicians."

I nodded. "Like that French nonassassination." The president's limousine was blown up in a visit to Algeria, and it turned out that neither president nor driver was actually there, actually human.

"My God." He stopped pedaling but his bicycle stayed upright; VR couldn't topple the exercise machine outside our illusion. "Could that be why they sent three soldiers?"

"To kill us if we broke the rules? That's ridiculous."

"In this brave new world? I don't know."

"Be realistic, Paul. If they wanted us dead, this powerful 'they,' they wouldn't have to send three assassins up into orbit. They could push a button and blow all the air out of Mars side."

He started pedaling again. "That's why I love you, Carmen. You're such a ray of sunshine."

I was sweating a little from the exercise, but a new patch of cold sweat broke out on the back of my neck:

What if we were twenty-four light-years away and decided to do something subversive, like surrender to the Others? The Earth couldn't do a thing to stop us.

But Namir and Dustin and Elza, for all their quiet and civilized manners, had once been trained to kill. And were presumably loyal to Earth.

What were their orders?

✸

We weren't headed out to the iceberg for a couple of weeks, but *ad Astra* itself—the habitat we'd be living in on the way to Wolf and back—was up and running, and we wanted to live in it in Earth orbit for a while. If something went wrong, we could always send out for a plumber.

Speaking of plumbing, we did have a week or so of roll-up-your-sleeves work before we took off. The large crew who'd set up *ad Astra* had the hydroponics working as they would in the normal one-gee environment, on the way to Wolf. But it would take at least a week of zero gee before we hooked up with the iceberg, and of course you can't have standing pools of water in zero gee. They turn into floating blobs. So we had plant-by-plant instructions as to what had to be done to keep root systems and everything moist en route.

(Good practice. We'd be doing it again at the halfway point, since we'd be in zero gee while the iceberg slowly rotated around to start braking.)

Quarantine rules made the transfer into the Space Elevator a little complicated. Every area had to be sterilized after we passed through—from Mars side through the air lock to the hub, then down the extension tube to where the Space Elevator was waiting. It took three trips, awkward in zero gee, especially for our spook pals, who didn't have a lot of experience. Finding handholds when your hands are full.

It wasn't too hard to say good-bye to Little Mars, as much time as I'd spent there. It was actual Mars, the Mars colony, that felt like home. Florida was a distant memory. Another world.

We spent four and a half days in the Space Elevator, first at zero gee, but with increasing gravity as we moved out to the end of the Elevator's tether.

About halfway, I started feeling heavy and depressed. For years, I'd been used to exercising an hour or more a day in Earth gravity, but it was always a relief to get back to Mars-normal. I'd get used to it in time. But it felt like carrying around a knapsack full of rocks, permanently attached.

There wasn't much to see of *ad Astra* as we approached, but we didn't expect anything dramatic. A big flat white box with a shuttle rocket attached. The rocket would maneuver us into rendezvous with the iceberg, then shut down till we got to Wolf, where it would be a landing craft. If the Others let us land.

Going from the Elevator into *ad Astra* was simple. They coupled automatically, and we walked through two air locks into our new home.

It was stunning. It was huge, at least to my eyes. The line of sight was about fifty meters, over the gym and swimming pool and hydroponics garden. I had trouble focusing that far away, and it made me grin.

Namir, Elza, and Dustin were not smiling. By Earth standards, this was not a big place to be locked up in for a large part of your life. The rest of your life, perhaps.

We stacked our boxes and suitcases there by the air lock, next to the life-support/recycling station, and sent the Space Elevator back down, to pick up our Martians. We went off together to explore.

The hydroponics garden was technically a luxury. There was enough dehydrated food in storage to keep us alive for twenty boring years, and plenty of oxygen from electrolysis. But fresh fruit and vegetables would mean more than just variety in the diet. The routines of growing, harvesting, propagation, and recycling had helped keep us sane in Mars, where we had fifteen times as many people, and more than fifteen times as much living space. Plus the chance to take a walk outdoors, which on *ad Astra* would be a short walk. Then light-years long. Eternity.

Everything was in a sort of early-spring mode, still a month or more from the earliest harvest. Grape tomatoes and spring onions, from a first look. They smelled so good—nostalgia not for Earth, where I never gardened, but for the Martian garden, where I'd worked a couple of hours a week.

The central space was larger than all the rest put together. There was a padded track for jogging or running around its hundred-meter perimeter. On the "southern" end of it (we decided to call the control room "north") there was a small Japanese-style hot bath and a narrow rectangular swimming pool, which could maintain a decent current to swim against.

South of that were the exercise and VR machines, similar to what we had in Little Mars, with a relatively large lavatory and an actual shower, and the infirmary, with an optimistic single bed. The lavatory had a zero-gee toilet exactly like the one on the Space Elevator, for the few days we'd be weightless.

Farthest south was the large and rather forbidding Life-Support/Recycling area, a bright room full of machines. Every metal surface was inscribed with maintenance instructions, I supposed in case the computer system failed. So we could stay alive until we died.

That was an interesting prospect if something did go wrong, and we went merrily blasting away for years, leaving Wolf 25 far behind. Paul said that if we just kept going in a straight line, without turning around midway to slow down, we had enough reaction mass to go more than a hundred thousand light-years. At which point, we'd be twelve years older, while the unimaginably distant Earth would have aged a thousand centuries.

Our seven cabins were in a north–south line along the hydroponics garden. We checked a couple of them, apparently all the same, but very malleable, with moveable walls and modular furniture. The wall that separated them from the hydroponics area was semipermanent, a lattice for vines.

The kitchen and dining room were twice the size of their Little Mars counterparts, where we did little actual cooking. Elza volunteered that Namir was an excellent cook, which was good news. I can just about flip a burger or scramble eggs, and we wouldn't have either of those.

There was a lounge next to the dining room, with a pool table and keyboard and various places to sit or, I suppose, lounge. I hadn't touched a piano keyboard in a dozen years. Would boredom drive me back to it?

Between the lounge and the Martian area was a meeting place that would be maintained at a compromise ambience—a little too cool and dark for humans; a little warm for Martians.

At the northernmost area, the lounge led into a library and study, with workstations but also wooden panel walls and real paintings. Then there was another air lock and Paul's control room. He sat down at the console and ran his hands over the knobs and dials, smiling, in his element.

The spies looked kind of grim. It was understandable. They were losing a whole planet, one the rest of us had written off a long time ago. I did feel sorry for them, especially Namir, shut off from his complex history.

Which he was also bringing with him.

II

GOOD-BYES

After our final briefing in New York, and before we flew out to the Space Elevator, Elza and Dustin and I had been given a few days to settle our affairs on Earth.

We didn't have to empty out our New York City apartment. Elza had made a clever deal with Columbia University, where they assumed the mortgage and will maintain the place for the half century we'll be gone. If we don't come back, it will be a unique small museum. In the unlikely event that we do return, we can either step back into the old place or leave it as a museum and negotiate an alternative—probably more comfortable—living space with the university.

I had to go say good-bye to my father, which I could no longer put off. He has two rooms in a Jewish assisted-living complex in Yonkers, which offers free room and board for people in his situation: he was in Israel for the first stage of the Gehenna attack, and so his body is suffused with the nanomachines that comprise half the poison. The second half could await him anyplace in Israel. People die every year when they return and open an old closet or something. I knew a man who went back and lived for years, then, for a reunion, put on his old army uniform and stopped breathing.

Father had been in New York, staying in my apartment, when the bombs went off in Tel Aviv. I was going to bring my mother back to join him for a tour of the American West.

Instead I brought her ashes, months later.

We have had few words since then, and none in Hebrew. When I greeted him with *Shalom*, he stared at me for a long moment and said, "You should come in. It's raining."

He made a pot of horrible tea, boiling it Australian style, and we sat on the porch and watched the rain come down.

When I told him what I was about to do, he crept away and came back with a dusty bottle of brandy and tipped a half inch into our teacups, which was an improvement.

"So you come to say good-bye, actually. God is too kind to give me another fifty years of this."

"You may outlive me. God can be cruel in his benevolence."

"So now you believe in God. Wonders will never cease."

"No more than you do. Unless living here has weakened your mind."

"Living here has weakened my stomach. A constant assault of bad kosher cooking. A good son would have brought a ham sandwich."

"I'll bring one if I come back. At 142, you'll need it even more."

He closed his eyes. "Oh, please. You really think those alien bastards will kill you?"

"They haven't been well-disposed toward humans in the past. You did see the moon thing?"

"Two nights running, yes. Some people here thought it was staged, a hoax."

He sipped his tea, made a face, and added more brandy. "I know bubkes about science. I couldn't see how they'd fake that, though."

"No." They could have faked the halo of dust, I supposed, but not the rain of gamma radiation. Orbiting monitors had pictures of the explosion, too, from farther out in the solar system. "It's real, and it demands a response."

"Maybe. But why you?"

I shrugged. "I'm a diplomat."

"No, you're not. You're a spy. A spy for a country that hardly exists anymore."

"They needed three military people in the crew. Our triune was perfect because we wouldn't upset the social balance—two other married couples."

"Your shiksa wife could upset some marriages. Your husband . . . I've never understood any of that."

I decided not to rise to that bait. "They got a diplomat, a doctor, and a philosopher."

"They got three spies, Namir. Or didn't they know that?"

"We're all military intelligence, Father. Soldiers, not spies."

He rolled his eyes at that. "It's a new world," I said, I hoped reasonably. "The American army has more officers in intelligence than in the infantry."

"I suppose the Israeli army, too. That did a lot of good with Gehenna."

"In fact, we did know something was about to happen. That's why I was called back to Tel Aviv."

"'Something' had already happened. If I recall correctly." His face was a stone mask.

Maybe love could get through that. But I'd known for years that I'd never loved him, and it was mutual.

He wasn't a bad man. But he'd never wanted to be a father and did his best to ignore me and Naomi when we were growing up. I think I'm enough of a man to understand him, and forgive. But love doesn't come from the brain, from understanding.

I so didn't want to be there, and he released me.

"Look. I can see you have a million things to do. I will take all my pills and try to be here when you come back. Okay?" He stood and held out his arms.

I clasped his fragile body. *"Shalom,"* he finally said into my shoulder. "I know you will do well."

I took the skyway across to the Port Authority and walked a mile through the rain back to our apartment. Saying good-bye to the city, more home to me than Tel Aviv or any other place.

Life without restaurants. Walking by so many favorites, the Asian ones especially. But it was less about missing them than it was all the ones I'd been curious about and put off trying. I read that you could eat at a different restaurant for every meal in New York City and never eat at all of them. Does that mean that three new places were opened every day?

A holo I recognized as James Joyce abjured me to come into a new place, Finnegans Wake, and have a pint of Guinness. I checked my watch and went in for a small one. A quartet was holding forth around the piano, with more spirit than talent, but it was pleasant. When I left, the rain was more forceful, but it wasn't cold, and I had a hat. I rather liked it.

Eleven years eating computer-generated healthy recycled shit. Well, I'd survived on army rations for some years. How bad could it be?

When Elza came home, we'd have to decide where to go for dinner, the last one in this city. Maybe we should just walk until we got hungry and take whatever appeared.

I was going to miss the noise and the crowds. And the odd pockets of quiet, like the postage-stamp park behind our apartment, two benches and a birdbath, running over as I took my last look.

Neither Elza nor Dustin was home. The place felt large without them. About twelve hundred square feet. In *ad Astra*, we'd have three cabins, each less than a hundred square feet.

Wrong comparison. How many square feet did I have aboard the *Golda Meir*? A hot hammock, shared with two other guys.

We were allowed to take fifteen kilograms of "personal items including clothing," though we'd be supplied utility clothing and one formal uniform. What would that look like? Tailor-made to impress creatures who live forever in liquid nitrogen. They probably dress up all the time. "Dress warmly, son; it's only going up to minus 253."

Books. I immediately picked out the slim leather-bound volume of Shakespeare's sonnets my first wife gave me, the only Passover we shared. I took a small drawing of her out of its frame and trimmed it with scissors so it would fit inside the book.

I took some comfortable worn jeans out of the closet, but then traded them for some newer ones—they will have to last thirteen years, or at least six and a half. A chamois shirt from L.L. Bean. Army exercise outfit. Comfortable leather moccasins.

There were hundreds of books I would have enjoyed having, but of course the ship would have all of them in its memory. Likewise movies and feelies.

I should take a few books I could read over and over, in case the library malfunctioned. A volume of Amachai, one of cummings. A large slim book with all of Vermeer.

I hesitated over the balalaika. It gave me pleasure, but the others probably wouldn't like it much even if I were talented. No one in the world except Elza thought that I was. It would probably wind up going out the air lock, and maybe me with it.

Three blocks of fine-grained koa wood and two carving knives, with a sharpening stone.

The bathroom scale said eight kilograms. I decided to leave it at that and let Elza make up the difference with clothes. That would benefit all three of us. She would never admit it, but she liked dressing up a little and was easier to get along with if she felt she looked attractive. To me, she would look fine in a potato sack.

I sat down at my writing desk, opened the right-hand drawer, and lifted out the 10.5-mm Glock, with all its reassuring and troubling weight. Illegal in New York City despite the state and federal permits clipped to the side of its shoulder holster. It would be a central exhibit in the apartment-museum. "With this weapon, Namir Zahari killed four looters who attacked him in the ruins of Tel Aviv." And no others, of course. No Others, certainly. It would not be that kind of diplomacy.

I wiped it clean with an oil-impregnated cloth. The breech smelled of cold metal and faraway fire. I'd last used it at a pistol range in New Jersey, first week of January. Elza'd been with me, with her little .32. An annual family custom that would not be welcome on *ad Astra*.

Putting it away, I had a familiar specific feeling of memento mori. Two of our team in the Gehenna cleanup committed suicide, both with Israeli-issued pistols like this one.

I used to wonder how much horror and sadness I could absorb before that kind of exit seemed attractive, or necessary. I'm fairly sure now it couldn't happen; I'm not set up that way. I'll keep plugging along until my luck runs out; my time runs out. Along with eight billion others, perhaps, at the same instant.

Though what does "at the same instant" mean in our situation? Twenty-four years later? Or perhaps the Others have a way around Einsteinian simultaneity.

My phone pinged, and it was Dustin. He was landing at Towers in a few minutes. He'd already talked to Elza, and they'd decided to meet for dinner at the Four Seasons, okay? I said I'd make an early reservation, for seven. An hour away, plenty of time to walk.

The rain was over and not programmed to resume until tomorrow.

I put on evening clothes and left the Glock in the drawer. Strapped the little .289 Browning to my right ankle. Called Security and told them the route I'd be walking. There was already someone on duty down the block, they said; the same one who'd followed me back from New Jersey. I walked the stairs to the basement and went out through the service entrance of the apartment building next door. No one in the alley.

It had been years since the tail had caught anyone, but that one time saved my life. I recognized this one, a small black man, as I passed him at the first intersection, but of course we didn't acknowledge one another.

That would be one nice thing about leaving the Earth behind. I wouldn't have to worry about bodyguards. Though I'd never faced a more dangerous adversary.

So much for my romantic stroll with Elza (and our usually invisible companion), ending in a random restaurant. I'd thought Dustin was going to be in Houston till the next morning.

"I was a fifth wheel down there anyhow," he explained as I sat down at the elegant table. "My two projects put on hold for half a century. They'll be political curiosities when I come back."

"We're political curiosities already," I said. "What's a spook without a country?" He politely didn't say that I should know.

We talked shop for a few minutes. I'd worked out of Houston for a year sometime back and made friends there.

When Elza showed up, I nodded to the human waiter, and he poured us each a glass of Pouilly-Fuissé and returned the bottle to ice.

I held up a glass. "To getting back alive."

"To getting *there* alive," she said, and we all touched glasses. "You wrote to Carmen Dula and the others?"

"It went up on the Elevator day before yesterday." Since *ad Astra* was technically part of the fleet, we weren't allowed to contact it electronically. So I sent a paper note telling them we'd be on the next Elevator.

"It's too strange," Dustin said. "We're going to spend thirteen years with these people, and we can't even chat beforehand."

"Worse for them. We can at least look up their bios and news stories—millions of words, for her and Paul Collins. But they shouldn't be able to find a single word about us."

"You enjoy being a man of mystery," she said. "Poor little Mars Girl won't have a chance."

"You doctors are all about sex. It hadn't crossed my mind."

Elza looked at me over her glass. "She's an old hag anyhow."

"Eight months older than you. But you knew that."

"Maybe we should have just snuck up on them," Dustin said. "This way, they'll have plenty of time to get dressed and put away the sex toys."

"Dream on," Elza said.

The maître d' came over, and we negotiated the complex combination of food-ration credits, legitimate currency, and hard cash that dinner would cost. Maybe by the time we got back, they'd have that mess straightened out. Meanwhile, it cost the same no matter what your entrée was, so I had pheasant under glass, very very good.

With the coffee and dessert, we mostly talked about what we were leaving behind.

We'd all been visiting family, Elza in Kansas and Dustin in California. I told them about the uncomfortable meeting with my father. Elza'd had a warm family reunion all weekend, but Dustin's parents were even worse than mine. They're old anarchists and have hardly spoken to him since he joined the service. Now they're deniers, convinced that the whole thing is a government conspiracy. They live in an Earthlove commune, surrounded by like-minded zealots. Dustin fled when he turned eighteen, eleven years ago.

"They claim to be self-sufficient," he said of the commune, "trading organic dairy goods for things they can't raise on the farm. But even when I was a kid, I could tell something was fishy. We all lived too well; there was money coming in from somewhere."

"Now who's paranoid?" Elza said.

"You could have them investigated," I said. "Section E audit."

"Well, they were, of course, back when I joined the Farce. I've read the file, but it doesn't go beyond a few background checks, my parents and the commune's leaders. All harmless nuts."

"You want them to be more interesting than that."

"Dad was always hinting that the commune was part of something big. When I was old enough, I'd be brought into the inner circle."

I'd heard the story. "But you ran away anyhow."

"Along with most of my generation. Not many people under fifty there now." He tasted his coffee and added more hot. "That's typical of cults, once the charismatic leader dies or leaves. That was Randy Miles Brewer; he was pretty senile when I left."

"Dead now?" Elza said.

He shrugged. "Technically not. He's composting away in some LX center in San Francisco." The Life Extension centers could keep you going past legal brain death, in some states, as long as blood or some equivalent fluid kept circulating. "So tell me, who pays for that? It'd be a lot of eggs and cheese."

"You could subpoena their records," I said.

He waved it away. "Don't want to cause my parents any grief. In fifty years, it'll all be in some dusty file in Washington, or Sacramento. I'll look it up then."

"They might still be alive."

"Not with natural medicine. *Your* dad has a better chance at, what, ninety?"

"Ninety-two. He says he'll try to wait it out, but I don't think he'll try hard. That age, if you don't really enjoy life, you won't get much more of it."

"It feels strange," Elza said, her voice a little husky. "Saying goodbye to my granddad and g-ma. If I were staying on Earth, I might have twenty more years with them."

"Think of it as being social pioneers," Dustin said. "The social protocols of relativity. When you come back, you'll be thirteen years older. But your parents and grandparents . . ."

She broke the moment of silence by laughing, with an edge of hysteria. "Like it'll make any difference. Chances are . . . chances are we're not . . ."

"Elza," I said, "sweetheart—we ought to make it a rule: We don't talk about the end until it's near. There's no use plowing the same field over and over."

"I don't think that's healthy," Dustin said. "Ignoring reality. When you were in combat, you guys never talked about dying?"

I tried to be honest. "In the Faith War, no, not much. But we were all eighteen and nineteen, and felt immortal. When someone got killed, it was like a supernatural visitation.

"Gehenna was totally different. I mean, there were bodies everywhere you looked, so after a while they were just part of the scenery. It was more dangerous, I guess, with all the loonies and looters. But the corpses, they were like a dream landscape, a nightmare. They weren't individuals; you didn't see yourself becoming one of them." They nodded, as if they hadn't heard all this before. Turning points in life bring out the same old stories. Even among relativity pioneers.

This was the wrong place. It was becoming a fashionable hour for the rich and famous; the Four Seasons was filling up and getting loud with background chatter, people wanting to be noticed. We three, arguably the most-talked-about people here, definitely didn't want to be noticed.

Our identities hadn't been revealed, and wouldn't be, as long as friends and relatives cooperated, until we were safely in orbit.

We took the Fifth Avenue and SoHo slidewalks back, less for the time saved than from a desire to be part of a crowd. We dawdled at the entrance and transfer point so my bodyguard could catch up. When we got to the condo door, I gave him the good-bye signal, stroking an eyebrow twice.

"Same old signal," Dustin said as he palmed the night lock.

"Yeah. I'd change it if I thought someone might actually be after me. If somebody really wanted my ass, they'd have it by now."

"So you're wearing flared trousers for the look," Elza said.

"Force of habit." Once we were in the elevator, I pulled the ankle holster off.

"A .289," she said. "Not with legal rounds, I hope."

"Neuros." I'd never fired one at a person, but they were impressive on a dummy. Smart round that finds an eye and blows a small shaped charge across the frontal lobes.

"Jesus," Dustin said. "You got them where?"

I laughed, thumbing the door open. "Jesus had nothing to do with it."

"Boys and toys." Elza went by me, flopped down on the couch, and slipped her shoes off. "So I get to take an extra seven kilos of clothes?"

"Only sexy ones," Dustin said.

"I don't *have* seven kilos of the kind you like. That'd be about a hundred outfits."

I sat in the easy chair and picked up the balalaika and plucked an arpeggio.

"Say you're not taking the banjo?" Dustin said, with hope in his voice.

"No. I'll be in my sixties when we get back. Take it up seriously then, as a retirement project."

Elza laughed. "You'll retire about a year after you're dead."

I had a sudden impulse to throw the instrument against the wall, just to do something unpredictable. Instead, I set it gently against the bookcase. "I don't know. In a way, this is early retirement. Cleaned out my desk to embark on a new life of travel and adventure."

"Or stay in one room for thirteen years, trying not to go mad," Dustin said.

"There is that. I wonder whether they've packed enough strait-jackets."

Elza got up and went to the refrigerator. "Wine?" She poured two glasses of white wine and a small glass of vermouth for herself. Bunched them together in two hands and brought them over to the coffee table. "I'm kind of torn," she said. "Maybe go out to the Galápagos early, do some snorkeling."

Dustin held his glass up to her. "I'll catch up with you. Say good-bye to London and Paris, maybe Kyoto. Come from the other direction."

"City boy."

"Don't care much for the water. Fish fuck in it."

She arched an eyebrow. "People do, too."

"I'll wait for zero gee." He looked at me. "You've been there."

"It was all men. None of them appealed to me."

"I mean the Galápagos. Diving."

"Wasn't recreational. Bomb threat to the Elevator."

"I remember. The note said something about Gehenna."

"Someone in Personnel must have sat down and entered Gehenna/skindive/license to kill."

Elza sighed. "And I'm still on my learners' permit."

"Well, you've got four days. I could get you a quick transfer to the Zone. You'd get more experience in four days than I've had in twenty years."

"I'll think about it. Did you see many fish there?"

"Not so many pretty ones. You want to go into the shallows, the reefs near the shore, unless you're after big sharks."

"Maybe, maybe not."

"They're protected. If one bites you and gets sick, there's a huge fine."

"But you were there before," Dustin said.

"Twenty-five years ago, first wife. I could hardly get her out of the water, sharks and all."

"You think of her a lot," she said.

I tried to be accurate. "Her image comes to me often. I don't sit and dwell on the memory of her."

"I know that. I guess that's what I meant." She shook her head. "Crazy time."

"We're all dwelling on the past these days," Dustin said. "Leaving everything behind."

There was so much I didn't want to say. She gave me the Shakespeare book in the morning; at noon, she took one breath and died. Was it more or less horrible that it happened to so many at the same time?

"You're the philosopher," I said. "I'm more an engineer, cause and effect." Elza was watching me closely. I don't think I'd ever raised this directly with her before. "We were crazy in love, like schoolkids, and although I know it was all blood chemistry boiling away, brain chemistry . . . still, we were addicted to each other, the sight and sound and smell of each other, like a heroin addict to his junk . . ."

"Been there," Elza said.

"But you never lost anyone the way I lost her. Like a sudden traumatic amputation—worse, because you can buy a new arm or leg, and it will do."

"So that's what I am? Your—"

"No. It's not simple."

She picked at a nail, concentrating. "I had a friend lost a leg before she was twenty, AP mine in Liberia. She said the new one did everything she asked it to. But it was never really part of her. Just an accessory." She stood up. "I better pack some clothes." She put her glass in the refrigerator and went into the bedroom.

"For a diplomat," Dustin said softly, "you don't have an awful lot of tact."

"I don't have to be a diplomat with you and her. Do I?"

"Of course not." He got up and went to the fridge. "Cheese?"

"I just ate a whole bird."

"A little one." He set out five chunks of cheese, including half a wheel of Brie, and put them on a platter with some bread and a knife. "They won't have cows in *ad Astra*."

I sliced off a piece of something blue. "Not going to keep for fifty years," he said.

"Not much will." I was still seeing her. "Gehenna will just be a history lesson to most people."

He broke the lengthening silence. "Her name was Mira?"

"Moira. My father approved of her, nice Jewish girl. I think he's a little scared of Elza."

"Who wouldn't be?"

"*I'll* give you something to be scared of," she said from the bedroom, bantering, the hurt gone from her voice.

"Best offer I've had today," he said.

I didn't hear her walking up behind me, barefoot. She put both hands lightly on my head and tangled my hair with her fingers. "I'll sleep with Namir tonight."

"Okay by me," I said.

"We have to talk." She rubbed my temples. "You can love her. You will love her, always. But you have to leave her here. Here on Earth."

"I think that's already done." Literally, anyhow.

"We'll talk about it." She went back to the large bedroom.

I joined her there an hour later and we did talk. Moira was my generation, a year older than me, but forever young to Elza, and not much I could do about that.

She wanted to know what Moira and I had done that I didn't do with her, and I tried not to think of it as an invasion of privacy. Of course the big thing she couldn't do was have me as a twenty-five-year-old lad, and there was another thing I didn't mention, to preserve the woman's dead dignity. But I did describe a trick Moira would do with her breasts, and we were both happy and relieved when she made it work. Elza's a little self-conscious about her small breasts, as Moira was about her large ones. I decided not to bring that up.

While we lay there entwined, the diplomat in me affirmed that I could leave Moira here on Earth. I didn't say that part of me would stay with her, too; neither of us buried, neither dead.

I pretended to be asleep, as always, when she slipped away to join Dustin. Thinking furiously about the lies that grace our lives.

12

GROWING THINGS

The Martians came up a week after we did. We helped them unload their few packages. Earth-normal weight was oppressive to them, and they clumped around with exaggerated care. Well, it wasn't exaggeration. Like having to carry around a weight one and a half times as heavy as you are. Carry it for thirteen years with no relief.

Snowbird didn't complain, but her voice was unnaturally high and reedy. I doubt that they spoke much English on the way up.

I put my arm gently around her shoulders. "It's very hard, isn't it?"

"Hard for you, too, Carmen. You haven't been to Earth in a long time."

"I exercise in Earth gravity every day."

"I should do that," she said. "Become Earth-strong. By the time we return, the quarantine may be lifted."

Fly-in-Amber, behind us, made a dismal noise. "I have a better idea. Let's just go home. We can't live this way."

She gave him a long blast and high-pitched growl in consensus Martian, and he squawked and clattered back.

She turned back to me. "Perhaps we should rest in Mars territory for a while." They plodded off, muttering.

"Before long, they'll be in zero gravity," Paul said. "He'll complain about that, too."

✸

The last thing we would have to do before Paul cut us loose was to tape things down, mostly chairs. When we were flung away from the Space Elevator, we'd be in free fall, like someone jumping out of an airplane. But we would plummet for eleven days. Jostled every now and then by steering jets. That would be tomorrow.

The habitat didn't have any independent propulsion, of course, but it was firmly attached to the ship that would eventually be our landing vessel, much smaller. It would fly away like an eagle clutching an elephant.

Before that, we had to water the plants. We'd spent six days following the directions the hydroponic engineers had left behind, making sure all the root structures could be kept moist without water surrounding them. There was a water-absorbent granular medium held inside a fine-mesh net for each plant or group of plants. There was no automation in this temporary arrangement, of course. Every morning we'd spend an hour giving each plant a measured shot of water from a portable hydrator, a water pump with a hose and syringe.

The first morning, still in gravity, I split the chore with Dustin. It was interesting to get him alone; he usually deferred to Namir or Elza.

I had to ask him about his weird family, growing up. "I never gave it much thought," I said, "but isn't it strange that a person who winds up in espionage should have grown up in a commune, with anarchist parents?"

He laughed. "Not so odd. Like a kid whose parents are lawyers or cops might want to escape and become a bohemian artist.

"I didn't want to be a spy, anyhow. A philosophy degree doesn't open many doors, though. The Space Force paid through my doctorate in exchange for four years' service, which I thought was going to be in communications. You go where they send you, though. They needed engineers for communication."

"And philosophers for spookery?"

"It's a grab bag, intelligence. Not that they'd ever admit it, but it's where you go if you have education but no useful skills. The personnel database says there are three other philosophy Ph.D.s in intelligence. We ought to get together. Form a cabal."

"Namir says there are more officers in intelligence than any other part of the military."

He nodded amiably. "As if that were a good thing? It's been that way for a long time."

"I've never known a philosopher before. If it wasn't for the Space Force, what would you be doing?"

"Staying out of harm's way! You know, sit around, think deep thoughts. Beg for scraps."

"And teach, I suppose."

"And write papers that two or three people will read." The bush he was watering had tiny white flowers with a penetrating sweet smell. He bent down and breathed deeply, and read the label. "Martian?"

"Martian miniature limes. They tweaked the genes so it wouldn't be all branch, growing tall in Martian gravity. We'll see what it does in one gee."

"The past year and a half, I've been assigned to a think tank in Washington. All the services, multidisciplinary. The Ethics of Military Intervention."

"Any conclusions?"

He made a sound I'd come to recognize, a puff of air through his nose: amusement, contempt, maybe patience. "Under the present conditions . . . it's hard to justify most wars, anyhow, that aren't a purely defensive reaction to invasion. But now, with the Others threatening the whole human race with casual destruction? How does anyone justify a war against any human enemy?"

"Is that a question I'm supposed to answer?"

"No." He growled a string of foreign syllables. "That's Farsi: 'There is some shit a man does not have to eat.' Adapted from American English, I think, though the principle is widely spread."

"But it implies there's another kind of shit that a man does have to eat. Glad I'm a woman."

He smiled at me. "See? You're a philosopher already." He sniffed the lime flowers again. "Though living on recycled shit is something I tried to become philosophical about, before we came up."

"Hunger helps." It dominated the menu in Little Mars. The pantry machine broke up all organic waste, and some inorganic, and put it back together to make amino acids, then protein. Mixed in with measured amounts of carbohydrates and fiber and fat, some trace elements, it could produce blocks of edible stuff in programmed colors, textures, and flavors. "Elza said that Namir is a good cook. I wonder what he can do with pseudobeef and pseudochicken."

"Make pseudo–Beef Stroganoff and pseudo–Chicken Florentine, I guess." He sighed and leaned back against the lattice that would be supporting bean vines. "Carmen, what do you think our chances really are? Are we just wasting our time? Intuition, I mean, not science."

"I don't think you can do science without data. I do have an intuition, though, or an optimistic delusion." I sat down on the edge of the tank. "Do you know the story of the lucky chicken?"

"Tell me."

"Well, suppose you had a flat of fertilized chicken eggs—that's one hundred and forty-four—and you dropped the flat from waist height or shoulder height. Some eggs would break. Discard them and do it again, and again, until finally you have just one egg."

"The lucky egg."

"You're getting it. You hatch it and collect *its* fertilized eggs—"

"Unless it's a rooster."

"Then you have to start over, I guess. But you do the same thing, dropping them over and over until one survives. Then you wait for it to mature and collect *its* eggs. And again and again."

"I see," he said.

"Eventually, you will produce the luckiest chicken in the world. The version I heard, the benefactor was the pope. He put the chicken in a fancy papal chicken basket, and it never left his side. So nothing bad ever happened to him."

"This is not the last pope we're talking about, then."

"Not a *real* pope. Me, actually. I'm the lucky chicken."

"They dropped your mother from a great height?"

He was so much like Paul I could smack him. "Not that I know of. But ever since I got to Mars, I've had the most incredible luck. All 'The Mars Girl' crap. All kinds of trouble, and I always seem to come out on top. So maybe my main qualification for this job is as a talisman. Stay close to me, the way the pope stayed close to his lucky chicken."

He was nodding, looking serious. "You do believe in luck?"

"Well, at some level I suppose I do. Not in lucky charms, talismans. But just as an observation, sure. Some people seem to be lucky all the time, while others seem to be born losers."

"That's true enough. Something that statistics would predict."

"I suppose you could pretend to be scientific, and put the whole population on a bell curve, just like you would for height or weight. Normal people bulking up in the middle, the unlucky ones off to the left, the luckiest trailing off on the right."

"Ah *ha*!" He grinned and rubbed his beard. "There's your fallacy. You can only do it with dead people."

"What? Dead people have all run out of luck."

"No, I mean, all you can say of someone is after the fact: 'he was lucky all his life' or 'she was unlucky'—but a living, breathing person always has tomorrow to worry about. You could be the luckiest person in the world, in two worlds, in the whole universe. But some tomorrow, like the day you meet the Others, boom. Your 'luck' runs out, like a gambler's winning streak. And in that particular case, so does everybody else's."

"Are you always such an optimist?"

He picked up his hydrator, and we moved on to the next patch. "By Earth standards, America anyhow, I really *am* an optimist. You can define that as 'anyone who isn't suicidally depressed.' There may be free energy, but that doesn't translate into universal prosperity. Most people work at unsatisfying jobs with ambiguous or worthless goals and low pay, and anyhow, they're just marking time until the end of the world. Namir and Elza and I, like you guys, are in the unique position of being able to *do* something about it."

I was still living in a kind of double-vision world, the sanitized version that was broadcast (and which I sort of believed for years) versus the grim reality that was in Namir's newspaper. And America was far from being the worst off. The front-page picture in the last paper showed the Ganges, a clot of corpses from shore to shore. A block-wide funeral pyre in Kuala Lumpur, within sight of the proud old Twin Towers.

These were beets, four small plants per net bag, 50 ccs water each. I wouldn't touch beets as a girl, but in Mars I came to love them. Red planet and all. I mentioned that to Dustin.

He laughed. "I grew up in a vegetarian family. Beets were the closest thing I had to meat until I got off the commune."

"Bothers you to go back to veggies?"

"No, I just eat to fuel up. Pseudo–hot dogs with fake mustard, yum. Elza's about the same. Namir might go crazy, though."

"He likes his meat?"

"Fish, actually. He doesn't like to be far from the sea."

"He better take a good last look."

"On Mars, you had actual fish."

We said "in Mars," usually. "A pool of tilapia." They lived on plant waste.

"He was hoping."

"Guess we're not a big enough biome. It was marginal on Mars, a luxury, and we didn't have to deal with water at zero gee." I clicked on the notebook. "Twenty kilos of dried fish in the storeroom." The storeroom was already in place on the iceberg. It had five hundred kilos of luxury food. Including fifty liters of two-hundred-proof alcohol, more than enough for each of us to have two drinks a day.

"He can do something with dried fish, Spanish. Some kind of fritters."

His smile was interesting. "You really like him. I mean, apart from . . ."

"There's no 'apart from,' but yes. We're closer than I ever was with any of my natural family."

I wasn't sure how to interpret that. I wanted prurient details. "You knew Elza first, though."

"By a few weeks, maybe a month. By then it was obviously a package deal or no deal.

"I'd heard of Namir professionally, and was curious anyhow. We first met without her, very American, shooting pool."

"You beat the pants off him."

"Not a chance. He's a shark. Shows no mercy."

"You knew about him and Gehenna."

"In what way?" he said without inflection.

"That he missed the first part, and so survived the second."

"Oh, sure. He was about the highest-ranking officer of the Mossad in Israel, certainly in Tel Aviv, who survived."

That was interesting. "I wonder why he didn't press his advantage with that."

"How so?"

"He's still with the UN, isn't he? If he'd stayed in Israel—"

He laughed. "Smartest thing he ever did was go back to New York. Lots of ruthless people jockeying for position in the Mossad, with three-quarters of them suddenly gone. His turf in New York was safe. Besides, it's the place he loves best."

We moved on to the delicate celery plants. "There's an odd chain of circumstance that winds up putting the three of us here. As if we're collectively a lucky chicken—or an unlucky one."

"What makes you say that?"

"Like this . . . the Corporation wound up agreeing that they needed no more or less than three military people on the mission. So they sent the computers out sniffing for three military people who could live together in close quarters for thirteen years, getting along with four civilians at the same time, people who had a certain amount of academic training and professional accomplishment. They didn't want three men or three women, so as not to have one gender dominate on *ad Astra*."

"And they had to be spies, of course. Don't forget that."

"In fact, the probability that they'd come from intelligence was high. A person who'd spent his professional life shooting down planes or disarming bombs wouldn't be too useful. They wanted one of the three to be a medical doctor, too, who'd done general practice."

"We all agreed on that. Someone who could work without consultation."

"That may be what happened. The computer pulled out Elza, and she dragged me and Namir along."

"That could be it," I said. But computers have to be programmed, and it would be easy to start out with Namir and his mates and make sure they would be the ones the program selected. "I'd hold them like this." He was picking up the plant by its stalk; I slid my hand under the ball of medium and lifted it out.

"Right," he said. "Have to be careful with the babies."

"Were you going to have any?" I asked. "Before you got orders to waltz off into outer space and tilt with monsters?"

"Well, neither Elza nor Namir wanted any children. They're not that optimistic about the future. Immediate or distant. If it were up to me, yes, I'd like to watch one grow up. Help it grow up."

"Sort of a social experiment? A philosophical one?"

"Cold-blooded, I know. You have two?"

"Technically. They were born ex utero, though, for which my 'utero' is grateful. And they're being raised by the community, in Mars. Which I don't like much."

"You're so right. Speaking as someone who was raised by a commune. With my mother and father warned not to bond too closely."

"You didn't have a mother figure or father figure at all?"

"No. There was a couple in charge of children. But it was obvious we were just a chore. They were pretty harsh."

"That must have been rough. The two in charge of our kids are nice people; I've known them for years."

"Good luck. Ours were nice to adults."

We moved on to the carrots, frilly and delicate. "Working in Washington, did you commute every day?"

"No, I had a little flat in Georgetown. Go back to New York on Thursday night or Friday. Sometimes bring Elza back to DC if our schedules allowed. Sometimes I'd just go up overnight; it's only an hour and a half on the Metro."

"Best of both worlds."

"Started out that way. Washington's falling apart. Both the cities, actually. Less comfortable, more dangerous."

"Did you go armed?"

"No, I'm fatalistic about that. Elza had a gun, but I don't think she carried it normally. Namir usually did, and he had a bodyguard as well. But he was threatened all the time, and attacked once."

"In the city?"

"Oh, yeah, right downtown. Stepped off the Broadway slidewalk and a woman shot him point-blank in the chest. Somehow she missed his heart. She turned to run away, and the bodyguard killed her." He shook his head. "He got hell for that, the bodyguard. No idea who she might have been working for. No fingerprints or eyeprints. DNA finally tracked her down to Amsterdam; she'd been a sex worker there twenty years before."

"No connection with Gehenna?"

He shook his head. "And Namir says he's never used the services of a 'sex worker,' not even in Amsterdam. Men lie about that, but I'm inclined to believe him."

"Point-blank in the chest. That must have laid him low for a long time."

"Had to grow a new lung. Takes weeks, and it's no fun."

Another bit of mystery for the mystery man. "He's made other enemies, obviously, since Gehenna. Being a peacekeeper."

"Mostly in Africa. Very few pale beautiful blondes."

"It's not my field. But I assume you could hire one."

"Yes and no. In New York, you could rent a beautiful blond hit woman and probably specify right- or left-handed. But you can't hire someone so totally off the grid, not in America. If she ordered a meal in a restaurant, she'd get a cop along with the check, asking what planet she just dropped in from."

"It's gotten that bad?"

"Since Triton, yeah. But even then, a couple of years before that, America was . . . more cautious than most places."

"A police state, my mother said. She calls herself a radical, though."

He laughed. "She's no more radical than I am. From her dossier."

"You've read my *mother's* dossier?"

"Oh, sorry. You thought I was a lepidopterist."

"No, but . . . I assumed you'd read mine and everybody's . . ."

"I'm just nosy. And seven days is a long time to kill on the Space Elevator."

"So what about my father? Was he banging his secretary?"

"Nothing personal. Just blow jobs." He smiled at my reaction. "Bad joke, Carmen, sorry. Sometimes my mouth gets into gear a little ahead of my brain."

"I like that in a spy," I said, not sure whether I did. "Not so Earl Carradine."

"You see the last one?" he said. "Where he solves your little problem with the Others?"

"Haven't had the pleasure. What, he takes his Swiss Army knife and turns a bicycle into a starship?"

"No, he discovers the whole thing is a hoax, from a corrupt cabal of capitalists."

"Oh, good. We can go home now."

"It actually was a little clever this time. Not so much gadgets and gunplay."

I had to laugh. "Unlike real life. Where a beautiful blond mystery woman nails the spy as he steps off the Broadway slidewalk. For God's sake!"

"What can I say?" He injected the last carrot bunch. "Life does imitate art sometimes."

❊

We could've just stayed in the habitat for launch, which might have been fun. Suddenly detached from the Space Elevator, we'd be flung toward the iceberg at a great rate of speed, but the sensation to us would be "oops—someone turned off the gravity."

For safety's sake, though, all of us climbed through the connecting tube into the spaceship *ad Astra*. (We should come up with a separate name for the habitat. San Quentin, maybe, or Alcatraz.)

We helped the Martians get strapped into their hobbyhorse restraints—with all those arms, they still can't reach their backs—and then got into our own couches, overengineered with lots of padding and buckles. But that was for the landing, 6.4 years from now, at least. Paul didn't expect any violent maneuvers on the way to the iceberg. There were two course corrections planned right after launch, and unpredictable "refinements" as we approached the iceberg.

Paul had said to expect a loud bang, and indeed it was about the loudest thing I had ever heard. No noise in space, of course, but the eight explosive bolts that separated the habitat from the Elevator made the whole structure reverberate.

"Stay strapped in for a few minutes," he said, and counted down from five seconds. The attitude jets hissed faintly for a minute and stuttered. Then the main drive blasted for a few minutes, loud, but not as deafening as the bolts had been. I suppose it was a quarter of a gee or so, not quite Martian gravity.

"That should do it. Put on your slippers and let's go check for damage."

Our gecko slippers would allow us to walk, as if there were weak glue on our soles, down the ship's corridor, and through most of the habitat. The sticky patches on the walls and floor and ceiling were beige circles big enough for one foot. (You could squeeze both feet into one if you liked the sensation of being a bug stuck in a spiderweb.)

Those of us used to zero gee just sailed through the tube into the habitat, the others picking their way along behind us. Namir was game for floating through but banged his shoulder on the air lock badly enough to leave a bruise. He'd had a little experience before, in the military and of course getting from the Elevator to Little Mars, perhaps just enough to make him too confident.

My immediate concern was the plants. A small apple tree had gone off exploring and made it almost to the galley, and a couple of tomato plants had gotten loose. Meryl unshipped the hand vacuum and was chasing down the floating particles of medium before we had a chance to ingest them. I returned the apple tree to its proper place and re-planted the tomato vines.

The three spooks were doing the various things people do when they're getting used to zero gee—except barfing, fortunately. They practiced pushing off from surfaces and trying to control spinning. Once you get the hang of it, it's not hard to eyeball the distance to wherever you're going, and do a half turn, or one-and-a-half turn, to land feet-first. You can also "swim" short distances, but nobody needs that much exercise.

There was a very distinct look in Dustin's eye, and Elza returned it. I hoped it worked for them better than it does for most. (Paul and I first had sex in zero gee, and it worked all right. My first time with anybody, whatever the gravity, so it was a double miracle for me.)

Snowbird and Fly-in-Amber were clumsy in zero gee. The gecko slippers were less effective with them, since they had more inertia than humans—if I'm moving slowly and put my foot down onto a beige spot, it will stop me. Snowbird has four times my mass, though, and will rip off and keep going.

I went into Mars territory with her to check their garden, since it was easier for me to move around and manipulate things. It was dark and cold, as it was supposed to be. Their garden was simpler than ours; Martian tastes didn't run to a lot of variety.

Trays of stuff that resembled fungi and a few stubby trees. As on our side, one of the trees had come loose, but it was easy to retrieve and fix with duct tape.

A screen all along one whole wall was a panorama of their underground city, which was almost all of her planet she had ever seen. Though Mars wasn't "her" planet the way Earth was ours.

They had known for thousands of years that Mars was not their natural home. They only learned recently that they were put on Mars as a sort of warning system for the Others: when humans had advanced enough technologically to come in contact with the Martians, they were advanced enough to present a danger to the Others, even light-years away. Which led to the Others' attempt to destroy us, thwarted by Paul and the Martian leader Red. The cataclysmic explosion that was supposed to sterilize Earth only rearranged the farside of the Moon. Killing Red in the process.

So from one point of view, the Martians were humanity's saviors. Another point of view, more widely held, says that it was all the Martians' fault. (And since I was the first to come into contact with them, I shared the blame.)

After taking care of the garden, we went into the "compromise" lounge, not quite as dark and cold. There was a bench for humans to sit on, not of much utility in zero gee, and a skillful mural of the aboveground part of our Mars colony, a mosaic of pebbles from both Earth and Mars. It was special to me, made by Oz, Dr. Oswald Penninger, who had been my mentor when I first came to Mars.

I told Snowbird about it. "I met Dr. Oswald," she said. "I breathed for him." Oz had spent some time in the Martian city, measuring the metabolism of the various families.

"I miss him," I said. "He was one of my closest friends." He and Josie might have been on this expedition if the Corporation hadn't been pressured into taking three military people.

"It is difficult for us to gauge human personality. But I can understand why you would like Dr. Oz. He is interested in everything. Or should I say 'was,' as you did? He will not live long enough to see us again."

"I should have said 'is.' As long as the person is alive."

"He told me about Norway," she said, "where he studied art. I'd like to go there someday. It sounds a little like Mars."

"Maybe they'll do something about the gravity by then."

"I hope so. This is nice." She pushed up gently, rose to the ceiling, and floated back down. "But you are joking."

"Yes. Gravity's like death and taxes. Always with us."

"Not always. There's no gravity here, nor death, nor taxes. Not for some time. And when we take off for Wolf 25, it will be the ship's acceleration that presses us to the floor."

"Homemade gravity. You can't tell it from the real thing."

"Ha-ha. Dr. Einstein's Principle of Equivalence. A good joke."

Was it I who had made the joke, or Einstein? I decided not to pursue it.

Dustin came into the lounge, sideways and a little fast. He crashed into a wall with a modicum of grace.

"Good aim," I said. "You want to work on the speed."

He brushed himself off, rotating toward the center of the room. "Good aim if I'd been aiming for this door," he said. "Good afternoon, Snowbird. What's up?"

"Carmen helped us with a tree. Now we are discussing general relativity."

That raised his eyebrows a few millimeters. "A little beyond me. The math, anyhow. Tensor calculus?"

I had to come clean. "Don't ask me. I'm just sitting around being impressed. What is tensor calculus?"

"To me, it was a big 'stop' sign. I withdrew from the course and changed my major to philosophy. From physics."

"Pretty drastic."

"I try to be philosophical about it. Snowbird, your family is both, right? Science and philosophy?"

"Not in the sense of being scientists and philosophers, no. We don't experiment, traditionally. Not on things and not on ideas. I am in a small group that wants to change that. Which I think is why the others were glad to see me go.

"Traditionally, you know, we learn by rote. It's not like human physics and chemistry and biology. Things and processes are described in great detail, but those descriptions aren't tested, and the underlying relationships aren't studied."

"We'd call that Aristotelianism, in a way. If you had an Aristotle."

"I know. It was studying the ways you classify different methods of thinking that made some of us want to change the ways we think."

"*Some* of us who are not completely grown yet." Fly-in-Amber came drifting out of Mars territory. "Not completely sane . . ." He gently collided with me, as I put my other foot down on the beige spot to anchor us.

"Thank you. Snowbird was not yet two when you humans came. The novelty of it made a huge impression on her unformed mind."

"You will never win this argument, or lose it," Snowbird said. "I know you're wrong, and you know *I'm* wrong."

"And since you *are* wrong, that settles it." Fly-in-Amber crossed all four arms in a human-looking gesture. "That's logic."

Dustin stayed out of it, but I didn't. "Why does it have to be one or the other, Fly-in-Amber? Your science was fine in the old days, but it wouldn't get you off Mars."

"And to the planet of the Others, where we'll be destroyed along with everybody on Earth, and perhaps in Mars as well? That's not progress, Carmen."

"Not the example I would choose," Snowbird said.

"But it's relevant," I insisted. "Human science explained everything pretty well until we met you, and found you had this energy-out-of-nowhere thing. Now we have to fit you into our universe, just as you have to fit us into yours."

"How can you say that? If you hadn't stumbled onto us, we could have happily gone on for an eternity, or at least until the cows came home. If we had cows."

"Was that a joke, Fly-in-Amber?"

"Of course not. I am only trying to adapt to your idiom."

"He pretends not to have a sense of humor," Snowbird said, "which makes him even funnier."

"Idiom," Fly-in-Amber repeated. "Idiom is not humor."

"What does the philosopher say about that?"

He grinned. "I have enough for a monograph already."

"Humans do not understand this, and neither does Snowbird." Fly-in-Amber made a complex gesture that started him rotating. I reached out and stabilized him. "Thank you. It's not a concept that I can express in English, or any human language." He rattled off about thirty seconds of noises in the Martian consensus language. I recognized three clear repeated sounds—one for negation, one for "human," and one that signals an "if . . . then" statement.

Snowbird was totally still, absorbing it. "Can you translate?" Dustin said.

"Not exactly . . . no. But I could try to say part of it."

Fly-in-Amber put his small hands together and made a slight bow, perhaps a parody of human gesture.

"It's about the social function of humor in both races. As if humans were one culture." Fly-in-Amber barked, and Snowbird answered with a series of clicks. "He points out that you are essentially one culture, in Mars.

"From the first time we communicated—with Carmen, after we decided to let her know we spoke human languages—it's been obvious that humor both unites and separates the two species. Martian humor is almost always about helplessness, about fate and irony. Humans also recognize this, but most of your humor is about suffering—about pain, loss, death. To us . . . that preference itself is beautifully funny, and is even funnier as you think about it. Like a hall of mirrors, the images fading off into infinity.

"I'm not saying this well. But for most of us, humor is absolutely necessary for survival—if you lived in a small hole in the ground, and knew there would never be anything else, you would perhaps feel the same way."

"Sort of like what we call 'gallows' humor," Dustin said.

" 'Ask for me tomorrow,' " Fly-in-Amber quoted, " 'and you will find me a grave man.' " He said it with a British acting voice. "That was a BBC radio production of *Romeo and Juliet* in 1951. Very Martian humor. Mercutio has been stabbed, and he jokes about dying. Most human humor is not so clear to me."

"Nor as funny," Snowbird said. "So many jokes about people falling down, which is hardly possible with four legs. Sex jokes aren't funny because we have to figure out what the people are doing, and why that's more funny than what they normally do." She turned to Fly-in-Amber and made the thumping laughter sound. "Only two people! Only two!"

"Some of us don't think that's funny," Fly-in-Amber said. "They can't help the way they're made."

"Do you tell jokes about Martian sex?" Dustin asked.

Snowbird pantomimed scratching her head, which was kind of funny, avoiding all the eyes up there. "No . . . no fate or irony or helplessness there. What is there to laugh about?"

"Trust me," he said. "Humans find Martian sex pretty entertaining."

"But it's so plain and innocent, compared to human sex. We don't hide away and do it in private, and kill people if they do it with the wrong person."

"You'd never have a Shakespeare," I said.

"I think we do have individuals like Shakespeare," Fly-in-Amber said. "Though it would be difficult to explain, to translate, what I mean by that."

"I should think so. Since you don't seem to have anything like drama."

"Nothing dramatic used to happen to us, before you came. I suppose we're going to need drama now."

"And psychoanalysis," Dustin said. "Social workers. Police and jails."

"We look forward to evolving."

PART 2

THE PLANT

I

GRAVITY SUCKS

On Earth we'd seen pictures of the iceberg, and so didn't expect it to look like an iceberg, glistening and pure. I was once stationed in Greenland in the winter; it looked something like that, cold and dirty. Elza said it reminded her of North Dakota in the winter—windstorms drive dark topsoil to mix with blizzard snow to make a black substance they call "snirt," neither snow nor dirt.

It was the fossil nucleus of an ancient comet. Billions of years ago, Mars had bent the thing's orbit around, turning it into a small asteroid of ice and impurities, never to be warm enough to have its day in the sun and grow a magnificent tail.

So it was a huge dirty snowball, somewhat out of round. White splashes where engineers and their robots had blasted and drilled to turn it into a huge fuel tank. It provided reaction mass for the main drive and an array of small steering jets, mainly for turning us around at midpoint—and evading rocks, if it came to that.

Everything had been tested out; the main drive fired for several days, stopped, turned around, and fired again. Now we coasted in to meet it.

It was a death trap in several ways. The sheer amount of energy blowing out behind was like a continual thermonuclear explosion, and although stars do that for millennia on end, no machine has ever done it before—let alone for thirteen years. And it wasn't as straightforward as nuclear fusion or matter/antimatter annihilation; it was just the magic Martian energy sources stacked up, or nested, for a multiplicative effect. I didn't have the faintest idea why it worked, and its designers were only a couple of baby steps ahead of me. All we knew for sure was that the scale model had worked, going out a hundredth of a light-year and back, with one pilot/passenger.

It was like successfully testing a motorboat, and saying, okay, launch the *Titanic*.

Which brings up another actuarial disaster waiting to happen: what if we hit something on the way?

It wouldn't have to be another iceberg, real or metaphorical. Going at 0.95 the speed of light, a fist-sized rock would be like a nuclear bomb. We did have an electromagnetic repeller to keep interstellar dust from grinding us down to a sliver. But it wouldn't work on anything as big as a marble.

Bigger things we could sense at a distance, and avoid with a quick blip from the steering jets, which explains our lack of fine glassware and china. Though if our cosmological models were right, such encounters would be rare. If we were wrong, it would be a bumpy ride.

There had been no serious problems with the test run. But we were going twenty-four hundred times farther.

Four engineers were still living on the iceberg. They would get us screwed down tight into the ice and connect our habitat with the storage area, where they'd been living the past ten months. Have to check the caviar and vodka supplies. (Actually, the modifications that allowed them to live there made the storage building a de facto alternate living area, if something made *ad Astra* uninhabitable, and if we somehow survived that event.)

We'd been talking with them for days, via line-of-sight laser modulation, and were glad to be able to aid them in a small conspiracy.

The plan was supposed to be that we not make physical contact with them, because they were all from Earth, and we were all quarantined because of exposure to Mars and Martians. They'd been talking it over, though, and decided to come say hello and be contaminated. Then they'd go back to Little Mars instead of Earth and wait for a chance to hitch a ride on to Mars. Which seemed like a better prospect than their home planet.

All four of our resident semi-Martians thought they'd be welcome, thumbing their collective nose at Earth. Of course, the two actual Martians didn't understand why anyone would want to live on Earth in the first place. All that gravity. Humans everywhere.

Paul brought us in smoothly, a couple of small bumps. The comet didn't have any appreciable gravity, of course, so it was more a docking maneuver than a landing.

The robots had carved out a rectangular hole in the ice, two meters deeper than the habitat was tall. Paul nudged us in there, and the robots slid blocks of ice and dirt in place over us, a kind of ablative protective layer. He detached the small lander and inched it onto the surface. A flexible crawl tube connected the ship's air lock with ours.

Paul swam through in a space suit, followed by the four engineers. We were all wearing our usual motley, so the five of them looked like an Invasion of the Space People movie.

They all popped out of their suits as quickly as possible, Carmen aiding Paul and the engineers unscrewing each other. They were two couples, Margit and Balasz from Hungary and Karin and Franz from Germany.

They were wearing skinsuits, of course. Margit filled hers in a spectacular way, but Karin was more attractive to me, compact and athletic like Elza. As if there were any scenario where that would make a difference. ("Oh, a Jew," she says in my dreams, speaking German—"Let me make up for World War II.")

Margit spread her arms and inhaled hugely, starting a slight rotation. "Ah! Martian air. I feel so deliciously contaminated."

We shook hands all around and made introductions, though we'd met on-screen. Snowbird and Fly-in-Amber came floating tentatively out of the darkness.

The four newcomers were somewhat wide-eyed at the apparitions, but Balasz croaked and whistled a fair imitation of a greeting.

"The same to you and your family," Snowbird said. "You are almost correct."

"Not bad for a human," Fly-in-Amber grumbled. High praise.

"This is so huge," Karin said, apparently of the farm. "How many species?"

"About three dozen," Meryl said, "with another dozen to be planted in a few months. And eight Martian varieties."

"It will make it easier," Franz said. "Playing with your food. The same meals over and over can drive you crazy."

Paul laughed. "Make you do irrational things, like give up Earth for Mars."

All four of them smiled. "Definitely," Karin said. "Though it might depend where on Earth you call home."

"I will miss New York," I said. "Though it's not exactly the simple life."

"Mars has plenty," Paul said. "Small-town life, but something new every day, every hour. Trade with you in a minute."

Karin shook her head. "No, I'm not that great a pilot. You can keep your starship."

"So when are you going to tell them?" Carmen said.

Karin and Franz exchanged glances. "Actually, we were waiting to get your opinion," he said.

"A pity we aren't a little farther out," I said. The outer limit for line-of-sight transmission was set at four hundred million kilometers, the maximum distance between Earth and Mars, and we were still within that.

"It is," Franz said. "They'll know we've been withholding the fact."

"You ought to wait until the last minute," Carmen said. "Don't give them time to round up a bunch of lawyers."

"The worst they can do is shoot you down," I said, "but I don't think they can afford to waste a spaceship."

Paul agreed. "They'll fine you the expense of decontamination and the flight to Mars. But since there's no money on Mars, all they could do is seize your assets on Earth."

"Which aren't much," Karin said.

"None from us, of course," Margit said. Hungary was part of the Cercle Socialisme.

"It would be courteous to give them enough warning, so they don't send up an 'uncontaminated' Space Elevator."

Moonboy held up a hand. He hadn't spoken before. "Wait. You're missing the obvious." Everybody looked his way. "Just lie to them. Make up some story about how you were forced to come aboard *ad Astra*. Medical problem or something."

"Of course," Balasz said. "Once one was exposed to Martian-ness, we might as well all be, since we all have to go back together."

"Could you cooperate with us in this ruse?" Margit said.

There was a general murmur of assent. "I cannot lie," Fly-in-Amber said. "It is not a matter of choice for me. My function is to record things as they happen."

"My function," Snowbird said, "is to sit on you if you open your mouth. You have to record everything, but you don't have to communicate it to everybody. Least of all to humans on Earth."

"True enough." He turned to the engineers. "I do not have lips. But my orifice is sealed."

Snowbird turned to Carmen. "See? He doesn't know."

So we manufactured a credible medical crisis, choosing Karin because she was the pilot. We gave her severe bronchitis that didn't respond to their ship's primitive treatment, and so she had to spend a few days in our infirmary. Actually, she was outside most of the time, helping the other three finish battening down the hatches.

We took pleasure in their company for the eight days they remained on the iceberg, enjoying the last contact with people from outside our circle. I'm sure that Elza enjoyed more than social intercourse with Balasz, a warm and handsome man. Dustin and I exchanged a raised eyebrow or two over it. Under the circumstances, it would have been surprising if she had kept her hands to herself.

(Dustin, I think, had more than a passing interest in Margit, but would never initiate a liaison himself. I've told him that if Adam had waited for Eve to ask, none of us might be here. But he remains diffident.)

We said our good-byes, and they "cast off," drifting a few kilometers behind the iceberg, well out of the line of fire. They were sending a record of our launch to Earth, and also to Paul—though if anything serious went wrong, I'm not sure what he could do.

It took all morning to secure the plants, some of which would be glad to have gravity again. Beans and peas were going totally schizophrenic in zero gee, with no up or down. Carrots had started growing beet-shaped.

After everything was secured and misted, we crawled and glided up into the ship and strapped in. I'd wanted to stay down in the habitat, taped into one of the chairs, but Paul talked me out of it with one pained expression. For the most daredevil pilot ever to elude a miniature supernova, he's an extremely cautious man.

We were all nervous when he pushed the LAUNCH button; only a fool would not have been. If there was any noise or vibration, I didn't sense it (though Snowbird said she did). Perhaps the sensation was too subtle compared to the sudden clasp of gravity. Acceleration, technically.

It seemed greater than one gee, though of course it wasn't. It also seemed "different" from real gravity in some indefinable way, as if (which we knew to be true) the floor was aggressively pushing up at us. Relativistic heresy.

After about five minutes, Paul said "Seems safe," and unbuckled. If something had gone wrong, we could theoretically have blasted off in this lander and left ad Astra behind. Go back to Earth and start over.

I undid my seat belt and levered myself up, trying not to groan. I'd been desultory on the exercise machines, which were awkward in zero gee. Time to pay the piper now.

Dustin did groan. "I'm going on a diet."

"We don't want to hear any Earth people complain," Fly-in-Amber said, inching painfully toward the air lock. "You are built for this."

"So are we," Snowbird said. That was true; they were overengineered for Martian conditions. But then they would have inherited the Earth, if the Others' grand plan had succeeded.

They had both been spending two hours a day in the Earth-normal exercise rooms in Little Mars, but that didn't make the change welcome. In an open area, we can help them get along, offering an arm or a shoulder, but in the spaceship aisle and the tube connecting the air locks, they had to crawl along on their own.

"I'll bet the Others have a way around this gravity," Snowbird said. "We should have asked them while we had their attention."

"We had our fill of their attention," Fly-in-Amber said. "Besides, they live in liquid nitrogen, floating like fish in Earth's water. They don't care about gravity."

I'd never thought of that. We didn't really know what they looked like, so my image was of crystalline or metallic creatures lying almost inert under the cryogenic fluid.

"I want to go to Earth and see the water," Snowbird said. "I want to wade in the sea."

"Things go well, you probably will," I said. "Surely the quarantine can't last another fifty-some years."

"For a spy, you're a hopeless optimist," Carmen said. "I don't suppose you're a betting man as well."

"If the odds are right."

"Then I'll bet you a bottle of whisky—good single-malt Scotch whisky, bottled this year—that the quarantine will still be in place when we return. If we do."

"A fifty-year-old bottle?" Maybe half a month's pay. "I'll accept the wager. Even against the Lucky Chicken—*especially* against her, so I can lose."

"You lose, and everybody wins. Quarantined, but alive."

After a few minutes of walking around, mostly checking plants for damage, all of us probably felt like lying down. I fought the impulse by going to the exercise machines. At least I could sit down on the stationary bicycle. Watch the water splashing into the pool. In a couple of hours, it would be full; I looked forward to cooling off in it.

I wondered whether the Martians would try it. Their underground lakes were shallow and muddy, and I couldn't remember any reference to their using water recreationally. It was pretty rare stuff.

They didn't wash for personal hygiene. They used flat scrapers, like ancient Roman athletes, the residue stirred into water that would be used for agriculture.

I got up and went back down the yellow corridor to the pantry, to see what I could put together for our first shipboard meal. (I hadn't attempted cooking in zero gee.)

It was cold, maintained about ten degrees above freezing in the main area. Forty below in the "freezer," which of course was heated up to that relatively balmy temperature, from the iceberg's ambient coldness, about three degrees above absolute zero.

I'd spent hours studying the pantry's organization and modifying it according to some logic and aesthetic that was arcane even to me. "This is the way I want it" was what it boiled down to. I would be the one spending the most time down here.

I took a basket and collected what I would need for a pasta dish that would resemble spaghetti and meatballs, comfort food, though there was no actual meat, and I assumed the spaghetti would have to be done in a pressure cooker. The air pressure was like Little Mars, about equivalent to nine thousand feet in altitude; boiling water wouldn't cook fast.

I filled bottles with olive oil and wine concentrate, which I'd keep in the kitchen. No sense in making wine out of it for cooking; the alcohol would just boil off anyhow.

It would be a month before I had any fresh vegetables or herbs. But I did have dehydrated tomatoes, mushrooms, and onions in resealable jars, and flash-frozen green beans and corn for a side dish.

Moonboy came in with two-liter flasks for wine. They had lines marked for 130 ccs of alcohol and 50 ccs of concentrate; he chose Chianti when I told him what we were having. Some bureaucrat had set up the alcohol supply so you had to type in your initials and the quantity dispensed—or you could type in "communal," as Moonboy did. Mr. Communal might wind up being quite a lush.

Nobody'd said anything about limits. Would you be cut off if the machine decided you were drinking too much for a pilot, or a doctor? For an out-of-work spy?

The wines we'd made in Little Mars that way weren't too bad. The water has more oxygen dissolved in it than normal air would provide, and the theory was that it gave it a "brighter" taste. Whatever, I could live with it. I enjoy fine wine but will take any old plonk rather than nothing.

(In the desert, we boy soldiers made a horrible wine out of raisins and cut-up citrus, with bread-making yeast. I still can't look at raisins.)

There was a lot of floor space beyond the pantry, which took up less than a quarter of the storage warehouse. The rest was a combination of replacements for things we knew would wear out, like clothes, and tools and raw materials for fabricating things we hadn't predicted needing.

Like weapons, I supposed. We made a point of saying that the mission was peaceful and unarmed. But when I floated through the warehouse and its large semisentient machine shop, I saw that it wouldn't take much inventiveness or skill to put together individual projectile and laser weapons and small bombs.

It was unlikely that any conventional weapon would have a nontrivial effect on the Others. But they might not be the only enemies out there. Sooner or later, we'd have to talk about that. I would just as soon not be the one to bring it up, though.

All that stuff waiting for something to go wrong made me wonder whether we might have traded in one of our xenologists, or even a spy, for a gifted tinkerer. We had engineers in a couple of flavors, and smart machines to do their bidding. But could any of those engineers take a blade to a piece of wood and carve a useful propeller out of it? An oar? I could, of course. But that's not like having someone who would say, "You don't need a propeller. This is what you need."

I added a frozen cherry pie to the basket and a quart of something supposedly resembling ice cream. By the time I got to the kitchen, everybody was relaxing with a drink in the dining room or the study. Moonboy was intently playing the piano, silent with earphones, studying a projected score. Snowbird was standing by the small bookshelf, studying one of the few physical books we'd brought along.

Had to get used to their standing all the time. There are no social signals in their posture that I can recognize. When are they relaxing? Does the term have any meaning to them?

I set the stuff out in proper order on the work island, and put the pseudomeatballs in the microwave to thaw, then poured a glass of reconstituted Chianti. Not really bad. Asked the screen for pressure-cooking directions, and it said at this "altitude" I didn't have to pressure-cook pasta; it just took longer. Okay; filled the pot three-quarters with water and added a little salt and oil, and put it on high.

My skin seemed to relax on my body, blood pressure coming down. I had so missed this plain thing. Whenever we were in a situation where it was possible, cooking was my main relaxant and restorer. Neither Elza nor Dustin did much cooking, though they had their specialties. Dustin's Texas chili was a possibility here, but Elza's skill with sushi was unlikely to be of use, unless we met some edible aliens. She could handle tentacles.

For two summers before I joined the kibbutz in Israel, my aunt Sophie hired me to do "dog work" in her New York restaurant, Five Flags. I did a lot of vegetable chopping and some simple *sous-chef* things, and was exposed to basic techniques in French, Spanish, Italian, Portuguese, and Chinese cooking. College and combat took me away from that world, and I never pursued it professionally, nor actually wanted to. That might make it too serious, no longer relaxing.

Meryl came over and refilled her glass. "Can I help?"

I measured some water into the dehydrated onions. "Nothing much to do, I'm afraid. I would love to have an onion to chop."

"Not for a month or so." She looked out over the hydroponic farm, more white plastic than greenery. "When we left Mars for Little Mars, I didn't think I'd miss it, working with the plants."

"No green thumb?"

"Well, no enthusiasm. I thought the 'ag hours' were somebody's bright idea for morale. But I did grow to miss it, in Little Mars. One thing to look forward to, here."

I nodded. "You're not looking forward to six years of leisure? Or twelve?"

"Sure." She retreated into thought, expression momentarily vacant. "I had an elaborate course of research planned, the thing we talked about the other day."

I remembered. "Delphinic and cetacean pseudosyntax."

"The more I think about it, the more futile it seems. No new data, no experimental subjects. I could work like a dog for twelve years while everybody else in the field is working for fifty. I come up with some brilliant insight and find it's been old news for thirty years. People are having tea with whales and sex with dolphins."

"Better than the other way around."

"If you haven't tried it, don't knock it."

The meatballs dinged, and I took them out. "It seems to me your work would have value as methodology even if people on Earth came up with different results, with newer data." I touched a couple, and they were thawed, still cool.

"Too abstract. I mean, you're right, but eventually it would be old data pushed around by outdated methodology. Xenolinguistics is moving fast now that we have actual xenos."

"None of us will be doing anything on the cutting edge." I poured a little oil into a large pan and put it on to heat. "Can't beat relativity."

Even if communication with Earth were completely unrestricted, you couldn't stay current with research. At turnaround, three years and a couple of months from now by ship time, twelve years would have passed on Earth. If you sent a message there to a colleague who answered immediately, the answer would get to Wolf 25 almost thirty-seven Earth years later. Not so much communication as historical record.

I shook the wet onion flakes into the oil, and they sizzled and popped. The cooking-onion smell was intense but faded in seconds in the thin air.

"Smells good." She leaned back against the island and took a sip of wine, then sighed. "I just haven't been admitting it to myself. I should table the cetacean stuff till I get back to Earth. Little Mars, anyhow. Join the crowd and study the Martian language."

"Makes sense," I said.

"I resisted it back on Mars because I didn't have any special talent for it. But neither did Carmen, and she's making headway."

"At least you'll be carrying your research materials along with you."

"If they cooperate. Fly-in-Amber isn't happy about being source material, I can tell that already."

I shrugged. "He's studying us. Turnabout's fair play."

"I'll point that out to him."

I shook the onions around in the pan and slid the meatballs into it.

She laughed. "They're subtle, the yellow ones. As he says, he can't lie. But he's very careful in the kinds of truth he shares."

"You've known him awhile?"

"Sure, since he came to Little Mars, '79. I'm not sure I know him any better than the day we met, though."

"He acts as if he's just a recording device."

"Yeah, that's his pose. But he's a lot more complicated than that. Mysterious. Talk to Snowbird about him sometime. He's more strange to her than *we* are."

"Really." I drew a liter of water and dumped the tomato and wine concentrates in it.

"That's what she told me, in those words. All the yellow family . . . she says they act as if they're the only ones who are really real. The rest of us, we're just a dream."

"They're *all* delusional?"

"Maybe. Snowbird thinks it may be true."

I smiled at that, but at the same time had a little twist of something like fear. "If you *were* a dream, would you be aware of it?"

She looked straight at me, not smiling. "Not if the dreamer knew his business."

2

YEAR ZERO

The Corporation asked us all to keep daily diaries, and gave us a program guaranteed to keep them private until fifty years after the last one of us has died. Our privacy guarded, I suppose, by the Tooth Fairy and Santa Claus.

I'll pretend they're telling the truth, and anyhow I don't have a lot to hide. I admit that I pick my nose when no one is looking. I don't like my body very much. I prefer masturbation to sex with my husband. I'm jealous, and a little bit afraid, of Elza, and trust her not at all. She will have every man on this boat, then come after the women. But it's not as if I don't have fantasies about her men. One of them, anyhow.

I've started writing because the trip has officially begun. We started blasting today. What a verb, as if we were miners. But it's accurate; we're standing on top of a matter/antimatter bomb that will keep exploding for 12.8 years plus.

Trying to get used to Earth-strength gravity. I asked Paul how long it would take if we accelerated with Mars-normal gravity. He said he couldn't do hypogolic cosines or something in his head, then fiddled with his notebook and said it wouldn't work; it would take umpty-ump years to get there; umpty-less-ump, but long, in our time frame. But we might get there with our backs intact. I can't find any way to stand that doesn't make my back hurt.

Part of the problem is associative dissonance, how nice to have a college education and have names for everything. My body feels this gravity and thinks I should be in the gym in Little Mars; an hour of sweat, then back to normal. But this *is* normal; all through human history people put up with weighing this much. So settle down, back, and get used to it.

(later) I heard splashing; the pool finally filled. Took a towel over. Namir had the current on and was swimming in place.

I'd never seen him naked. He looks good for a man his age. Solid muscles and only a little paunch. A lot of hair. He's circumcised, something I'd only seen in pictures. It makes him look vulnerable. It also makes his dick look longer, or maybe it just is longer. I'll have to ask Paul. Or maybe not.

The timer rang, and he got out. I would like to report that his vulnerable penis sprang instantly erect when I stepped out of my robe, but alas it just sat there. Perhaps he's seen a naked woman or two before. Maybe even one with tits.

The water was cold but felt good, and I warmed up fast with the current at six knots. Turned it down to one for the backstroke. Namir did glance at my frontal aspect, cunt-al, but then politely turned away. I had a wicked impulse to tease him but don't feel that I know him well enough. Which is odd, after all these weeks. But he's a formal, quiet man. He jokes and laughs when it's appropriate; but when he's by himself, he looks like he's thinking about something sad.

Which of course he must be. He walked through Tel Aviv right after

Gehenna, millions of his countrymen dead and rotting in the desert sun. What could anyone learn, or do, or believe, to get over that?

He told us that two of the men under his command killed themselves that first day. Shot themselves. He said that like he was describing the weather.

But I think his calm fatalism gives us all a kind of strength. We will probably die on this trip. The trick is to say that without being brave or dramatic. We will probably have powdered eggs for breakfast. We will probably die in five years and three months. Pass the salt, please.

Namir cooked his first dinner last night, and it was pretty good, considering the restrictions he's working under. Spaghetti with meatless meatballs, with reconstituted vegetables that weren't too mushy. Before long we'll all be staring at the hydroponic garden chanting "grow, grow."

Actually, we'll all be doing something more or less constructive. We talked about that after dinner. Paul's continuing his VR course work for a doctorate in astronomy and astrophysics, to complement his geology degrees. Elza is studying trauma medicine, and also does abstract needlepoint and God knows what kind of bizarre sex. Dustin says he doesn't have to actually *do* anything. A philosopher by training, he might burst into thought at any moment. He's also practicing trick shots on the pool table, though I don't know how long that will last. Elza asked him to limit the noise to ten minutes at a time, preferably once a year.

Moonboy is a good pianist, huge hands, but he usually plays silently, with earphones. He's writing a long composition that he began when he left Mars. He's a xenologist, of course, like Meryl and me, so we have plenty to do, getting ready to meet the Others. Meryl also does word and number puzzles with grim seriousness. Taped to her wall she has a crossword puzzle that has ten thousand squares.

Namir does woodwork as well as cooking; he brought some fancy wood and knives from Earth. He also studies poetry, though he says he hasn't written any since he was young. He works with formal poetry in Hebrew and Japanese as well as English; his job title at the UN before Gehenna was "cultural attaché." I wonder how many people knew he was a spy. Maybe they all did. He even looks like a spy, muscular and handsome and dark. He moves with grace. I sort of want him and sort of don't.

The Martians weren't in on the after-dinner conversation; they rarely join us for meals. They don't eat human food and perhaps they're uncomfortable watching us consume it. But I'm pretty sure that their answer to "What do you plan to do for the next six and a half or thirteen years?" would be "Same as always." They're born into a specific social and intellectual function and don't deviate much.

Fly-in-Amber's yellow family are recorders; they simply remember everything that happens in their presence. They're weirdly acute and comprehensive; I could fan a book's pages in front of Fly-in-Amber and immediately afterward—or ten years after—he could recite the book back to me.

Snowbird's white clan is harder to pin down. They classify things and visualize and articulate relationships. They're naturally curious and seem to like humans. Unlike Fly-in-Amber's family, I have to say.

Every kind of Martian has remarkable verbal memory. They're born with a basic vocabulary, evidently different for each family, and add new words just by hearing them. They have no written language, though human linguists are making headway on that. Meryl and Moonboy and I are adding to an existing vocabulary of about five hundred words and wordlike noises, with help mainly from Snowbird. Meryl is best with it; she worked with porpoise and whale communication, inventing phonemelike symbols for repeated sounds.

We'll never be able to speak it; it's full of noises that people can't make, at least not with the mouth. But Moonboy believes he can approximate it with a keyboard in synthesizer mode, with percussion, and fortunately Snowbird is fascinated by the idea and willing to work with him hour after hour, tweaking the synthesizer's output.

This doesn't read much like a diary. I remember my freshman year, on the way to Mars, studying the London journals of Pepys and Boswell. But Pepys was wandering around his ruined city, and Boswell had Dr. Johnson to write about, then going down to London Bridge for his whores. The professor said Boswell had a condom made of wood. That's stranger than Martians.

We need a Boswell or a Pepys instead of, or along with, this ragtag bunch of scientists and spies. The huge tragedy of London's collapsing under fire and plague is small, compared to eight billion human beings snuffed out for being human.

3

RECORD

The sponsors of the Wolf 25 expedition required that each of us keeps a record of our experience, but left the form of that record up to the individual. Mine will be a note to you, my imaginary friend. You are very intelligent but don't happen to know what I'm about to say, and so are eternally interested.

This is the record kept by General Namir Zahari, originally commissioned by the Mossad, an intelligence arm of the Israeli army. I am joined by American intelligence officers Colonel Dustin Beckner and Colonel Elza Guadalupe, to both of whom I am married.

There are no other military personnel on the mission. There are two native Martians, Snowbird (of the white clan) and Fly-in-Amber (of the yellow), and four humans with Martian citizenship. The pilot, Paul Collins, resigned a commission in the American Space Force in order to come to Mars. He is married to Carmen Dula, who was the first person to meet the Martians and is circumstantially responsible for the complications that ensued.

Though let me record here that any contact with humans would ultimately have resulted in the same unfortunate sequence of events; the Others apparently had the whole scenario planned for tens of thousands of years.

If you look at this as a military operation, which in a sense it is, it is the most ambitious "attack" ever launched. All of the energy expended in all of the wars in modern history wouldn't propel this huge iceberg to Wolf 25 and back. Even with free energy, it's more expensive than World War II.

If it's the most expensive such project, it may also be the most ambiguous. We don't have the slightest idea of what we will face there, or what we will do. By far the most probable outcome will be that the Others will destroy us long before we're close enough to harm them.

But we cannot do nothing. Once they realize we thwarted their attempt to destroy humanity, they will simply do it again, even if it takes centuries.

The fact that the Others are so mind-numbingly slow does not really work to our advantage. Our experience with them in the Triton "demonstration"—and what the Martian leader Red found out about them—indicates that they plan ahead for many contingencies, and their machines react automatically when conditions are right. The concept of "Wait—hold your fire!" probably is not in their repertoire.

The small robot ship that precedes us may be our best hope. It will start broadcasting from right before turnaround, and so the message will get there long before we arrive. It will explain in detail what our situation is and plead that they let us approach and talk.

We hope they will not vaporize it as soon as it is detected.

We do know they understand and "speak" English, though there would be no such thing as a conversation between one of them and one of us. You could ask a yes-or-no question and would have to wait half an hour for a reply, unless they had a machine set up to interpret the question and deliver a prerecorded or cybernetically generated answer.

The last message we got from Triton was evidently one of those: "I am sorry. You already know too much." Then Triton exploded with sixteen hundred times the energy output of the Sun, a fraction of a second after the Other sped back to Wolf 25 with tremendous acceleration. Then it tried to use Red in a delayed-action attempt to destroy life on Earth. But the Martian gave up his own life instead.

(It was not so great a sacrifice, in an absolute sense, since he would have died anyhow, along with life on Earth. But it's touching and heartening that he would go against the will of his creators in our favor. He was able to defeat his own programming to make a moral choice, which gives us a small wedge of hope.)

Carmen is of the opinion that even if the Others destroy this vessel, the *ad Astra*, the fact that we came in peace could work in the human race's favor. I didn't publicly disagree with her, but that's naively optimistic. The flag of truce is at best an admission of weakness. It can also be the first warning of a desperate attack, when your opponent has little strength and nothing to lose.

I think that if they allow us to approach their planet, or some surrogate planet, it will be to evaluate our strength. Probably just prior to destroying us.

But that's a human soldier talking. Soldier, diplomat, and spy. I have no idea what action their godlike psychology might produce. Carmen could turn out to be the pessimist. They'll apologize for trying to exterminate everybody—"What were we thinking?"—and send us back home laden with treasure and praise. And pigs will fly.

At any rate, they hold all the cards, and we don't even know the name of the game. We have a little over five years to think about it and agree on a course of action. If we don't agree, I suppose the majority will rule.

Or the strongest minority.

4

WEIGHTY MATTERS

The humans said I must keep a written diary of this expedition, which I complained was ridiculous, since all I am is a living, breathing diary. But what if I died? they asked. I never think in those terms, since when I die the nonredundant parts of my memory will be passed to my successor. But in fact I might be physically obliterated out here, something that has not happened to a member of my family for 4362 ares. A certain amount of knowledge was lost that day, unrecoverable. So I have to agree with them, and am writing this down, though it is unutterably slow and imprecise, and includes the labor of translation, since we have no written language.

English is their language, so I will use it, though French and Russian are easier for me to speak, since they have more sounds like our own.

Not speaking my own language depresses me. Snowbird is missing her "white" language, too, perhaps more than I miss mine; theirs is prettier, if less accurate. The consensus language we're constrained to use lacks both qualities. And English is unspeakable. Namir, my favorite human here, can converse with me in Japanese, which is the most pleasant human language I know.

This is the first of May, 2088, the last day when our clocks and calendars will be the same as those on Earth and Mars. When we reach turnaround, halfway to our target, it will be August 13, 2091, on the ship, but back on Earth it will be July 2, 2100, almost nine years later. They say this is because of general relativity, though it makes no sense to me. They say our clocks run faster because we are moving, and although I know it's true, it also makes no sense to me. Snowbird seems to understand it somewhat. She told me that little t, which is our time, is equal to c over a times the hyperbolic cosine of a over c times Earth time, which is big T. I suppose it's true, but all I have to do is remember it. I think if I had to understand it, my brain would overheat and explode.

We have been accelerating for eight hours, and I think it will be eight *years* before I get used to it, if ever. It is like carrying more than your own weight on your back. The instant it started, I had to shit. That's an impolite word, for some reason, but is the closest human word to what we do. I went as fast as I could, which was slowly, into our living area, to the patch of dirt we use for recycling our toxins. Snowbird was already there, being younger and stronger, but she respected my seniority and allowed me to step in first. The extra gravity did accelerate the process, which is the only good thing I can say about it.

I told the pilot, Paul, that I thought it was unfair, and asked him why we couldn't accelerate at Mars gravity, so everyone would be comfortable. He said it would take us more than two years longer to get there. I said if we're all going to die when we get there anyhow (as Namir says), then I should think he would want to take more time, not less. He laughed and said I was right, but he didn't turn down the acceleration. Perhaps he can't. It's all very strange, but I have been dealing with humans almost from the beginning, and nothing surprises me anymore.

I should say something about the Others, toward whose planet we are recklessly speeding. They created us Martians, evidently twenty-seven thousand Earth years ago. We are biological machines, as are humans, but humans are not in agreement as to who designed them.

The Others had observed humans evolving into tool-using creatures, then fire-using, and thought it was only a matter of time before they had starships and would present a danger.

Often this is not a problem, the Others say, because when a race discovers nuclear energy, it usually destroys itself before it develops starflight.

I take it we Martians were a mistake, overall. We did fulfill our major function, which was to notify the Others that humans had developed the ability to go to a nearby planet. Then we, the yellow family, did as we had been programmed and delivered a coded message to the humans, which gave them the basic facts about the Others.

One individual Other had been waiting in the solar system for twenty-seven thousand years. His main function was to watch how the humans responded to this new knowledge and decide whether to let them live. He decided they should not live, but the automatic device that should have destroyed them didn't work. Humans moved it to the farside of their Moon, and when it exploded, it hurt no one but the one Martian who was carrying it.

Then the humans studied us Martians. Among other things, they figured out how we tap free energy from another universe. No Martian understands how that works, and I don't think any human actually does, either. But they can use it, and it gave them starflight, which I don't think was in the Others' plans.

The Others say they have either destroyed or spared hundreds of intelligent races in this part of the Galaxy, and have no record of having failed before. But I don't know about that.

We of the yellow family specialize in memory, not original thinking, but I do have a theory about the Others: I think they're lying. We do have evidence that they are capable of marvelous things, like inventing us and modifying a part of Mars so that we had a place to live before we inherited the Earth. We know they can make a small bomb powerful enough to eliminate life on Earth. But that doesn't mean that everything they say is true.

We have three sources of information about the Others. The primary thing was the coded message, which was like an ancestral memory in the yellow family. But it was not a regular memory; we had no access to it until we looked at a triggering light that came from the Other who was watching us from Triton, the satellite of Neptune. I saw that light and fell down and started babbling, and so did every other yellow Martian who saw it. We all said the same thing; three separate recordings give exactly the same nonsense sounds.

A human researcher discovered that there were two simultaneous messages in our stream of nonsense. One was amplitude modulation, and it was like a pattern of ones and zeros, modeled after a method that humans had used, attempting to communicate with other stars, what they call a Drake diagram. It told the humans something about the Others—how long they had been in the solar system, the fact that they had a body chemistry based on silicon and nitrogen, and the fact that we were made by them.

But there was a much more complex message hidden in the frequency modulation, an extremely concentrated burst of information that was in the language of the red Martian family. There is only one red individual at a time, and he or she is our leader.

The red language is the most complex Martian language, the only one that has a written form. Our leader only had a couple of days to live—the bomb was inside him—and he had no time to analyze and write down the long message. But he had it in his memory, and translated most of it into our consensus language, talking constantly to Mars as he sped to the farside of the Moon to die.

I wish he had lived long enough to discuss the truth of what the Others had told him through us. His replacement will be able to, but she won't be old enough to have mastered the language for many ares.

So we go off to meet our mortal enemies, and most of what we know about them is from the pack of lies they told our leader just before they murdered him.

5

SWEET MYSTERIES OF LIFE

Paul and I looked at the various cabin configurations and decided to put both beds together in my cabin and open a sliding door between the two spaces, while closing off the exterior door to what was now the bedroom. So in his cabin, now our living room, there was a worktable with two chairs facing each other, and a lounging chair that reclines. One VR helmet, but we could always borrow another from the gym or lounge.

I didn't have to tell him that I liked the arrangement because he sometimes tosses and turns in his sleep so much he wakes me up. This way, I'll have a place to tiptoe off to, to lie down in peace.

We put both windows on the wall by the worktable. Set them for adjacent views of the Maine woods, an environment we often use for biking or running.

Once we had everything the way we liked it, we celebrated our new nest the obvious way. We started with him on top, but he was too heavy—it was like fucking in the exercise room on Little Mars, which we never felt the need to try. I guess we'll get used to the gravity before too long. But for now it's doggy style, arf arf.

(I want my Mars gravity back so I can be a Hindu goddess again, holding on to him lightly with my arms and legs while he rises to the occasion.)

We panted for a while with the unaccustomed exertion—we'd never made love except in zero gee and Mars-normal gravity—and giggled over the new canine aspect of our relationship, and how superhuman our parents had been, to conceive us.

"If you don't mind," I said, "I never want to think about that again."

We pulled the covers up and rearranged the pillows facing each other, trying to recline comfortably in this gravity. "I do want to think about something else, though," he said. "Our spy buddies."

"So you've got a hard-on for Elza. Go on; she'll eat you alive."

"Yeah, right. Did you see Namir and Dustin practicing martial arts yesterday?"

"I saw a little of it—I was in the study and heard them throwing each other around. He's not bad for an old guy."

"He's not bad for anybody. Dustin is almost as good, but Namir is stronger and quicker—I did kapkido at the Academy for two years." He shook his head. "Either one of those guys could kill me. I mean literally. In a split second."

"So you better not offer to . . . Oh." I saw what he meant. "Literally."

"Maybe that's their mission. They could kill all of us in seconds, without weapons. Remember? We talked about this right after we met them."

"Yeah, vaguely . . . in VR, exercising. So why on earth would they want to?"

"On Earth, they wouldn't have any reason. But you read that thing in Namir's *New York Times*, the two-page debate about *ad Astra*."

"Sure. The idiots wanted us to just floor it and ram the planet like a doomsday bomb. As if the Others would just sit there and let us do it."

"That wasn't the part that worried me. It was the business about surrender. Something like 'We're not going to all that trouble and expense just to have them kneel down and grovel.' Did you see who signed that?"

"No. I vaguely remember it."

"It was a four-star American general, Mark Spinoza. Ring a bell?"

"Not really."

"He's on the Committee. Liaison to the American military. Who, incidentally, had a big part in designing and building this machine . . . and choosing the crew."

"But he couldn't *order* them to do that. Namir's not even under his authority."

"Neither are Dustin and Elza, technically. They all had to suspend their commissions, remember? Nobody can give them orders, in theory, any more than they can give the rest of us orders."

"Okay. So what are you worried about?"

"Just that they might agree with him. And do it on their own."

"No. They're not right-wing loonies. They're not killers, either, even though they're soldiers, ex-soldiers."

"I know Namir has killed, at least as a young man in wartime. And we don't really know anything about their politics. They seem reasonable, but they could just be following a script—and it wouldn't have to be from General Spinoza or the Corporation or anybody. They've lived together as men and wife for five or six years. They might have devised their own plan."

"Which would include killing us in case of cowardice. I don't think so."

"Or just overpowering and confining us. Then using the ship to try to destroy the Others."

I turned his head and held his chin between thumb and forefinger and stared. "I never really know when you're kidding."

"What would you say if I asked you to take Namir to bed and coax the truth out of him?"

"I would say 'I never really know when you're kidding.'"

He kissed me suddenly, a soft peck on the lips. "The secret of an exciting marriage." He turned onto his side and stretched out, readying for sleep. "Keep 'em guessing."

6

PRIVATE PARTS

The first room configuration we tried was to leave Elza's cabin the same size but move an extra bed into it. Then we almost doubled the size of the middle cabin, as a common room, with the third cabin the smallest possible bedroom, for whoever was the odd man out. The common room had all three windows together in one panorama, currently the beach at Cannes at the height of the tourist season.

As sexy as that scene was, I felt no real inspiration when I joined Elza in the double bed. I'd sparred for an hour with Dustin and then swum at six knots for an hour. When I got out I sympathized with the poor Martians in all this gravity. I felt like a large animal that had been run into the ground when I fell into bed. Elza seemed tired, too. Maybe that was why she asked for me, the first night with gravity.

"I've never seen you swim so much in a gym," she said sleepily.

"Set the thing for an hour. I was about to get out early, then Carmen came over. I offered to let her have it, but she said no, no, finish your hour. So I was kind of stuck."

"Stuck showing off your bare ass to a pretty girl."

"She's not a girl, not particularly pretty, and I was doing a side-stroke."

"Okay, showing off your bare side. To the most famous woman on two planets."

"Well, you know me. I really wanted her autograph."

"Is that what they call it now?"

I poked her in the ribs. "Where is that off switch?"

"I'll be good." She put her head against my shoulder and was asleep in a couple of minutes, her warm breath regular against my skin. So familiar and so unpredictable.

Her jibing made me think about Carmen. I was attracted to her, not because she was The Mars Girl. Probably not a smart course to follow, though I didn't think it would bother Elza a lot. Carmen's relationship with Paul was not monogamous on either side. Fly-in-Amber told me that when he was asking about our triune. She "mated" (his word) with several men who stayed in Little Mars waiting to go on to Mars, and he knew from talking with Carmen that it was with Paul's blessing, and that Paul was casually involved with a couple of women on Mars. This was before the one-gee shuttle, so going between the two planets was a complex affair taking months of zero-gee coasting.

Speaking of complex affairs. Trapped inside this small box together, we all know that the wise course would be to treat one another as friends and not let it go beyond that. But it probably would, even if the mission were prosaic, because it's so damned long. Add the desperate knowledge that we will all probably die at Wolf 25, or before, and the impulse to be impulsive is hard to resist.

I've heard Carmen denigrate her body as unwomanly three times, which is too often for it to be a casual remark. But in fact her supposed shortcomings are what make her so alluring to a man like me. I suppose her slight, tomboyish body reminds me of the young schoolmates who were the first focus of my teenaged passions—who never said yes, but have never quite relinquished their hold on me. Maybe they never said yes because I never had the courage simply to come out and ask.

Odd to think that they're old enough to be grandmothers now, those who lived past Gehenna. I'm sure that none of them remembers the plump Jewish boy whose hair wouldn't stay put. Or maybe one of them is obsessed by plump Jewish boys and can't figure out why.

Today was the first time I've seen her completely nude, and I looked away quickly so as not to make my interest too obvious. Then I got a glimpse as she turned around and swam on her back, as I was saying good-bye. No apparent tattoos except for the functional timepiece on her wrist. No obvious scars. Her pubic hair is shaped so as to accommodate a brief bathing suit, which is odd, since there are no bathing suits within a hundred million miles. In fact, she probably hasn't worn one since she left Earth, twelve or thirteen years ago. Maybe it's permanent. I'll have to work it into a conversation somehow. "I couldn't help but notice, as I was scrutinizing your pubic region . . ." Perhaps not. I shall be patient, and wait for a time and place when it will be natural to ask.

7

KAMIKAZE

8 May 2088
Instead of a regular diary entry, I'm going to put in part of a transcript of the meeting we just had.

Namir suggested that it would be a good time, starting the second week, for all the humans and Martians to get together and record a consensus of what we think we're headed for. We met at 0900 in the "compromise" lounge, at the entrance to the Martian area.

Part of it became a little dramatic. My husband would have said "annoying."

Namir: My proposal was that we record a kind of "baseline" report on what we expect to happen when we arrive at Wolf 25. Our ideas will change over the next six years, naturally.

Paul: One possibility is that there will be nothing there. The one on Triton said that's where they live, and took off in that direction. But we lost track of him after a few minutes. He could have gone anywhere.

Snowbird: Why would they do that?

Paul: They may have misrepresented their strength, or rather their vulnerability. If we were to attack swiftly, they might not be able to react in time.

Namir: Possibly. Doesn't seem likely. We have ample evidence of their strength.

Me: They had hundreds of centuries to plan ahead.

Paul: That's what I mean. They don't want to confront us in real time.

Fly-in-Amber: They have planned ahead for this. We will not surprise them.

Elza: We have to try.

Dustin: I'm not convinced that that is true. As you know, Elza.

Elza: Pacifist swine. (Note: said smiling.) Explain, for the record.

Dustin: This mission is predicated on two things: one, that they know they did not destroy us; and two, that they care. But we know almost nothing about their psychology. Maybe they are so confident they won't bother to check, in which case, showing up on their doorstep may be a disaster. Or they might know they didn't destroy us but feel the spectacular demonstration was enough to keep us out of their hair. So again, don't go bother them.

Namir: Dustin, even if the mission *is* a mistake, we can't turn around and go home. The die is cast.

Me: It's still a good viewpoint to put in the mix, trying to predict what they're going to do.

Paul: Let's get a sense of the timing. From the Earth's point of view, the Other left Triton in July of 2079. At its rate of acceleration, it will take only about twenty-four and a half years to get there, assuming it decelerates at the same rate. Say it gets there in January 2104.

In the worst-case scenario, they find out the Earth hasn't been destroyed and turn around to finish the job. Which they do in the middle of 2128.

Namir: That's not the worst case.

Paul: What is?

Namir: You assume that the Others have to obey the same speed limit as we do. Suppose they can go a lot faster than the speed of light and are due here tomorrow?

Paul: Relativity won't let them. They'd be traveling into the past.

Namir: (Laughs.) And show up tomorrow. They've done other impossible things.

(Namir and Paul argue fruitlessly for a few minutes. Never argue science with a lawyer, I told Paul.)

Meryl: Let's assume there's no magic superscience involved, all right? (She looks at her notebook.) If they go straight to Wolf 25, they'll get there around 2104, by the Earth calendar. We won't be there until eight years later. And they'll have our "ready or not, here we come" message months before that. Which I was so enthusiastic about.

Can we agree that the probability they won't be ready for us is almost exactly zero? (General agreement.) And at any rate, if we did surprise them, there's not much we can do about it. Short of using the *ad Astra* as a huge kamikaze bomb?

Snowbird: What is that?

Fly-in-Amber: It's a Japanese word meaning a suicide airplane.

Snowbird: Oh. Well, that would make sense, wouldn't it? We're expecting to die anyhow.

Fly-in-Amber: Most humans won't do that. Not if they have a chance of living.

Snowbird: But they don't live that long anyhow.

Namir: I'm glad you brought that up, Snowbird. We ought to consider it.

Elza: I'm not sure I can. We would be murdering a whole planet, besides ourselves.

Meryl: That's right.

Namir: Which is what they tried to do to us.

Dustin: He wants you to think like a soldier, love, not a doctor.

Moonboy: What if we had to do it to save the human race? What if we got a message like "Fuck you and the planet you came from"?

Paul: We never could save the human race, if they decided to destroy it. We could never catch them. We could only take revenge, after the fact.

Namir: I could do that.

Dustin: You would. Definitely.

Moonboy: I would, too. It's not as if they were human.

Me: Namir, it would be like Gehenna. There could be innocent races on that planet. For all we know, the one who attacked us was a lone lunatic, who claimed to represent the Others but actually did not.

Namir: With due respect, Carmen, I have been there, and you have not. Genocide is not murder. You can forgive a murder and go on with life. But if we had found a country responsible for Gehenna, we would have had no mercy. We would have leveled it, in retribution. Which is not the same thing as revenge.

(There was a long silence.)

Paul: The kamikaze thing is not going to happen. I'm the only one who could do that, and I won't. Besides, if our intent had been to launch a huge relativistic bomb, there would be no need for a crew. One kamikaze pilot, perhaps.

Dustin: (Laughs.) Now that does make me nervous. You *would* need a crew, if only to keep that pilot from going mad during six years of isolation. But of course the crew wouldn't know they were all going to die.

Paul: Are you a philosopher or a story writer?

Dustin: Sometimes the difference is moot. Are you lying? Don't answer; we covered that one in freshman logic.

Fly-in-Amber: Are you two joking? Sometimes it's hard to tell when humans are serious.

Dustin: Sometimes jokes are serious, Fly-in-Amber.

Paul: Not this time. He's just playing games.

Dustin: One of us is.

Snowbird: This is making my brain hurt. I have to leave.

So everyone laughed, and talked Snowbird into staying, promising that they would keep things straight. And the rest of it was pretty much a recital of what we already knew.

But no one here knows Paul as well as I do, and I know he has a deep reserve of seriousness, which sometimes frightens me. I'm a little frightened now.

A few days ago, out of the blue, before we went to sleep, he suggested that Namir, and perhaps the other two, were under orders to kill the rest of us if we tried to surrender, and use the *ad Astra* as a kind of 9/11 on the Others.

But a starship isn't a jet plane. They wouldn't know how to do it.

There's only one person here who does.

8

WATER SPORTS

Last night when all the humans were in bed, I walked quietly out past the hydroponics to the gym. I touched the water in the pool—it was very warm—and decided to try floating in it. See whether it indeed would give Snowbird and me some relief from all this gravity/acceleration.

There was no easy way for a four-legged person to get in. Humans just sit on the edge and slide in. We can't quite bend that way.

In retrospect, I realized I should have waited until at least one human was around. But there is a dignity factor about clothing, and I was not sure how to interpret it across species.

They almost never appear without clothing in front of one another—like us, they take off their clothing in order to prepare one another for reproduction, and like us it is indecorous to look at another without clothing except under special circumstances. Swimming was one of those for them. Would they feel the same about us? I have only appeared unclothed before humans as part of a scientific investigation, and even that was uncomfortable. But they certainly don't want people to go into their swimming pool with clothing on.

Finally, I took off my cloak and simply jumped in. It made more of a splash than I had expected. A light came on, and I heard human footsteps coming around the hydroponic trellises.

It was a most strange feeling. The water was only a little more than a meter deep, but it had splashed all over me. I had never been completely wet except in the process of being impregnated, so with the approaching footsteps I felt somewhat indecent, and was also embarrassed that I had splashed so much precious water out of the pool.

I did feel lighter, even though my feet were on the floor, which is to say the bottom of the pool. Then I moved sideways and tipped over—I was suddenly floating and had no weight at all! I inhaled some water and had a little coughing fit, but of course was in no danger, since my breathing spiracles are distributed evenly around my body surface. The noise did upset Carmen, though, who was the first human on the scene. She cried out my name and Snowbird's—of course she couldn't tell us apart without our clothing—and seized my head and pulled me upright.

She was yelling, asking if I was all right. The water was doing strange things with my hearing, and when I spoke, my voice sounded hugely amplified.

"I am all right, Carmen, and I am Fly-in-Amber, and I'm sorry to waste water and make a mess."

"Don't worry about water; we're riding a mountain of it. Did you have an accident?" Paul rushed up and said more or less the same thing.

"No, no. I just wanted to try floating, but didn't want to bother any humans while they were using the pool." In fact, although several could have stood in the pool with me, there wouldn't be room for anyone to swim.

"Want to try it with the current?" Paul asked.

"Please, yes." He stepped on a button and it was marvelous, like thousands of tiny fingers wiggling over your skin. It also felt deeply obscene. "That is very good."

Snowbird appeared and addressed me in the consensus language, which we don't normally use among humans. "Fly-in-Amber! You . . . I find you naked!"

"Speak English, Snowbird. Yes, I am naked, and so are humans when they do this. You should try it."

"Not at the same time," Paul said quickly. "You displace too much water."

"I'll get out, then, and let Snowbird—"

"I'm not ready to be naked in front of all these people! I have to think about it."

"It doesn't bother us," Carmen said. "It's proper, for being in the water."

"But the whole idea—'being in the water'! You can't even say it in our language. It's like 'breathing in outer space.' It should not be possible."

Carmen gestured toward me. "You'd better come up with a word for it. I don't think Fly-in-Amber wants to come out."

"In fact," I said, "I'm not sure *how* I'm going to get out. I can't jump high in this gravity."

Namir had come up. "You don't have to do anything. I'll get a couple of planks." He went off toward the storeroom. I wanted to tell him not to hurry.

"We'll improvise a ramp," Carmen said. She stepped out of her robe and slid into the water. Her body was strange, warmer than the water, and soft. "We should have made this bigger. We weren't thinking about you guys."

"We hadn't thought of it either, Carmen. It's such an odd idea."

"Fly-in-Amber," Snowbird said, "are you losing part of your skin?"

I had a moment of panic. There was an iridescent sheen on the water, evidently oil from my skin, and small floating particles, perhaps flakes of skin. Carmen was looking at the water with alarm.

"I'm sure it's nothing." I bent over and looked at it closely. "It's just been two days since I scraped."

"Of course," she said, though her smile did not look normal. She of all people might have reason to fear, since she had been the first human to catch a disease from us, and, of course, no human had ever bathed with us.

"Humans do catch skin diseases from other humans," Snowbird explained, "like athletes' foot and herpes. But we have never had skin diseases."

"That's, um, reassuring."

"There would have been no reason for us to be designed with skin disease," I said. "The difference between intelligent design and random evolution, I'm afraid."

"We ought to build a special pool for you two," Paul said. "Deeper, so you have maximum buoyancy. Not as wide, since you probably won't be swimming."

"That would be most kind of you. Perhaps with colder water?"

"If we put it in your area, it will be plenty cold."

"That's wonderful. Carmen, you could come over anytime and enjoy the cold."

"Thank you, Fly-in-Amber, but we really prefer the warmer water." She was shivering a little. "In fact, I think I'll go take a nice hot shower right now."

Going from a swim to a shower seemed redundant. But nothing about them surprised me.

Namir returned with the plastic boards then, and looked at her in what I think is a sexual way when she got out of the water. I wondered if they'd begun mating but had learned not to ask.

Over the next four days, they used boards like that to build us a big waterproof box, large enough for both of us to stand in, and improvised a pump that circulated the water and filtered it.

It will make the gravity so much more manageable. And Snowbird and I will be the cleanest Martians in history.

9

ADULTERY FOR ADULTS

1 June 2088

Gone for a month now. A real-time view to the stern shows the Sun as the brightest star in the sky; the Earth is of course invisible.

The only milestone of note, dear diary, is that Elza has apparently made her first sexual conquest—I say "apparently" because who knows? Though if it had been Paul, I think he would have told me, or politely asked me first.

It was Moonboy. Meryl told me after we finished an especially frustrating session with the Martians, tracking down their elusive and totally irregular verb forms.

We were alone at the coffee tap. "So do you know about Moonboy and Elza?"

"No, what?" I knew it wasn't billiards, of course.

"Well, they got together yesterday. In the fucking sense, I mean."

An odd choice, I thought, but she had to start somewhere. "Is it, um, I mean, is it a big deal to you?"

"More so than I let him know when he told me. It's always been theoretically okay. But this is the first time . . . for him."

"Not for you?" I pretended I didn't know.

She smiled and shook her head. "Back on Mars." I knew of two men, one of them married, some years ago. Mars is like a small village with no place to hide.

"Think it's a one-time thing?"

"It was already a two-time thing when he told me." She looked around. "It may be becoming a three-time thing as we speak. But no, I don't think they're going to get married and run off to the big city."

"I've been waiting for that shoe to drop myself," I said. "The way Paul looks at her when he thinks I'm not watching."

"But you've always been, what, open?"

"Sure, for years, he was in Mars and I was in Little Mars. We didn't actually marry until we got the lottery and were going to have children. Before that, we both had considerable variety."

"I bet you did." She grinned. "Being famous and all."

"Well, guys had long layovers on their way to Mars."

"Layovers."

"Probably half of them just wanted to be able to say 'I fucked The Mars Girl.'"

"The price of fame. And Paul the most famous pilot in history? He was not exactly a monk, if I recall correctly."

"But we'd talked it through before either of us was famous, long before we were married. I thought fidelity was a holdover from old times, when women were property."

"Do you still?"

"Not as strongly. But yes." It wasn't something I'd put into words. "Things are different, now that we've had children, but really there's no reason for that. Parenthood in Mars is so detached from biological reality."

She nodded. "You don't go through all the physical grief. And then you don't raise them by hand."

"Which I sort of regret. They have my genes, and Paul's, but we're more like an aunt and uncle who play with them now and then." I had a cold feeling, deep. "Under the circumstances, of course, that's for the best."

"When you get back . . ."

"They'll be older than me. Fifty years pass for them, twelve for us. In the unlikely possibility that we survive."

"Yeah." She leaned back and closed her eyes; she was dead tired. "I shouldn't be so concerned about where Moonboy puts his weenie. Let him have whatever pleasure he can find."

"For symmetry, you ought to go after Namir. He's old, but not *that* old. And good-looking."

"If good-looking was important to me, I wouldn't have grabbed Moonboy. Besides, if Namir is interested in anyone aboard, it's you."

"Really."

"Don't act surprised. It's pretty obvious."

"We've liked each other from the beginning. But not that way."

"Man, woman. It's the basic way."

"He's never made any kind of . . . gesture."

"I don't think he ever would. He's the kind of man who waits for you to ask."

"Well, he's got a long wait, then." Or maybe not.

10

SWEET MYSTERY OF LIFE

Elza was late coming to bed. I'd just turned off my book and the light when the door opened and closed and I heard her slip out of her clothing. I touched her shoulder as she eased into bed. Cool and damp with sweat.

"Exercising this late?"

"In a way. Moonboy."

"Ah." I didn't know what to say. "Meryl know?" They have both their beds together in one large suite.

"No. She was with the Martians."

"A . . . sort of a milestone, I suppose."

I could feel her smile in the darkness. "The first act of adultery outside of the solar system."

"That presupposes an abundance of virtue on the part of extraterrestrials. We'll put up a plaque anyhow."

"You're too sweet."

There was a long pause. "So how was it?"

"It was Moonboy. Men don't normally reveal hidden depths."

"Or lengths?"

"Men." She made a quarter turn and pressed her back into my chest, spoon fashion. "Get some sleep."

"What, I don't get sloppy seconds?"

"Thirds. Get some sleep." I didn't press the issue, though I found the situation curiously stimulating.

※

I hadn't brought along my balalaika because I knew it annoyed Dustin, and it was unlikely that the four "Martian" humans would care for it. (Most of the actual Martians seemed indifferent to music; it was background noise to them, neither pleasant nor unpleasant.) But I hadn't thought about all the room in the warehouse, where the four workers had lived before we arrived. It was a little cold, but large and totally isolated from our own living quarters. You could back up your balalaika with a brass band, and no one could hear you.

So I set out to make a thing like a balalaika. I could have just described it to the automatic shop machine, but there was no satisfaction in that.

No wood around to work with except the blocks of koa I brought for carving, so I asked the machine what it could simulate. My balalaika at home was made of rosewood, light and dark, and ebony. I found a picture of myself playing it, and so was able to measure it precisely from the image. I found instructions for making your own balalaika in Russian, no problem.

The three strings were easy, carbon fiber and nylon wires. The "wood" had the right color and density but wouldn't fool a termite. The thinnest stock it could generate was two or three times too thick. So my first order of business was to take a strip of it and see whether I could plane it down.

No luck. No fibrous structure, so the hand plane would just bite out a chip at a time. But I blocked it in place and used a sander to bring it down to two millimeters' thickness. It was still strong and stiff; I clamped it to the edge of the worktable and plucked it, and it made a satisfying twang.

I experimented with scrap and decided to forego tradition and cut the "wood" by laser, which left a more accurate, smooth edge than any saw in the shop. And with modern glues, I didn't have to improvise the elaborate clamps that the Russian plans called for. I also cheated on the tuning pegs, bridge, and tailpiece, by describing them and letting the shop turn them out robotically. So it only took a couple of days, and a lot of that was learning. If I wanted to put together another one, I could probably do it in an afternoon. Give it to Dustin, so we could do duets.

It looked identical to mine at home except for the inlaid red star and "Souvenir of Soviet Olympics 1980," which made mine a fairly valuable antique, in spite of being very ordinary in a musical way. A gift to my father on his tenth birthday. His parents had gone to the Olympics before he was born.

I was working on the finish when Fly-in-Amber came in and addressed me formally in Japanese. I set the instrument down and stood, and returned the greeting with a slight bow, which he had tried to do.

"Snowbird should be asking you this," he said, "since human behavior is her area of expertise, but she was unsure about politeness."

"And you don't care."

"Of course not. I am not human."

I chose not to pursue the obvious there. "So what does Snowbird want to know?"

"Oh, I want to know as well. But my interest is not professional."

"Fire away."

"Pardon me?"

"Please ask the question."

"It is more than one question."

"All right. Ask them all."

"It's about your wife Elza mating with Meryl's husband Moon-boy."

Good news travels fast. "Well, they weren't mating. There was no possibility of offspring."

"I know that. I was being polite. Should I say 'fucking'?"

"With me, either one is fine. But your instinct is right."

"Snowbird wanted me to talk to you in private, which is why I am bothering you here. She wants to know if this causes you pain, the adultery."

"Not really. I've been expecting it." I didn't want to get into a definition of adultery.

"Is there symmetry? Are you going to mate with one of the other women?"

I had to smile. "Not immediately. It doesn't always work that way."

"Are you not attracted to any of them?"

"I'm attracted to all of them, in varying degrees. I just don't act on that attraction as directly as Elza does."

"Is that because you are old?"

"I'm not *that* old. It's less youth on Elza's part than impulsiveness. I want to know someone well before I am intimate with her."

"Always 'her'? You are not intimate with men?"

How honest do you have to be with a Martian? "Not in many years. Not since I was boy."

"Not with Dustin Beckner?"

"No. Definitely not Dustin."

"Yet you are married to him."

"Yes, and I love him, but in a different way. You can love without mating." He was silent for a moment, so I asked, "Do you feel love? Do you love Snowbird, for instance?"

"I don't think so, in human terms. She says there was a word in ancient Greek, *agape*, that approximates the way Martians feel about one another."

"You wouldn't have erotic love."

"No. That wouldn't make sense. There is pleasure in mating, but you often don't know ahead of time who will be involved, or how many. And, of course, you don't know which of you will be the female until the contest is over. The female feels it more strongly."

"Well, 'erotic' means more than that, if you go back to Snowbird's ancient Greek. It's an intense feeling one has for another, whether or not sex is involved."

"Humans do that?"

"Some. Most."

He hugged himself, which I knew signified thinking. "We are simpler, I think. I feel especially close to the other members of the yellow family. But they are the only ones I can speak to plainly, in the language I was born with."

"Is that the same with all Martians?" I knew the yellow ones had a reputation for being standoffish, but I hadn't met any Martians except our two.

"Oh, no. Blues cooperate with everybody; they were the example Snowbird used, to explain *agape* to me. My family is less open than the others, but that's appropriate to our function."

"Impartial observers."

"Yes." He switched to Japanese and apologized for the intrusion, and backed out.

He was often abrupt like that. As if he had some internal timer.

I finished polishing the balalaika and admired its strangeness. From a distance, it was a pretty close copy. The "wood" was exactly right in color, but it had no grain, close up, and it had the cool smoothness of ceramic.

The strings were not easy to mount, my big fingers clumsy with the knots. I almost called Elza but didn't want to interrupt her at her needlepoint, a fractal pattern that apparently required intense concentration. Finally, I got all three in place and taut, but the two nylon strings (both tuned to the same E note) kept relaxing out of tune. Then I remembered a young folksinger in Tel Aviv, replacing a string in the middle of a performance. He pulled it dangerously taut and released it with a snap, over and over, flattening the tone, then tuning it up. After a couple of minutes doing that on both nylon strings, they were remarkably stable.

I played a few simple tunes from memory, and scales in the four keys I used, then some arpeggios, working through the left-hand pain until my joints agreed to loosen up.

As sometimes happens, I felt my audience before I saw her. I turned, and there was Elza, leaning in the doorway behind me. She was holding two glasses, a wineglass with red in it and a cup of clear liquid with ice. I must have subliminally heard it clinking.

"It sounds good," she said. "I've missed it."

"I hope you didn't hear it inside."

She set the wine down next to me. "You buy the next." She folded into a graceful lotus, not spilling a drop of her vodka. "No, Fly-in-Amber told me you were almost done with it. I went into the pantry for a drink and heard you. Peeked and saw you didn't have anything."

I sipped the wine. "Mind reader."

"So what were you talking to Old Yeller about?"

"Old Yeller?"

"It's a Texas thing. Thang."

"Gossip and biology. He wondered about you 'mating' with Moonboy."

"For a Martian, he has a very dirty mind."

"I don't think that's possible. Anyhow, I think he was asking on Snowbird's behalf. She wasn't sure what would be polite."

"And he doesn't care."

"Well, he approached me in Japanese, with an apology. But that was for interrupting my work, not for asking about my wife's extramarital affairs. Still, politeness."

"I don't suppose you told him it was none of his business."

"Slapped him with a glove and said 'lasers at dawn.' It's not personal with him, of course."

"I know. So why didn't he just ask me?"

"You don't speak Japanese." I set down the balalaika and picked up the wine. "I think he likes me. Or likes talking to me. Maybe being oldest male has something to do with it."

"Did you tell him any gory details?"

"I don't *have* any, dear. I'm not that close to Moonboy, and you haven't shown me the feelie yet. Did he know something I don't?"

She shrugged. "All men do. Have something no other man has. And I'm saving the feelie for our old age."

"In case we have one?"

She nodded, silent for a few moments, looking at the floor. Then she knuckled her eyes. "Could you play me that silly love song? The first, the first time . . ."

"Sure." I picked up the instrument and tuned up the flatted E strings, then plucked out the simple melody. *"Shteyt a bocher, shteyt un tracht . . . tracht un tracht a gantze nacht . . ."*

It's a song about a man finding a smart woman to marry.

II

HEROES

Paul had always questioned the necessity for radio silence between Earth and *ad Astra*. It assumed the Others were so inattentive and stupid that they wouldn't know we were on our way. Of course, our presence would be obvious after turnaround, with a gazillion-horsepower matter-annihilation engine blasting in their direction. The little probe that preceded us would deal with that by sending a warning and a message of peace well before we turned around and started blasting, decelerating.

What if they destroyed the probe before it delivered the message?

What if it delivered the message, and the Others destroyed us anyway?

What if they weren't on a Wolf 25 planet after all?

We went along with the order and were resigned to not hearing from anyone on Earth for another 3.4 years. Paul kept the radio on, though, in case things changed.

On July 10, 2088, things did. A fifty-two-second message came from

Earth. He called us all together in the lounge, Martians and humans, and played it back for us.

"This is Lazlo Motkin, just elected president of the world. One reason I was elected was that I wanted to change your mission and make it more in line with what the Earth's people really want.

"You are the finest heroes in Earth's history, hurtling into the unknown on a mission that will almost surely end with your deaths.

"We ask that you make this grim probability a glorious certainty. Rather than slowing down, we would ask you to continue accelerating. Going at almost the speed of light—and invisible until the last moment— you will strike the enemy planet with ten thousand times the force of the meteorite that brought about the extinction of the dinosaurs.

"Even the ungodly science of the Others cannot protect them from this apocalyptic assault. Please answer that you have heard and are willing to give your life in this noble enterprise.

"God bless you and keep you."

We all just stared at each other. "Who is that guy?" I said. "Lazlo what?"

"Motkin," Namir said. "He's a cubevangelist."

"Powerful signal," Paul said. "Pretty tight laser."

Namir shrugged. "He has lots of money, or did when money meant something, and a powerful broadcast site in the Atlantic, beyond the seven-mile limit. He could do it once."

"Once?" Paul said.

"They'll have people like me in the water in thirty minutes. Homeland Security. Unless Reverend Motkin really is president of the world, he's about to have a serious accident."

"Or had it about a week ago," Paul said.

"It's hard to get used to that. He was arrested or dead before that message was a tenth of the way here."

"What if he really is king of the world," Moonboy said, "or president or whatever. Some pretty loony people have made it to the top, even in normal times."

"I still wouldn't feel I had to kill myself on his behalf," Dustin said.

"Besides, the order is stupid," Paul said. "We don't know for certain which planet in the Wolf 25 system is their home world." There was a "cold Earth" planet that seemed likely, but also two gas giants with Triton-sized satellites.

"As we get closer, we might be able to tell which one it is," Moonboy said.

"It probably would be the one with all the missiles rising up to greet us."

"Maybe not," Namir said. "If we stopped accelerating the last month or so, we'd be coming in cold. They might not detect us until it was too late to respond. We'd still be going at 99 percent the speed of light."

"You're not arguing in favor of this kamikaze scheme," Elza said.

"Not this particular one. President of the world. But it's always been a possible strategy."

"As I said before," Snowbird said, "if we're going to die anyhow, we could still exercise some control over the situation that way."

"No," I said. "I didn't sign up for a suicide mission. Besides, even if we knew what planet they were on, we don't know who else might inhabit it. It might be like destroying Earth just to get Lazlo what's-his-name."

"Which might be happening even as we speak," Namir said. "Or after however long it takes his message to be picked up by the Others."

"Comforting prospect," I said.

"And an interesting thought experiment," Moonboy said. "If they did destroy the Earth, should we try to destroy them in turn? Or should we go someplace safe and try to restart the human race?"

"I'm a fearsome interstellar warrior," Namir said. "I'm not changing diapers."

"I don't think we have any diapers aboard," I said, "nor ovulating women."

"I can fix the ovulation," Elza said. "And we could improvise diapers and such. But really, where could we go, to play Adam and Eve, if we couldn't go back to Earth?"

"Mars," Fly-in-Amber said. "It's a nicer place anyhow."

※

We got the ersatz news broadcasts from Earth, but of course they weren't beamed, and were too weak and distorted by noise to be worth everyday amplifying and cleaning up. Namir had some experience and expertise to apply to it, though, and eventually had decoded about six hours of broadcasts prior to noon of July 3, when Lazlo Motkin had made his imperial request. All we found were two small stories, one a pro forma announcement that Lazlo was going to run for president of the United States on a third-party ticket, and the other a human-interest story about how he and his wife formed the Free America party and, working through several religious denominations, got enough signatures and funding to put himself on the ballot in several Southern states.

So how to interpret the tight-beam message to us? Probably just a crazy rant. But suppose the rest of the news was sanitized, and there really had been a theocratic revolution in the United States?

Paul raised that possibility during dinner, rehydrated mushrooms fried with pretty convincing butter over corn cakes, with actual green onions from the farm, our first crop.

"Doesn't make sense," Dustin said, "unless it's a very levelheaded theocracy. Why would they censor the news of their victory?"

"Maybe they're not idiots," Namir said. "Even theocrats might not want to invite the Others to their victory parade."

"The real question is what our response should be," Paul said. "I'm inclined to play it straight; tell them thanks, but no thanks. We're going to stick with the original plan."

"Which is to make it up as we go along," I said.

"Or just don't respond at all," Namir said. "He sent that a week ago. He knows our answer would take a week or eight days. If he's still in control of that powerful laser transponder a couple of weeks from now, that tells us something."

Meryl shook her head. "You're presupposing that the Earth authorities are aware that he's done this. I think he's just a rich fruitcake out in the middle of the ocean with his laser transponder and delusions of grandeur."

"In which case," I said, "we ought to send the message back to Earth and ask whether anyone can vouch for Mr. Lazlo."

"We could do that," Paul said, "but no matter what we hear back, we should stick to the original mission. If we'd wanted to just cannonball into the planet, there wouldn't be any need for a human crew and all this lovely life support." He held up a forkful of mushroom. "We could've just put an autonomous AI pilot on the iceberg and set it loose. But we *are* on board, and in charge, and we'll do what we're supposed to do."

He looked around the table. "So I second Carmen's idea—send the message back and see what the reaction is. But continue on regardless. Is everyone in favor of that?"

People nodded and shrugged. Moonboy said, "It's not as if they could do anything to us, right? I mean, there's no way they could set up another starship and have it overtake us before we got to Wolf 25."

"No," Paul said, "even if they had an identical iceberg in place, and all the people and resources. They couldn't catch up with us. We're already going two-tenths the speed of light."

"They couldn't catch us with a starship and crew," Namir said. "But they could catch us with a probe. A bomb."

"Always Mr. Sunshine," his wife said.

12

MEDICAL HISTORY

1 September 2088

So Elza thinks Moonboy is a little crazy. Maybe more than a little. He'd been acting more odd than usual for a couple of weeks, I saw in retrospect, but it hadn't made a big impression. He'd been moody as long as we'd known him; so now he was a little moodier, withdrawn.

I'm somewhat snoopy, but then that is what I'm paid to do. So when Elza said she was going down to the kitchen for a snack and set down her notebook without turning it off, I did what was natural for me and leaned over to take a look.

It was Moonboy's medical file, open to a confidential psychological evaluation, eighteen years ago. It was in a folder labeled "Aptitude for long-term assignment, Mars Base."

The box the psychiatrist had checked said "marginally acceptable," with a scrawled "see attached" alongside. I tapped on it, and the document was fascinating. Disturbing.

Moonboy had had inpatient psychiatric treatment, on Earth, for assault and claustrophobia. When he was eleven, a stepfather had gotten angry with him for crying and taped his mouth shut, then bound his arms and legs in tape, too, and pushed him into a dark closet for punishment. He choked on vomit and died, but was revived on the way to the hospital. He never saw the stepfather again, but the damage was done.

"Pretty interesting?" I hadn't heard Elza come back.

"I'm sorry. Compromising professional ethics."

"Well, I'm not a psychiatrist, and Moonboy wouldn't be my psychiatric patient anyhow. I really shouldn't have had access to the file. But I saw a thread to it and just asked, and it opened. You could have done the same thing."

"I'm surprised they accepted him for Mars."

"Hmm. A married pair of xenologists probably looked like a good package deal, and Mars itself isn't too bad for a claustrophobe. The base is big, and you can go outside. Unlike here."

"There are other factors for his moodiness," I said. "You're sitting on one of them, I must point out."

She shook her head. "I don't think so. But I should talk to him." She picked up the notebook and tapped through a few pages. "Meryl's okay with it. I talked it over with her. She hasn't been a saint."

"That's not too relevant."

"I know, I know."

"Are you still . . ."

"No, not really. We haven't closed any doors, but . . . yeah, I should talk to him."

"Would it do any good for me to talk to him? Give my okay?"

"No. He knows you're not bothered by it. Besides, you're an authority figure to him."

That was comforting. "Authority figures might be a problem, if one had tried to murder you at age eleven."

"Didn't just *try*. Though he doesn't remember dying. He passed out, puking, and was revived. He still doesn't know he died." She shuddered. "What a bastard."

"He does remember the incident up to that point?"

She tapped some more and shook her head. "Guy doesn't say whether he learned that from Moonboy himself or from hospital records." She put it down and leaned back, hands behind her head. "I ought to see whether I can get him to talk about his childhood."

"As his doctor?"

She gave me a look. "I'm always his doctor. Yours, too. But no; I don't want him to see me as a shrink."

"What as?"

She looked back at the notebook. "Why don't you and Dustin play some pool after dinner? A nice long game?"

13

TRAUMA DRAMA

I was headed for bed after watching a bad movie—Paul had given up halfway through—when the door to Elza's suite burst open and Moon-boy ran out, naked, carrying his clothes. That did get my attention. He hurried straight to his room, I think without seeing me.

Then Elza appeared, also naked, hand over her lower face, blood streaming from her nose, spattering her chest, a rivulet running between her breasts. I took her by the elbow and led her to the bathroom. Tried to seat her on the toilet, but she got up and inspected her face in the mirror, a mess, and gingerly touched her nose in a couple of places, wincing. "Broken," she said, though it sounded like "progen."

"What can I do? Get Namir?" He and Dustin were playing pool in the lounge.

"Just stay a minute." She was carefully packing her nostrils with tissue, her head bent over. "Hurts. More than I would think." She turned and got to one knee and spit blood into the toilet, and convulsed twice, holding back vomit. Then she sat on the floor, holding the scarlet wad of tissue over her nose.

"Moonboy?"

"Yeah. If you see him, would you pitch him out the air lock for me?"

"What happened?"

"We were just talking." She dropped some tissues into the toilet, and I handed her fresh ones. "Well, we sort of fucked, I guess that's obvious, and I was talking to him, reassuring him . . . and, I don't know. I must have blinked. He was starting to sit up, and he whacked me a good one with his elbow. Said it was an accident, but no way. Had all his weight behind it." She shuddered and rocked a couple of times. Another woman, I would have held, comforted. Elza wouldn't like that.

"Glad my martial arts instructor isn't here. She would slap the shit out of me."

"Was it something you said?"

She looked up at me, ghastly but a little comical. "Yes. But I'm not sure what, exactly. I'll talk with him after he's . . . after we've both calmed down a little."

"Maybe you should slap the shit out of *him*. I mean, just as therapy."

She nodded. "Therapy for me, anyhow."

Namir appeared in the doorway, galvanized. As if a silent lightning bolt had struck. "Blood," he said. "What?"

"An accident," Elza said, standing carefully. "Stupid accident. Get outa here and let us clean this mess up."

"It's broken," he said. Dustin had come up behind him and was staring.

"No shit, it's broken. But a doctor has already looked at it."

"You were with—"

"An accident, Namir. Make yourself useful and get me some ice.

And a drink, while you're at it." He backed away, and Dustin followed him.

I wet a handcloth with cold water and handed it to her. She dabbed and rubbed at the blood one-handed. The stream had pooled at her navel and gone on to mat her pubic hair. I gave her another cloth and rinsed the first one out.

"What are you going to tell them?"

She scrubbed her pubic hair unself-consciously. "They know I was with him. Namir, at least, knew I was going to raise some . . . delicate matters. For the time being, I'm going to stand behind doctor-patient confidentiality." She threw the rag into the sink. "Help me get dressed?"

She pulled a brown shift out of a drawer and wriggled into it, switching arms to keep the wad of tissues in place. She went back into the bathroom and spit out a clot and retched.

"Ugh." She sat heavily on an ottoman, elbows on her knees.

Meryl tapped on the doorjamb and stepped in. "Moonboy *hit* you? Elza?"

"Said it was an accident. Pretty well aimed."

"I don't understand. I can't imagine a less violent man."

"Wonder how often people say that. After ax murders and such."

"Where is he now?" I asked.

"In bed." They were set up with separate bedrooms currently and a small shared anteroom. "I haven't talked to him. I was reading in the kitchen, and Namir came in."

Elza peered up at her. "He's never, um?"

"Never even raises his voice, no."

"Well, he's sitting on something. A powder keg." She looked at the tissues and replaced them. "At least he didn't break any teeth. 'Dentist, heal thyself.' "

"I . . . I'm sorry," Meryl said with an odd tone of voice, like "I'm kind of sorry my husband hit you while you were fucking, but not really."

"Look," Elza said, "it probably was an accident. Let's leave it at that. I'll talk to him after he's rested."

"I suppose accidents aren't always accidents," Meryl persisted. "Maybe it wasn't you who was the actual target."

"Maybe not." She shook her head. "Probably not. But not you, either. Childhood thing."

"He had a *happy* childhood. He adores his mother."

"And his father died?"

"Left. But it was amicable, no-fault."

"You might talk to him about that. Or no. Let me talk to him. It's something we were . . . closing in on."

Namir came in with a tall drink and a plastic bag of chipped ice. "Thanks. Carmen, do we have a clean washcloth left?"

"Sure." I handed it to her and she wrapped it around the ice, dropping the bloody wad, and pressed the cold pack to her nose.

She sipped the cold drink, holding it at an awkward angle. "Thanks. Look. I don't think he knows how badly he injured me. Let's not make a big deal of it?"

Dustin shook his head. "No. He's got to know he—"

"Trust me, no, darling. This is something I have to control, whether he knows it yet or not."

"I could," Namir began.

"No. You boys get back to your game. Please. Just be normal."

Sure, a normal family full of Martians and spies, hurtling toward its doom a contracted quarter of a century away.

Paul stepped into the doorway, rubbing sleep from his eyes, and stared at the sight of all the blood. "What the fuck?"

"A reasonable question," Elza said.

14

LOVE AND BLOOD

I lay in the dark holding a pack of tissues, listening to Elza's ragged breathing as she went in and out of sleep. I passed her a tissue whenever a stoppage woke her. Then the pills would carry her back to sleep.

When people stopped falling out of the sky, the day of Gehenna, I took an embassy car and drove out to the suburb past Neve Tsedek, where my parents lived. Driving was difficult downtown, streets clotted with cars that had gone out of control as their drivers died. Some automatic cars were stalled, pushing against piles of metal and flesh. I tried not to drive over bodies, but it was impossible. I saw perhaps fifty people walking or standing in all of downtown Tel Aviv, sharing with me the inexplicable gift of life.

On the thruway there were long stretches of uninterrupted pavement, and then immense pileups, surrounded by empty undamaged cars. Of course people would stop, then open their doors and take one breath of unfiltered air.

My mother's neighborhood looked unaffected, except for a few cars oddly parked in yards or in the middle of the street. There were no people about, but that could have been normal.

The front door was unlocked. I called for her, and, of course, there was no answer.

I found her in the kitchen, lying on her back in a tidal pool of blood. The door to the garden had been kicked down from the outside.

A nurse by training, combat nurse by politics, she had rushed to the knife rack and snatched a razor-sharp Toledo steel paring knife, a souvenir from Spain that she used daily and kept keen. A straw in her left hand, she had tried to give herself an emergency tracheotomy. Then nicked an artery, a carotid artery. Of course the tracheotomy wouldn't have helped.

She wrote in blood on a white plastic cutting board CAN'T EX-HALE, with a drying fingerprint apostrophe. She had always been careful about grammar.

Too much blood in this life.

15

SEX AND VIOLENCE

This was a very interesting day for observing humans. I didn't witness the precipitating incident last night but have reconstructed it from several accounts, including Snowbird's interpretation. She is closer to Carmen than I am, and Carmen saw much of it.

Apparently Elza and Moonboy were mating (or "fucking," to be more accurate), an intimacy outside their traditional pairing and tripling but not forbidden. Something went seriously wrong, and Moonboy struck Elza with such force that he caused a serious injury to her face. Then he went back to his own area, leaving Elza alone and bleeding.

Carmen saw that she was in trouble and came to her aid. Elza is a doctor, but perhaps with only two hands had trouble treating herself.

I heard the noise when other humans became involved and watched from a distance I hoped was polite. It was fascinating.

Much of human action is, of course, predicated on passion, but for all the indirect evidence I have of this from reading and cube, I had never before seen one person injure another out of emotion. He hit her face with his elbow, which makes me think they must have finished mating. In all the postures they use for mating, there are some where the female might surprise the male that way, but not vice versa. The elbow is not as complex as our joints; it is more or less a bony hinge that connects the upper and lower parts of the arm.

Evidently Carmen helped her give "first aid" to herself. Her two husbands showed up, and Dustin, at least, wanted to "discuss" the matter with Moonboy, which implied a desire to inflict reciprocal injury, a natural human trait. Elza insisted that he not do that.

Meryl, Moonboy's wife, showed up and argued that he had never done anything like this before, which Elza accepted, but said it didn't help her nose. Pilot Paul, who had been asleep next door, joined them, and so everything was explained again. So now every human knew what was going on, or at least part of it.

Namir and Dustin had been playing pool, and they obeyed their wife when she asked them to resume. The rest dispersed, Carmen staying behind to comfort Elza.

That is when the second phase began. Namir and Dustin were playing their game and talking when Moonboy came out of his room, staggering from the effects of alcohol, and asked them, or commanded them, to quiet down.

This seemed unreasonable to Dustin, at least, and he attacked Moonboy with the stick they use to propel the pool balls around. Namir moved in quickly to intervene, perhaps to prevent his spouse from murdering the young man. He is larger than either and was able to separate the two men and disarm Dustin and throw him into the swimming pool, which was probably wise. I know how calming that is.

Moonboy had sustained a wound to the top of his head, from the pool stick, which was bleeding even worse than Elza's nose. I saw this.

Blood covered his face and much of the front of his shirt. He fainted, and Namir carried him to the infirmary.

A comical scene ensued, which I suppose would be the third act of the play, in human terms. Moonboy's wound had to be sewn up with stitches. Namir started the process, cleaning the wound and removing hair from around it, but before he could start stitching, his wife came in and took over. So she sewed the wound closed while Carmen held the ice pack to her nose, both of them laughing over the absurdity of the situation. Along with Namir and Meryl, they carried the patient back to his bed.

Then the three women moved into the kitchen and drank alcohol and laughed for some time. The men either weren't invited or felt they wouldn't be welcome.

Altogether, a complex display of interactions, which I could not pretend to understand. It will be interesting to record the changes this causes in attitudes and actions.

It's a pity that we will probably not live to return to Mars and discuss all this. The starship is like a small laboratory, with us nine organisms sealed within. But there's no scientist to peer at us from outside, and draw conclusions.

16

INJURIES

Namir suggested a meeting the morning after, while Moonboy was still under sedation. It was natural for Elza to lead the discussion.

"For me, it could have been a lot worse." She touched her bruised nose gently. Both eyes were dark, too. One nostril was open, the other packed with gauze. "The break is simple, not 'displaced.' So it will heal without surgery. What's broken inside Moonboy is not so easy to heal."

"What do you know about his . . . condition?" Paul asked.

"More than I can say, ethically. It does involve anger that's been suppressed for years, though. Unfortunately, it's associated with claustrophobia."

"But this starship is huge," Snowbird said, gesturing with all four arms.

"Snowbird," Paul said, "you've always lived inside a big room, a cave. Moonboy grew up in Kansas, a large flat state. You could look around and see forty kilometers in any direction."

"I don't know that that's a factor," Elza said. "This was a very small space, involuntary confinement.

"Anyhow, as well as the sedative, I've given him a mild antipsychotic medication. For his protection and ours."

"Good," Dustin said.

"I should give you one as well, darling. You have not been a model of rational behavior."

"He came after me."

"You could have fought him off with a pillow, not a pool cue. Try to leave your balls on the table next time. So to speak."

"Yes, Doctor." Obviously a familiar response.

"So do we have to keep him doped up for the duration?" Paul said. "Do we have enough drugs for that?"

"I can synthesize things that simple. I could keep us all doped to the gills for the whole mission. Which has crossed my mind."

"That would not be practical," Fly-in-Amber said. "Would you be able to eat, and drink, and excrete?"

"All in the same place," Namir said.

"I've been to parties like that," Dustin said.

"They're kidding," Elza said to the Martian. "So am I. Meryl, he's never lost control like this before?"

"Not since we've been married; not on Mars." She hesitated. "He got in trouble when he was a kid. That involved fighting, I remember. At the time, I thought how unlike him that was. But I never asked him for any details."

"I'll see if he wants to talk about it."

"To you?"

"To a doctor. He ever say anything to you guys? About being a wild kid?"

The men all shook their heads. "I don't remember him ever talking about his life on Earth," Paul said. "Funny, now that I think of it. Everybody has Earth stories."

"He's odd that way," Meryl said. "He talks about his mother, when he was little, and he talks about college, but not much in between."

"That's not so unusual," I said. "Paul never talks about that time in his life. Do you?"

"Boring," he said. "Dealing drugs, child prostitution, day in and day out."

"Child prostitution?" Fly-in-Amber said.

"Kidding," he said. "They were all over eighteen."

"Paul . . ."

"I'm sorry, Fly-in-Amber. It's disrespectful of me to kid you."

"On the contrary," the Martian said. "I learn from your humor. If you had actually been a bad boy, you wouldn't joke about it. Your feelings are ambiguous, are they not? You wish you had been more bad?"

"Got me there," he said. "Elza, you're both victim and professional observer. What if it had happened to someone else—"

"Paul, that's not relevant," I said. "There are only two other women here."

"It might be relevant," Elza said, "on various levels." She touched her nose and grimaced. "I'd just asked him about his father, sort of out of the blue."

"What about his father?" Meryl said. "He never talks about him."

Elza studied her for a moment. "I know some things I shouldn't. Maybe because of my security clearance, I don't know, I . . . I was given access to confidential psychiatric records."

"About his father?" Meryl said.

"I'm on thin ice here," she said.

After a pause, everyone started to talk at once. "Wait, wait." Paul had the strongest voice. "Elza, you don't have to violate your political principles . . ."

"Yes, she does," Dustin said.

His wife smiled at him. "The philosopher speaks."

"All right. The principle of doctor-patient confidentiality is a luxury we have to forego."

"Like the luxury of anger?" she said, still smiling.

"We are seven people, or nine," he plowed on, "who may have the fate of the entire human race, both races, depending on our thoughts and actions. Our freedom to think and act can't be constrained by tradition. By law or superstition."

"I think he's right," Namir said slowly. "At least in terms of information."

Elza looked at him, then away. "Maybe so. Maybe so." She sat up straight and spoke to the middle distance, as if reciting. "This is something Moonboy doesn't remember, because it was repressed by court order: When he was eleven years old, his father killed him."

"Tried to?" Dustin said.

"Killed him. Not on purpose. Tried to stop his crying by taping his mouth shut. Then bound his hands and feet with the tape and threw him in a dark closet."

"Holy shit," Dustin said.

"When his mother came home from work, probably a few minutes later, she asked where the kid was, and got into an argument with dear old dad. When she opened the closet, Moonboy was dead. He'd choked on vomit and stopped breathing.

"The rescue people got his heart and lungs going again. But what if his mother had not come home in time? He could have died permanently or suffered irreversible brain damage."

"What happened to the father?" Namir asked.

"The record doesn't say."

"Moonboy thinks his parents got a no-fault divorce when he was eleven," Meryl said, "and his father dropped out of his life. Probably into prison or some rehab program, judging from what you say. With an ironclad restraining order." She shook her head. "It . . . explains some things. It's a lot to assimilate."

"The white hair?" I said. He had a tangled nimbus, like Einstein. "I know a person's hair doesn't turn white overnight."

"Old wives' tale," Elza said. "But continual stress can cause premature graying."

"Maybe that memory wasn't completely erased," Meryl said, "and he dwells on it at some level. His hair was almost completely white when we met. I think he was twenty-two."

"Is that why he's called Moonboy?" Namir asked.

I knew about that. "No, he was born during an eclipse, a total lunar eclipse." I cringed at the memory of a cheap magazine article when I was famous, putting us together: Moonboy and Mars Girl.

"His mother's an astrology nut," Meryl said. "We don't get along too well. *He* thinks she walks on water, though."

Dustin laughed. "Well, she did bring him back from the dead. Even if he doesn't know it, she does. It could make for an interesting relationship."

Meryl nodded. "It does explain a lot."

"His voice," Elza said. It was a soft, hoarse rasp. "That could be damage to his vocal cords from stomach acid. As he lay there dead."

Namir broke the silence. "We have to tell him. Now that we all know."

"Not 'we,' " Elza said. "I have to tell him. I started the whole damned thing, with my curiosity."

That was a delicate way to put it, I thought. Her curiosity about Moonboy's medical record came after her curiosity about his body. If that was what it was, her need for different men.

Of course the only man left now was mine.

17

THERAPY

I didn't want my wife alone in a room with the man who had assaulted her. But she felt they had to talk one-on-one, and besides, she would have no trouble overpowering him under normal circumstances. As a compromise, she let me sit in an adjacent room and watch the interview on a notebook, ready to rush in and save her. It wasn't necessary, as it turned out. But it was educational.

He knocked tentatively and walked in, looking sheepish and uncomfortable. She sat him down next to her desk and inspected his stitches, dabbing at them with an alcohol swab. He winced, and her expression was not one of empathy.

"You'll live," she said, and sat down facing him.

"I'm sorry, so sorry. Don't know what got into me." His speech was slightly slurred.

"That's what we have to talk about." She took a deep breath. "What happened yesterday started twenty-nine years ago. Do you know the acronym SPMD?"

He shook his head. "No. When I was eleven?"

"Yes. It's Selective Precision Memory Dampening. Not done very often anymore; it's controversial."

"When I was in the hospital so long, with pneumonia?"

"Yes. But it was a lot more than pneumonia."

For several minutes he didn't speak, while she recounted in unsparing detail what his father had done and what happened afterward. When she was through, he just stared into space for a long moment.

"They could have told me," he said in a flat, hurt voice. "Mother should have told me." He hit the desk with his fist, hard enough to hurt.

"She should've," Elza said. "I would have, at least when you were an adult."

"What did you say," he said slowly, "when we were in bed?"

"I asked you about your father."

He leaned forward and spoke through clenched teeth. "You asked me whether I loved him." I rose from the chair, ready to go next door.

"Let me see your hand." She took it in one hand and, with the other hand, pressed the inside of his wrist.

He sat back slowly and looked at his wrist, and touched the small flesh-colored circle there. "What's that?"

"It's a relaxant." She must have had it palmed. "It'll wear off quickly."

"I . . ." He looked at the wall. "I was upset because I couldn't, I couldn't come."

"You did all right."

"No—I mean it happens all the time. I thought with you, with a new sexy woman . . ."

"It's all in the head," she said gently. "It's always all in the head. You were nervous."

"When you said . . . that about my father, I suddenly couldn't breathe. I mean I tried, and it was like someone, someone was *choking* me. I must have lashed out. I don't remember."

"You got in a lucky shot."

He smiled for the first time. "Thank you for not killing me. I've seen you throw Daniel and Namir around on the mat."

"It took some restraint. How is the elbow?"

"Still hurts a bit."

She stood. "Hmm. Take off your shirt and get up on the examination table." He did, and she moved his arm around and palpated his elbow. "That doesn't hurt?"

"Not really, no."

She pressed behind his shoulder. "This does, though?"

"A little."

She nodded and looked at him for a moment. "Take off your shoes and lie down on your back." He did, while she watched and nodded.

"I want to check your reflexes," she said, starting to unbuckle his belt. She stopped partway. "This wouldn't be ethical on Earth. But we're playing with starship rules."

"Okay," he said, smiling broadly. She unzipped his fly, and his reflexes appeared more than adequate.

I'll have to ask her about that patch. I turned off the notebook. It was time to start dinner. Go pull some carrots.

18

ANNIVERSARY

Namir is baking a cake. It's everyone's anniversary: we took off exactly one year ago, and everyone is still alive.

The notebook says that on Earth it's 16 July 89, so relativity has shrunk about seventy days off our calendar.

It does feel like twelve months have gone by, though, rather than fourteen, so a time for taking stock. In one year:

Only the one day of violence, back in September, when Moonboy broke Elza's nose, and Dustin parted his hair with a pool cue. For a long time now, Dustin and Moonboy have been civil with each other, and Elza has lost her nasal accent.

Elza also has fucked every man aboard except Paul (if he's telling the truth), and Meryl as well, in a three-way with Moonboy, though that seems to have petered out.

The avocado tree has blossomed, but set no fruit in spite of assiduous pollination. We've asked Earth for advice, but they're half a light-year away, so it will be a while.

Most of the other crops are thriving. We've almost doubled the floor space allotted to tomatoes, trimming the real estate from leafy greens and legumes. Namir needed more Italian plum tomatoes for sauces, and no one complained. I wish we'd brought more fruit trees, myself, or more acreage. Enough grapes to make our own wine; the idea of waiting for it to ferment is attractive; something to look forward to. Can't have everything.

The planners were wise to design such a large hydroponic garden, even though we could survive without it. Having regular menial chores helps keep us sane; caring for living things promotes optimism. Even in our situation.

In the sports news, I'm now swimming two kilometers a day. There's a new house rule in billiards: Namir has to shoot left-handed, or no one will play with him. He still wins, but not all the time anymore.

On Saturdays, we move all the lounge furniture to the walls, string a badminton net across the room, and work up a good sweat. The Martians come out and play for the first few minutes, one on each team, though they overheat quickly and are handicapped by the gravity, not to mention lacking the concept of "sport." We compensate for their relative lack of mobility by letting them each use two racquets. They're ambidextrous four ways.

Meryl's wall-sized crossword puzzle is about a third finished. She'd better slow down. Elza put away her needlepoint for a while, but has started a new one, another fractal chromatic fantasy.

Moonboy spends an hour or two a day on the piano, composing silently, and sometimes plays all night, haggard but happy in the morning. I don't read music too well, but noticed the other day that *Composition 3: Approach/Retreat* is thirty-five pages long.

Paul spends most of the mornings drinking coffee and cranking out equations, which he sometimes tries to explain to me. He won't be through coursework on the doctorate for another year and a half. Then he'll write a dissertation and send it off to Earth. So maybe in fifty years he'll get a doctorate in Quaint Astrophysics from Stanford, if there still is a Stanford.

Namir is working on another balalaika, a long one with low notes, and is slowly carving a bust of Elza, which is at a creepy stage—half of it still a block of wood and half a mostly finished sculpture, as if she were being pulled out of the material. Straight on, I think her expression is one of stoic acceptance; from another angle, her lips slightly apart, she looks like she's on the verge of an orgasm. He knows her better than any of us, of course. Maybe that's what she looks like all the time, to him.

I've taken up drawing again, using the texts Oz recommended when I was first on Mars. No paper, but it was a lifetime ago when I last had paper to spare. I can adjust the stylus and notebook to simulate pencil, ink, or wash. I'm copying some faces from the actual book that Namir brought along, all of Vermeer. His *The Geographer* looks a lot like Moonboy, though his hair isn't white.

Our brand-new spaceship is getting a little worn around the edges. The air recycler started making a noise like a person whistling through her teeth, barely audible. Paul described it to the auto-repair algorithm, and the noise stopped for a few days, then came back. Meryl did it a slightly different way, and it stayed quiet. But it was a scary time. Can't send out for parts.

The Martians' swimming pool has to be continuously recaulked. Long hours of immersion—totally unnatural, of course, for Martians—must do something with the chemistry of their skin, which makes the water react with the caulking compound. Try to get those two out of the water, though.

Along with Meryl and Moonboy, I'm chipping away at the Martian language. Snowbird is more helpful than Fly-in-Amber, but even so it's a frustrating experience.

Moonboy is developing a good ear for using the synthesizer to simulate Martian sounds, and in a real sense he's the only one of us who can "speak" Martian with anything like a useful vocabulary. With merely human larynx and vocal cords, I can do about three hundred words that Snowbird can recognize consistently, but many of those, like "swimming," are neologisms derived from human sounds.

Moonboy can play more than ten times my number of words, but a similar problem is emerging: we can only talk about experiences that humans and Martians share. Most of what they do and think is hidden from us.

Some may even be hidden on purpose. We have no idea what their secret agenda might be. *They* might not even know.

When the lone Other communicated to us from Neptune's satellite Triton, it did so at first through a long rote message that Fly-in-Amber and other members of his family recited after a hypnotic stimulus. They translated it for us, but how complete was the translation? How honest?

We must always keep in mind that the Martians were created by the Others for the sole purpose of contacting us after we developed the ability to go to Mars. We were no danger to them until then.

This is the only thing that lone Other said to us in a human language, in response to our first message:

Peace is a good sentiment.

Your assumption about my body chemistry is clever but wrong. I will tell you more later.

At this time I do not wish to tell you where my people live.

I have been watching your development for a long time, mostly through radio and television. If you take an objective view of human behavior since the early twentieth century, you can understand why I must approach you with caution.

I apologize for having destroyed your Triton probe back in 2044. I didn't want you to know exactly where I am on this world.

If you send another probe, I will do the same thing, again with apologies.

For reasons that may become apparent soon, I don't wish to communicate with you directly. The biological constructs that live below the surface of Mars were created thousands of years ago, with the sole purpose of eventually talking to you and, at the right time, serving as a conduit through which I could reveal my existence.

"Our" existence, actually, since we have millions of individuals elsewhere. On our home planet and watching other planets, like yours.

This is a clumsy and limited language for me, as are all human languages. The Martian ones were created for communication between you and me, and from now on I would like to utilize the most complex of those Martian languages, which is used by only one individual, the leader you call Red.

When the Other sent this message to us, it must have known that within a few days the delayed-action bomb within Red would go off and destroy all higher forms of life on Earth.

So why did it bother?

Most of us think it was hedging its bets in case, as did happen, the human race figured out a way around the doomsday bomb. Namir believes it *assumed* we would solve the puzzle and survive, a subtle difference.

Red might have figured it out before he died. He had talked with the Other, or at least listened to it, and on his way to the Moon and doom, he talked nonstop about it for almost twenty hours. Every word was recorded, but it hasn't yet been translated—only one Martian, his successor, will be able to comprehend it, and when we left she was still studying the language.

(The long transition period between one leader's death and the education of the succeeding leader was never a problem before humans came along. Martian daily life was simple and predictable, and if something came up in the dozen or two ares while they were leaderless, it would just have to wait.)

We had dessert in the compromise lounge, so the Martians could comfortably join us, even though the human "year" is irrelevant to their calendar.

We had taken a plastic bottle of tej, Ethiopian honey wine, out of the luxury stores. It went well with the coffee-and-honey cake recipe Namir remembered from his childhood, some Jewish tradition.

Either would be poison to the Martians, of course, but they brought out some special purple fungus and what looked and smelled like sulfurous swamp water.

I held up my glass to them and croaked out a greeting that was traditional for such occasions, which roughly translates as "Well, another year." Snowbird and Namir exchanged toasts in Japanese and bowed, which in the case of the Martian looked weirdly like a horse in dressage. Plastic glasses were clicked all around.

The cake was sinfully excellent. "We should have this every day," Elza said. "In five years, we'll be bigger than the Martians."

"That would be attractive," Fly-in-Amber admitted, "but I don't think you have that much honey."

You can never tell when they're joking. They have the same complaint about us.

Moonboy had his small synth keyboard, and he played a few words for Snowbird, who responded with a thrumming, crackling sound, then the thump of laughter.

"I told her she was looking slim," he said, "and she answered that the food here was lousy."

That was actually a pretty subtle joke. Martians don't much care what they eat, but she knew about that attitude from humans.

After we finished the cake and tej, we switched to regular wine and other alcohol, and Snowbird asked whether Namir would bring out his balalaika and do a duet with Moonboy. Namir asked Dustin whether he could stand it, and he said that once a year wouldn't kill him.

By the time Namir had retrieved the balalaika from the workshop, Moonboy had figured out how to simulate a primitive accordion, and with his sensitive ear he had no trouble squeezing out chords that matched the Eastern European and Israeli tunes Namir knew, and did an occasional simulated-clarinet solo, what he called klezmer style. Most of it was new to me, and I was glad of the Martian request.

When we went to bed, Paul and I made love, even though it wasn't Saturday (badminton brings out the beast in him).

Afterward, he was restless. "I'm the most useless pilot in history."

"I don't know. The guy in charge of the *Titanic* didn't exactly earn his paycheck."

"This morning while you were gardening, I went up to the shuttle and put it through some simulations for landing."

A few years premature. "Practice makes perfect?"

"I could do them in my sleep, which is the problem. There are really only four basic situations in the VR—Earth, Mars, Moon, and zero-gee rendezvous. I can fiddle with the parameters. But I'm not really learning anything."

"Well, it's not rocket science, as they used to say. Except that it is rocket science. And you're the best. I read that somewhere."

I could feel his smile in the dark, and he patted my hip. "The best within a half light-year, anyhow. But we should have thought to make up some weird simulations, like a dense, turbulent atmosphere. A dusty one. You'd never land in a dust storm if you had a chance. But I'll have to take what I get."

"Well, it's just software, isn't it? Describe what you need and tight-beam it to Earth. They could develop and test it, and send it to you after turnaround."

He paused. "Sometimes you surprise me."

I resisted the impulse to reach down and actually surprise him. It was already late, though, and I didn't want to give him any more ideas.

19

YEAR TWO

8 May 2090

Our second year began with a smaller useful crew, and perhaps reduced efficiency from those of us who are left.

We've essentially lost Moonboy. Whenever he's not in VR, he's locked into earphones. He doesn't even take them off to eat. If you ask him a question, he hands you a notebook; write down the query, and he'll write a short response, or nod or shrug, usually.

It started with noise coming from the air-conditioning. At first it was a high-pitched whistle. We were able to program the self-repair algorithm and reduce it to bare audibility, but in the process introduced a varying frequency component: if you listen closely, it's like someone whistling tunelessly in another room. I can hardly hear it at all, but Moonboy said it was going to drive him mad, and apparently it did.

We can still use him after a fashion, to try to translate if one of the Martians says something incomprehensible. But it's hard to get his attention, and impossible to make him concentrate.

Elza says he's apparently in a dissociative fugue. His medical history is dominated by dissociative amnesia, not being able to remember a murderous assault by his father when he was a boy.

Medication isn't effective. A dose large enough to give him some peace knocks him out, and when he wakes up, the noise is still there, and he claps on the 'phones.

Meryl is of course, depressed, with Moonboy such a wreck, but everyone else seems stable, if not happy. Elza seems resigned to Paul's obstinate monogamy. I should thank him.

Memo to the next people who staff a mission like this: make sure nobody in the crew is fucking crazy.

Of course, we may all be, in less dramatic ways.

Other than the noisy life-support system, the ship seems shipshape. In December I spent a couple of weeks in advanced menu planning— we've been too conservative in using the luxury stores. We could use more than half of them on the way to Wolf. If we do survive the encounter with the Others, we'll probably be content with anything on the way back. Morale's only a problem on the way there.

I talked with Paul about this, but not with the others. The last thing I need in the kitchen is a democracy.

I'm continuing my study of first-contact narratives in human history. Usually less destructive than the Others' contact with us, though the ultimate result is often extinction, anyhow.

There aren't really close analogies. Aboriginal societies didn't send off diplomats to plead peace with their high-tech conquerors. What would have happened if the Maori, on learning where their invaders came from, had taken a war canoe and paddled around the Cape and up the Atlantic and the Thames to parley with Queen Victoria? She's atypical, actually. Reports of Maori military performance led her to offer them at least symbolic equality in the governance of New Zealand. The Others would probably just have nuked them all. With the wave of a hand.

Of course, we don't really know anything about their psychology or philosophy, other than the fact that they observed us, judged us, and tried to execute us all, with no discussion. When I was a boy, I watched my father spray a nest of wasps that had grown on the side of our house. You could see in their frantic paroxysms how painful an end that was, and my father laughed at me for crying. Maybe some few of the Others will mourn our necessary extinction.

In a way that I would hesitate to call mystical, life becomes more and more precious as we ply our way toward whatever awaits—and I mean that in the most prosaic sense; I wake up every morning eager for the day, even though I do little other than cook and read and talk. A little music, too little.

I swim almost every day, trying to reserve the pool for the half hour after Carmen swims. I can legitimately show up a few minutes early and look at her.

How do I really feel toward her? We talk about everything but that. If I were closer to her age, I might move toward romance, or at least sex, but I'm almost as old as her father. She brought that up early on, and I have no desire to appear foolish. Besides, I'm married to the only certified nymphomaniac within light-years. Another woman might be too much of a good thing.

But I do feel close to her, sometimes closer than I am to Elza, who will never let me or anyone else into her mysterious center—a place I think she herself never visits. Carmen seems totally open, American to the core, even if her passport says "Martian."

I think my foreignness attracts her, but at some level frightens her as well. The opposite of Elza, in a way. The fact that I've been a professional killer thrills Elza, I think, though she would be less thrilled if she knew how many I've killed, and how, and why.

PART 3

THE FLOWER

I

YEAR THREE

8 May 2091

This is the end of the third Earth year of our voyage to Wolf 25, to meet with the Others and learn our fate. Humans being superstitious about anniversaries, they asked that we each write up a summarizing statement for these occasions.

For me it's pointless, since I recall everything whether it is important or not. But I will do it. (Snowbird is more intimately involved with the humans than I am. That's natural; the white family is more social, even among Martians. We yellows are better observers.)

The most interesting thing about the year to come is that we're approaching the midpoint, turnaround time. The past year has been more or less uneventful for Martians, though it could have been our ending. The brown pyatyur fungus almost stopped growing, which would eventually have been fatal for us, but Meryl and Carmen figured out what was wrong. It was lacking nitrates—that is, the pseudo-Martian ecosystem was not properly recycling nitrates. We only need trace quantities, so the lack wasn't obvious. Human agriculture needs large amounts, though, and they are full of it. A day's production of human urine gives us a year's worth.

Snowbird continued working with Meryl and Carmen on their language lessons, and I sometimes participated, though it has become steadily more difficult. We seem to have covered all of the easy vocabulary, and it's hard to explore the more difficult words and phrases without Moonboy's synthesizer. They can't even approximate many of the sounds. Moonboy could do well within the range of his hearing.

(I think he might be able to help us more if the other humans weren't so afraid of him. Snowbird says that some of that fear is reflected fear of their own potential for not-sane behavior. Moonboy scares them, and he knows he's scaring them, which reinforces the behavior. Meryl explained this to Snowbird, but being able to explain it is not the same as coping with it.)

Namir and I have been playing chess, a variation of the game called Kriegspieler, where neither player is allowed to look at the board; you have to keep the positions of the pieces in your memory as you play. That requires no effort on my part, of course; like any other yellow Martian, one glance will fix the board in my memory for the rest of my life. Namir makes up for his occasional memory lapse by what he calls "killer instinct," and he wins almost every time. (I think it's less killer instinct than the fact that his moves are sometimes based on a board that doesn't exist, and so are impossible for me to anticipate.)

Kriegspieler is normally played with a third person, a referee who keeps track of the progress of the game with a physical board, out of sight. The referee tells you whether a move is impossible (blocked by another piece) or whether you've successfully captured a piece. We started out with Carmen as a referee, but I pointed out that she was supernumerary. I could tell Namir if a move was not possible or had been successful, and of course would not lie.

Snowbird plays a board game with the humans, too, a word game called Scrabble, which Meryl had brought along as part of her weight allowance, indicating that the game is important to her, and she is skilled at it. Carmen also plays, and they have a list of Martian words that may be used, and count double. I have played the game but find it maddeningly slow.

Badminton, on the other hand, is plenty fast enough for us in this gravity. Snowbird enjoys it, and I do not. Jumping around like that is ungraceful and painful. But a certain amount of exercise is necessary, as is the appearance of working with the humans as a team.

Whose side will we be on when we get to Wolf 25? The Others did make us, and (speaking as an individual) I can't pretend to be a free agent, independent of their will. I had absolutely no control over myself the one time the Others needed me to do their bidding, when I suddenly parroted their message in 2079. There could be a large variety of complex behaviors they are able to trigger with a word. Or just a particular beam of light, as happened then.

Suppose they ordered me to open the air-lock door?

But I suspect the fact that we haven't yet been obliterated means that the Others know where we are and what we're doing. The humans' efforts to keep the mission secret probably amuse them.

If they are capable of being amused. There are so many basic things we don't know about them, or have just inferred from incomplete data.

One thing that does seem inescapable is their lack of concern for human life, and probably Martian life as well. When we meet them, we will need to come up with some reason for their allowing us to live— something that doesn't have to do with the immorality or injustice of exterminating us.

What is important to them? Is there anything we can do that would make them happy? Whatever "happy" means. Maybe destroying planets is the only thing that pleases them.

We inhabit a different world of time. They seem glacially slow to us, and we must seem like annoying insects to them—buzzing around with our inconsequential lives, our tiny and evanescent concerns. (That was the way Namir put it. There are no glaciers as such on Mars, and no insects other than the ones that humans brought along for agriculture.)

In a few months, the charade will be over. No sense in trying to hide our existence once we've pointed our matter-annihilation jet directly at the Others. Prior to our turnaround, a small fast probe will broadcast a description of what we're planning to do.

Though it's not much of a plan. "Please don't kill us before you hear what we have to say."

As if we could really understand each other.

2

TURNAROUND

Paul has been at loose ends ever since he finished his dissertation—and it really was "finished" more completely than most scientific theses, since he couldn't make new measurements or read current research on the topic, which was *Data Granulation in Surveys of Gravitational Lensing in Globular Clusters, 2002–2085*.

So the approach of turnaround was a great outlet for his stalled energies. He had a checklist with nearly a thousand items, compiled before we left, and he added a few himself. The original list didn't say anything about making sure the balalaikas were secured.

We will be in zero gee for a little over two days, while our dirty iceberg slowly turns to point its jet toward the Others. The Martians will love it. I'm looking forward to the novelty myself. Good memories.

Taking care of the plants won't be the big project it was before we took off. Just keep everything damp. Try not to crash into anything while cruising from place to place.

I do have one big irrational worry. Nobody has ever stopped and restarted a huge engine like this one—the test vehicle was hardly a thousandth this mass. What if it doesn't start? Nobody *really* knows what makes it work, anyhow.

Maybe they do by now, on Earth. But if it didn't restart, and we radioed "What do we do now?" it would be more than twenty-four years before we got the answer. "Slam the doors and try again."

⚙

Even Fly-in-Amber, who wouldn't blink at the Second Coming, seemed a little excited about turnaround. Well, it *will* be the journey's midpoint, as well as a brief respite from the burden of Earth-style gravity. He was not happy that we had to drain their makeshift pool (and Paul was not happy about having to recycle the water separately, to keep all their germs and cooties in their own ecosystem). Our own pool came with a watertight cover.

We had the furniture secured and the plants taken care of a couple of hours before Paul was to shut down the engine. Namir prepared a luxury feast, lamb chops baked with rehydrated fruit and Middle Eastern spices, served over couscous. We opened one of the few bottles of actual wine.

After a pastry dessert, Paul checked his wrist and got up from the table. "Forty-eight minutes," he said. "I'll turn it off at 2200 sharp. No need for a countdown?"

We all agreed. "I'll go remind the Martians," Namir said. "When will you start the rotation?"

"After a general systems check, maybe an hour. Don't think we'll feel anything. Six degrees per hour." Two small steering jets on opposite sides of the iceball's equator would get us slowly spinning, then stop us twenty-eight hours later.

I had a queasy feeling that maybe I should have dined on soda crackers and water instead, Paul's reassurances notwithstanding. It was a little more than waiting for the other shoe to drop. I went back to the bathroom and found a stomach pill.

It didn't help that Moonboy sat there with his drugged smile, listening to the music of the spheres. When Meryl told him what was about to happen, he typed out LOOKING FORWARD TO IT. NOISE MIGHT STOP. Sure, if life support stops.

To distract myself, I went to the bicycle machine and took a VR ride through downtown Paris, trying to hit every man with a mustache.

At about five minutes to the hour, I joined the others in the compromise lounge. Everyone had filled squeeze bottles with water and other things to drink in zero gee, good idea. I went to the storeroom and drew six liters of water in a plastic cow, and concentrate for two liters of wine, which made a red light blink next to my name. Paul's light wasn't blinking, so I drew a couple of liters for him, too. He must have been too busy, hovering over the OFF switch.

I returned to the lounge with my armloads of water and wine. "You are ready for a party," Snowbird said. I croaked out a catchphrase that meant something like "I wish the same state for you." She clapped lightly with her small hands.

We were all sort of braced for it when 2200 came, but of course it wasn't like slamming on the brakes. Gravity just stopped. I pushed off gently and floated toward the ceiling. Namir and Snowbird followed.

"I guess nothing went wrong," Meryl said, rotating by in a slow somersault.

Moonboy hadn't moved. He took off the earphones and listened intently for a couple of seconds. "Still there." He put them back on, hovering a foot off the couch.

Elza floated up to join Namir, clasping him with her arms and legs. Well, he wouldn't be able to shoot pool; have to do something for two days.

Paul came out of the control room walking on the floor with his gecko slippers. He had a strange expression. My stomach fell as he spoke: "Something's screwy." He shook his head. "The proximity—"

There was a faint metallic sound. Then three more.

"The air lock," Namir said.

Surprise, then terror. Inappropriately, I laughed, and so did Meryl.

"Has to be the Others," Paul said.

"Might as well let them in," Namir said, "before they just blow it open."

The people who designed the ship should have put a camera out there. But we hadn't expected callers.

We all followed Paul, all of us but Moonboy, floating various trajectories toward the air lock. Paul opened the control box and pushed the OPEN SEQUENCE button. A pump hammered for less than a minute, fading as the air was sucked out of the lock.

The outer door opened onto total darkness. There was a moment of terrible suspense. Then a man in a conventional white space suit used a navigating jet to float in and stopped by touching the inner door window.

"I'll be damned," Dustin said. "They caught up with us this soon?" We'd talked about the possibility of Earth's inventing a speedier spacecraft, which would catch up with us. Turnaround would be a logical place to meet, when our engine was turned off.

"No," Paul said, "if they were from Earth, they would have radioed." He pushed the CLOSE SEQUENCE button, and the outer door closed and air sighed back into the little sealed room. The inner door opened and the stranger floated out toward us.

He or she or it undid the helmet clasps and let the helmet float away. A male in his twenties or thirties, no obvious ethnicity.

"Good for you. You didn't try to kill me."

"You're an Other?" Paul said.

"No, of course not." It wasn't looking at Paul, just studying each of us in turn. "They couldn't speak to you in real time. Your lives are trivially short and swift. I'm an artificial biological construct, like you two Martians, created to mimic a human rate of perception and reaction.

"I'm a tool made by a tool. The one who communicated with you from Triton—"

"Who tried to destroy the Earth," Paul said.

"Only the *life* on Earth, yes. I was made in case you survived that. As I believe you know, the one who made me lives slower and longer than humans or Martians, but is still a mayfly compared to the Others."

"It left Triton, though," Paul said, "just before the explosion."

"Yes. It is here now, in a small habitat near your air lock. Fastened to the iceberg by now. We've been nearby for some time, within a few million miles, but of course did not physically connect until your engine stopped."

"Why are you here?" I asked. "To keep an eye on us?"

"That, yes. And to help decide whether you should be allowed near the Others' home planet."

"Then you're set up to destroy us, as Red was?"

"Not at all. It's not necessary." His expression revealed nothing. It was not neutral, exactly, but more controlled than the serving robots at McDonald's.

"Because the Others themselves won't let us get close enough to hurt them," Namir said.

"That's correct. We have already begun sending them information. I think the more you let me know, the better your chances will be."

"Do you have a name?" I asked.

"No. You may call me whatever you please."

"Spy," Namir said.

"Considering the source," it said, "I am honored."

"You know a lot about us?" I said.

"Only what has been public knowledge on Earth. Namir, Elza, Paul, Carmen, Dustin, Meryl, Snowbird, Fly-in-Amber." It pointed. "That would be Moonboy."

He was facing away from us, floating halfway to the kitchen, listening to music. "Yes," Meryl said. "He's not feeling well."

"Perhaps none of you are." It looked around. "I will be as small a burden as possible. I will spend most of my time in my quarters, with the Other. Conversation necessarily takes a long time. Once we have deceleration, I can walk back and forth at will. The external airlock control is simple; I didn't use it this time because I didn't want to frighten you with an alarm."

"That was neighborly," I said. "Can I offer you something to eat or drink?"

"Oh, no. I don't want to burden your life support; I can take care of that in my own ship. Like the Martians, I consume very little."

"We were made by intelligent design," Snowbird said, "not haphazard evolution." She had been studying the history of human science. But it was correct; Martians needed only a third of the life-support mass humans required. (Being indifferent to what you eat or drink is a factor, too—if we were willing to live on hardtack biscuits and water, we could save a lot of reaction mass.)

"You took a chance coming over here," Paul said. "One course correction, and you'd be adrift."

"I'm replaceable. How often do you do that?"

"Every few days." Enough to keep us from going outside.

"A reasonable risk." It looked around. "I would like to have a tour of your ship, if you don't mind. Then you may tour ours."

Paul nodded slowly. "We have nothing to hide."

"I can speak consensus Martian," it said, turning to Fly-in-Amber. "Would you guide me?"

Fly-in-Amber trilled a "yes" sound, and they headed off toward the Martian rooms. A logical starting place, but both Paul and Namir looked unhappy. "Wish it had chosen you," Paul said to Snowbird.

"I wish that as well," she said. "I'm curious."

And more communicative, I didn't bother to add. Fly-in-Amber might remember every detail, but we'd have to drag it out of him if he didn't feel like talking.

"Well . . . come into the control room," Paul said. "We'll see what their ship looks like."

I put on my gecko slippers and followed him. We waited at the door for the others.

"General," he said as he walked in, and the control surfaces morphed to that configuration, a lot more dials and knobs and switches than the set he'd been using. He strapped himself into the swivel seat, and said, "Outside view."

There was a flatscreen a meter square in front of him, and it darkened to a velvet blackness with a thousand sparks. He twiddled a joystick, and the angle veered around dizzyingly until it came to rest on a familiar view of the iceberg surface, with a decidedly unfamiliar visitor.

It didn't look like a spaceship; it didn't look like a machine at all. It looked kind of like a starfish with seven legs, pebbly skin that was mottled red and black, with filaments like cilia or antennae wiggling on ribs that ran down each leg. It would have looked right at home on the ocean floor if it were hand-sized. But it was easily half as big as the *ad Astra* landing craft.

"I wonder what makes it tick," Namir said. "It can't be carrying enough reaction mass for interstellar travel."

"Well, if it's the same thing that left Triton, it took off at twenty-five gees," Paul said. "That argues for something more exotic than we've got. Spy says they've been following us, for who knows how long . . . so I guess it went out far enough to be undetectable, then just watched and waited. Then tailed us at its leisure." He cranked up the magnification and slowly examined the thing. No obvious portholes or gunports or wheels or grommets. I suppose if you examined a starfish with a magnifying glass, you would see about the same thing.

"Maybe it's alive, too," Meryl said, "the way Martians are, and Spy claims to be. Grown for a specific purpose."

"I would vote for that," Snowbird said.

"Looks like a relative?" Dustin said.

"In a way. If the Others have an aesthetic, and our design reflects it, so does the vehicle's design. Don't you think?"

"See what you mean," I said. Though "aesthetic" isn't the word I would have chosen. It was almost ugly—but then so were the Martians until you got used to them.

I went back to my workstation and considered the pictures of the ship, thinking of it in terms of a living organism. I'd studied Terran invertebrates, of course, and remembered a seven-legged starfish. I clicked around and found the one I remembered, a pretty British creature, nicely symmetrical and less than a foot wide. There was also a seven-legged one from New Zealand waters, almost a yard wide, that looked octopoid and menacing, and in fact a footnote warned that if it grabbed your wet suit, it was almost impossible to pry loose. But it was the slender British one, *Luidia ciliaris*, that resembled the starship.

Nothing but its shape was relevant, of course. The only other creature I could find with seven legs, other than sadly mutated spiders, was the extinct *Hallucigenia sparsa*, a tiny but mean-looking fossil.

The only picture we had of the Others was a simple diagram they sent that we interpreted as having six legs and a tail. Maybe they did have seven legs, instead. So built a starship in their own image.

It was an odd shape for a vehicle, counterintuitive, but maybe my intuitions would be different if I had a seven-based number system.

Zero gee isn't conducive to abstract thinking, which may be one reason space pilots have not distinguished themselves as philosophers.

Another reason may be that they are basically jocks with fast reflexes. I pinged my pilot and said I was going to nap for a while, and he joined me in the bedroom for a few minutes of not napping. Then we did doze together, floating in midair with a sweat-damp sheet wrapped around us. I dreamed of monsters.

3

THE GRAND TOUR

The humans of course wanted to interrogate me as soon as Spy went back to its ship. But I hadn't learned all that much about the creature. It asked all the questions.

We first went to the Martian quarters. It already knew the basic principles of our recirculating ecology; in fact, it knew more about some of the science and engineering than I did. It appears to have a memory like mine, perfect, but it had studied Martian physiology, for instance, with more depth than I was ever exposed to.

Part of what we discussed there is not translatable, because it has to do with an intimacy between Snowbird and me that has no human counterpart. To answer the obvious (to humans) question, it is not a sexual relationship, nor does it have anything to do with emotional bonding. It is a practical matter that has to do with being ready to die.

The pool that you built for us interested it; it wanted to know what humans gained by this demonstration of friendship. Altruism was difficult to explain, but it understood about doing favors in expectation of eventual return.

Then I took it around to all the crops. This took the most time, because for some reason it needed to know details about the propagation and maintenance of every species.

(I would call this a hopeful sign. Why would the Others need this information other than to help humans survive after some life-support mishap?)

Similarly, I took it through the warehouse area, which is mostly human food storage. It was interested in Namir's homemade musical instruments. Music seems not as mysterious to them as it is to Martians; it asked me some questions that I could not answer; I said to ask Namir.

It also asked questions about the shop area that I could not answer, mostly about the weapons that obviously could be made there. They can't be thinking that we will be making swords and pistols to attack them. I expressed this thought, and Spy said of course I was right. But I assume the situation is more complex than that and recommend that Paul or Namir, with their experience as warriors, engage him on this topic, to reassure them.

(I did not say anything, of course, about our conversation, our group meeting, on 8 May 2085, where we discussed the possibility of a kamikaze attack, using all of *ad Astra* as a high-velocity bomb. I assume that is no longer a possibility, so there was no need to discuss it.)

It was very interested in the swimming and exercise area, with the virtual-reality escape masks, or helmets. It looked at the exercise log carefully, perhaps to have a picture of each person's physical strength. There was a long and odd discussion about the physical differences between humans and Martians, which covered things it must already have known. I think it was examining my attitudes (or mine and Snowbird's) toward you humans.

I think that when we arrive at Wolf 25, the Others will want to exploit the difference between the two races and take advantage of the fact that we are, in some abstract essence, their children. As you know, from several conversations over these past three years, our allegiance is with you. Of course, that is exactly what I would say if I were lying, especially if I were on its side.

It wanted to investigate some private quarters. Since I am closest to Namir, I prevailed upon him. I explained to Spy about the sexual relationship among him and Dustin and Elza, as well as I can understand it, and how that mandates the arrangement of the sleeping area of each.

Of course, Namir's bedroom is small (as is Dustin's, since they are just for sleeping), and its walls are a constantly changing art gallery, thousands of reproductions from the great museums of Earth. Spy had difficulty understanding this, as do I. One thing Martians and humans have in common is a preference for darkness and quiet when we sleep. So what does it matter what's on the walls? Dustin's room is plain, with only an abstract picture he calls a mandala on one wall.

In Elza's bedroom there is a large cube for showing movies, which usually are depictions of humans mating in various ways, which Namir explained as being an aid in their own mating, or I should say "fucking," since I understand that Elza, like the other females, has suspended her reproductive function for the duration of the flight.

Of course Spy knew enough about human nature not to be surprised by that, as it was not surprised when we then visited the kitchen, where Namir pleases himself and the rest of you by preparing your food in various original ways. Neither we nor the Others see the point in changing the appearance and flavor of fuel.

I think we shared a thing like humor over your counterproductive need for variety in these commonplace aspects of life. I don't think its motives regarding me are friendly, though, or simple; it seemed to be testing me. Perhaps it will do the same with you humans at a later date.

We heard Namir and Dustin making noise down by the swimming area, and backtracked to watch. They couldn't play pool in zero gee, so they had improvised a three-dimensional variant, more gentle and slow than the original. I could not quite understand the rules, which amused them. Dustin said they had to make up the rules as the game progressed, since nobody had ever played it before.

This may be important: Spy revealed that the Others have a similar activity. Much of their time, like yours, goes to individual contests that have only a symbolic relation to real events. The compact way it described those contests did not reveal much, except that the physical actions are not accomplished by individual Others; they are done by beings like Spy, biological constructs that are autonomous but obedient. And the point of the game is not to win, but to discover the rules.

We completed the circuit by investigating the lounge and work areas, where most humans spend the waking hours that are not given over to strictly biological activities.

When Spy began to put on its helmet, Paul came over to operate the air lock. One person can do it alone, but it's simpler to have someone outside the lock pushing the buttons. He told Spy he would start to fire the steering jets at 0230; best to be inside by then.

Before the outer door was even open, Carmen and the others were bearing down on me with questions.

4

OTHER-NESS

Fly-in-Amber let us grill him for exactly one hour. Then he said he would submit a written report tomorrow and went off to rest.

Namir wondered aloud how he would do that. Lying down is irrelevant in zero gee, but they never actually lie down, anyhow. Hard to sort out all the legs.

Having a conversation was odd, too, without a physical up and down. By convention, most people tried to stay upright, but if you didn't hang on to something, you could start to drift. Paul let himself go every which way, I supposed to demonstrate how natural the state was to an old space hand.

We were in the compromise lounge, and it was cold. I told Snowbird we had to move into the dining area. She said she would come along for a little while.

Namir had put a collection of ration bars in a plastic bag with a drawstring. I took a peanut butter one and passed the bag around.

Snowbird bounced gently off the refrigerator and grabbed onto the dining-room table with three arms. "You were not too pleased with what Fly-in-Amber remembered?" she said to me.

"We could wish for more. But we'll have years."

"The next time it visits, we'll have plenty of questions," Paul said.

"Can you establish a radio link?" Meryl asked. "Or would it be better not to?"

"No reason not to," Namir said. He looked around with a stony expression. "It's a good thing we have nothing to hide. They're probably hearing every word we say."

"Through vacuum?" I said.

"Any Earth spook could do it. Spy could have dropped a microtransmitter in here while it was walking around, but you could be even more direct than that—attach a sensor to the hull and have it transmit the vibrations it picks up.

"I don't think that would work once the main drive starts up again," Paul said. "The vibrations would overwhelm your signal."

"Maybe so." His expression didn't change.

"They'd have something like S2N," I said. It's a spook program to coax out data that's buried in noise.

That brought a little smile. "How on earth do you know about S2N?"

"I haven't been on Earth since '72," I kidded him, "but you can learn a thing or two in orbit." It was an unpleasant memory. Dargo Solingen had used S2N to spy on Paul and Red and me, overhearing our whispered conferences under loud music. A day later, our secrets were headlines on Earth, and the Others decided it was time for us all to die. Sort of a turning point in one's life.

"What it said about the Others playing games," Dustin said, "to find out the rules. I want to know more about that."

"They might view us as contestants?" I said.

"Or pieces," Namir said. "Pawns."

"Anything but rivals," Meryl said. "If they perceive us as a danger, we won't even get close to them."

I nodded. "No matter what Spy says, we have to assume it can destroy us if it thinks we present a danger to the Others."

"We ought to figure out a way to talk to its buddy," Paul said. "The speeded-up Other."

"Hard to visualize a conversation," I said. "Eight minutes passing for us, for every minute it experiences."

"Say something, play a round of poker, then listen and respond," Dustin said. "Spy will always be our intermediary anyhow."

Namir nodded. "We could do something like that. We just have to find a way to present it so it appears to give them an advantage."

"Home team?" Dustin said. "We agree to go over there to talk?"

"That would be our advantage," Namir said. "Get a look inside their ship."

"Wait," I said. "We're not *fighting* them. It's the opposite. We want them to feel safe, cooperating with us."

Namir laughed. "Like a mouse negotiating with a python."

"She's right," Meryl said. "We can't see it as a contest. We already know what the result would be, in a contest of strength, or will."

"I don't know about will," Namir said.

Elza snorted. "Spoken like a true man. You have balls, darling, but they're no advantage here."

There was a loud ping from the control room. Paul launched himself in that direction, somersaulting in midair, and slipped through the door. I could hear him saying a few words, responding to the radio.

He walked back, with his gecko slippers, looking thoughtful. "Interesting coincidence. We have an invitation from 'Other-prime.' To come over for an audience with His Nibs."

"All of us?" I asked.

"Just four. You and me and Namir, and Fly-in-Amber."

"Any danger?"

"Well, we'll want to be tethered down on the way over and back, in case of a course correction blip. I can fix that easily with a guideline. Once we're over there . . ." He shrugged. "We'll be at their mercy. Exactly as we are here."

❋

Paul put off the turnaround rotation, even though it probably would make little difference. He got a roll of cable and a couple of pitons, ice spikes, out of the workshop, and I went along as fetch-and-carry. It was the first time either of us had been outside in over three years; we'd all done it as a safety drill before the engine started. You wouldn't want to do it during acceleration. Like being perched on top of a rocket. One misstep, and you'd slide off and drop forever.

Hammering in a piton wasn't simple in zero gee. There was nothing to hold him to the "ground," so after each swing, he would rotate away from the spike. He'd foreseen this, of course, and brought along a hand drill to make a preliminary hole.

I held a light for him but looked away from it to preserve my night vision. The sky was beautiful, the stars brighter than on Earth, the Milky Way a glowing billow across the darkness. I wished I knew the constellations well enough to tell whether they were different. Orion looked about the same. Paul pointed out where our Sun was. A bright yellow star, but there were brighter ones.

We had safety tethers attached to the air lock. After the piton was secured, Paul jetted across first, unreeling the guideline behind him. I followed him hand over hand, trying not to tangle the three lines.

The air lock on the starfish-shaped craft was a barely visible lip. Paul drilled and hammered a piton right in front of it. He secured the guideline to give it about three or four feet of slack; if you held on to it, you could walk, after a fashion, from one air lock to the other.

We returned to our own ship to relax for a few minutes and ensure we'd be going over with full air tanks and empty bladders. There was no strategy to discuss; we'd just keep our eyes and minds open.

Fly-in-Amber went over between us, moving with characteristic caution. I didn't mind going slowly. It was a long way down.

When we got to the air-lock lip, Paul opened the radio circuit—I heard a slight click—but before he could say anything, Spy's voice said, "Come in," too loud and too clear. The lips parted to reveal a red glow.

"Returning to the womb," I said. We went in, and the lips closed behind us. The small red light inside my helmet, an air warning, glowed green.

"Is this safe to breathe?" Paul asked on the radio.

"If I wanted to kill you," Spy said, "I wouldn't have to go to this much trouble. This is exactly the same pressure and composition as you breathe over there." He stepped in out of the gloom and made a circle with one hand. "Paul, get your feet under you. I'm going to turn on some gravity." As the light increased, so did the feeling of weight. It was very feeble, though; much less than Mars.

"What kind of gravity?" Paul asked.

"Triton. About one-twelfth Earth's gravity; less than a third that of Mars."

The room was organic in a mildly disgusting way. I had to take a colonoscopy before they would let me go to Mars, but they did let me watch, and the walls here looked like the inside of my large intestine then, pink and slippery. That gave me a whole new attitude toward the air lock. There was no furniture in the room, no windows except for two portholes, one on each side of the air-lock lips. Not a sound.

"I will introduce you to the Other-prime, though of course it cannot respond directly." He touched the wall, and a dark oval appeared, like wet glass. We stepped forward.

I'm afraid I made a little noise of alarm. It was, in a word, a monster. A word that shouldn't be in a xenobiologist's vocabulary, but there you have it.

The creature was all chitin and claws, hard shiny brown with yellow streaks and blobs. Six smaller claws, about the size of human arms, circled the thorax. A seventh one, twice as big, curled over the top like a scorpion's tail. A powerful serrated vise.

The biologist in me immediately wondered what was in its environment that required such armor and strength. "How big is it?"

"About twice human size," Spy said. "It won't hurt you, though. Too warm out here for it to survive.

"It is looking at you through me and wants to say something. I will relay the message in a few minutes."

I studied the creature while we waited. It looked more like a huge crab than any other terrestrial animal. No crabs on Earth were that big, I thought, except maybe the long spindly ones that live on the bottom of the ocean, spider crabs. This guy could eat them alive.

Which again raises the question, why? None of our speculations about its environment, living in liquid nitrogen, considered the possibility of strong, fast predators.

Of course, it couldn't react fast, which would explain the armor.

Maybe our assumptions about body chemistry were wrong. Temperature chauvinism. The fact that this species is slow doesn't mean that all nitrogen-based cryogenic life-forms are slow.

So that's the next question. If the environment has swift, strong predators, what did the Others evolve from, when a snail could run circles around them? Well, just because they're smart doesn't mean they're at the top of the food chain. There are plenty of environments on Earth where the crown of creation would be lunch.

It would be fascinating to investigate the Others' planet and see whether it was biologically as complex as Earth. Mars never had been, or at least we've never found any fossils you could see without a magnifying glass.

Maybe the Others' planet had a whole phylum of smaller and less complex crablike creatures, culminating in this beautiful example.

It was beautiful, in its way.

"It wants to congratulate you," Spy said, "on having made it halfway. The odds are good you will continue on to Wolf 25 and arrive intact.

"It currently has no interest in destroying you. It reminds you of the obvious, though: this ship you are in has an autonomous intelligence that thinks faster than you can and won't hesitate to destroy you, and us, whenever that might be necessary for the protection of our home planet.

"You are here on our sufferance. We are curious about you and wish to study you."

"Why should you let us live?" Namir said. "You've already tried to destroy us once—why should we expect you will let us survive now?"

"Is that a question you wish me to ask Other-prime?"

"Yes," Namir and Paul said simultaneously.

I wasn't sure about that, and started to say, "Wait." But it was too late when my lips formed the word.

What if it said, "You're right," and we all were simply doomed? It could flick us away like a speck.

Fly-in-Amber expressed my misgivings: "Perhaps that was not wise. We should preserve our options and not compel it to make a decision."

"Now or later," Namir said. "It will be easier to work with it if we know we have a chance of surviving."

It occurred to me that the room had no smell of its own. Standing next to Paul, I could smell the peanuts on his breath. But there was nothing from the ambient environment. Martian rooms had a characteristic smell, like damp earth; nothing like that here. It was like a VR background with the smell turned off.

Other-prime answered in less than a minute. Probably a prepared response; the question was no surprise. "That is fair. We do not think the same way as you, but let me try to put this in human terms.

"You averted worldwide catastrophe by moving our device to where it could not harm you. There were other things that you could have done, but that was sufficient. If you wish, you may think of that as a test that your species has passed. Contacting me here would be the second test.

"How many tests might be necessary for your assurance, I cannot say. The home planet does not yet know anything, of course; it will be more than a decade before my last communication from your solar system reaches them.

"I can say that other races have attained this degree of rapport with us, and many of them were allowed to go on their way. Some were not.

"None who resorted to aggression were allowed to survive. You must have deduced this already."

"That's all?" Paul said after a few seconds.

"Yes."

"I showed you around our facilities," Fly-in-Amber said. "Will you reciprocate?"

"Not now. I will discuss this with Other-prime. Right now it is resting."

"It takes a lot of energy for it to communicate with us?" I said.

"That is not something you need to know at this time. Be careful when you leave. There is no gravity on the other side of the air lock."

Paul snorted. "'Don't let the door hit you on the way out.'"

"It will not do that," Spy said. Fly-in-Amber nodded. Two species with but a single sense of humor.

5

TURNAROUND

I sat (or hovered) with Carmen, Paul, and Fly-in-Amber for an hour, with most of the others looking on, and we recorded all of our impressions from the half hour we were in the alien spacecraft. Of course we had all of the conversation in there recorded, too.

It was pretty straightforward. Even my Elza was a little optimistic. "It could have been a lot worse," she said. "Even an ultimatum is a kind of communication."

Paul, floating upside down, put on his slippers and did a gymnast's tuck to land feetfirst. "I guess we're safe as long as we remain interesting," he said. "For God's sake don't anybody be boring." He went back to the control room to start turnaround.

One of us did become less boring. Moonboy joined us and took off his earphones.

"Has the noise stopped?" Elza said.

He shook his head. "I've been sort of listening since the Spy one appeared. Are we in more danger now, or less?"

"Less, in a way," she said. "I mean, they were always out there. They didn't have to reveal themselves."

"Why not reveal yourself to a specimen you're studying?" I said.

He nodded slowly, looking at the space between me and Elza, not quite focusing, drifting slightly.

"Are you feeling better, Moonboy?" Carmen asked.

"I'm feeling more sane. For what that's worth." He looked directly at her, then away. "I'm sorry I've been . . ."

"You've been sick," Elza said. Did she not see how transparently he was trying to manipulate her and Carmen? I wanted to tell him to put his earphones back on and go sit someplace out of the way. There's a time and a place for everything, and for this it was months ago and billions of miles away.

Meryl gazed at her newly talkative mate in stunned silence. It was clearly time to leave them alone. "Good you're feeling better." I excused myself and geckoed over to the kitchen. From the pantry I got a tube of reconstituted gorgonzola paste and some crackers, tucked a squeeze bottle of wine under my arm, and stepped into the warmer human lounge. I asked it for quiet random Mozart and hovered near the bookcase, extracting the large book of Vermeer prints.

There's a kind of art to situating yourself in weightlessness. The cheese, crackers, wine, and book were all hovering within an arm's length. As long as I was careful in picking things up and replacing them, I wouldn't have to chase them down. Carmen and Paul did it automatically, with months of experience, but I still had to think things through and move with caution.

While I hovered contemplating this and Vermeer's faces, I gently collided with the bookcase. The cheese and wine and book all inched toward me. I was disoriented for a moment, then realized that Paul had begun turning the iceberg around. My satellite objects and I weren't attached to anything, but our frame of reference was moving fast enough to go through a half circle in, what, thirty hours? This seemed faster than that. I'd ask the notebook later.

The cheese wasn't bad, considering. The "wine" was pure plonk, but better than nothing.

So we were one-quarter of the way to the next wine shop or liquor store. That put the trip into a certain perspective. Or maybe halfway to dying, which put it into another.

"Penny for your thoughts." Carmen had drifted up behind me, stopped herself with a toe to the wall. "We've started moving," she said, her face at my level but sideways.

"Just noticed." I handed her the wine bottle, and she squeezed a dash of it into her mouth, from an impressive distance.

"Owe you one. What about our silent partner?"

I looked over toward the other lounge, and he wasn't there anymore. "I'll wait and see. One swallow does not make a spring."

I offered her the cheese and crackers, but she waved them away. "I gain weight in zero gee just thinking about food."

That made me smile. "Weight?"

"Mass, inertia, whatever. Turns into weight." She looked back to where Moonboy had been. "You're not . . . not too sympathetic."

"Aside from the fact that he broke my wife's nose? That he's acting like a sullen child?" She made a helpless shrug. I tried to choose my words carefully. "His madness, or behavior, is not his fault; I understand and agree with that. He was treated abominably as a child, and I wish his father could be punished for that."

"Stepfather."

"If this were a military operation, he would no longer be part of it. We can't leave him behind or send him back—"

"Or kill him," she said quietly.

"No. But we could lock him up. Take him out of the equation."

"That would destroy him, Namir."

"I believe it would. But his is one life versus billions."

She shook her head. "If I could wave a magic wand and make him disappear, I would. But imprisoning him would affect us as well as him."

"You don't think it affects us to have him moping around like some *demented* . . ." She flinched, and I lowered my voice. "He's already wearing us down. Three more years?"

We'd had this argument before, from various angles. Her response surprised me. "It could be a long three years. Let's see how he acts when we have gravity again. See whether this recovery lasts."

"I'm glad you can see it that way."

She smiled and touched my shoulder. "Don't want *two* crazy men aboard." She kicked off from the bookcase and floated toward the kitchen.

6

ADJUSTMENTS

I was jangled but way behind on sleep, despite the sweet nap with Paul, so I took a half pill and went zombie for about eight hours. When I woke up, Paul was snoring upside down in a corner, naked. Zero gee can do funny things to a penis, but I decided his need for sleep trumped my curiosity. And he might be low on energy. I closed the door quietly and drifted toward the gym, where Moonboy was tumbling.

It may have been weightlessness as much as the appearance of Spy that had shaken Moonboy out of his sullen isolation, into impressive gymnastics. He's Paul's age, but was bouncing around like a kid.

Well, not exactly like a kid. There was an element of grim determination in his constant motion, getting a maximum of exercise while honing his zero-gee gymnastic skills. I had seen him studying Paul, then trying to duplicate the ways he got from place to place. He was never as graceful but became almost as fast and accurate.

Not a particularly useful life skill, unless he planned a midlife career as a laborer in orbit. But I was hoping all the jumping around was a kind of transition back to a normal life. Or "normal," in quotation marks.

Meryl was watching him from a distance as he practiced floor-to-ceiling, ceiling-to-floor rolls. I floated over to join her.

"He's getting good," I said.

"That he is." She didn't look at me.

"Have you talked?"

"Said hello." She took a breath and let it out. "What should I say to him? I mean really."

"Welcome back?"

"I don't know that he is back. I'm not sure where he's been." There were beads of tears on her eyelashes. She rubbed her eyes and left wet spots on her cheeks.

"Maybe you want to wait until the gravity comes back."

"Maybe." Our thighs touched, and she put a hand on my knee. "You're so lucky with Paul."

"Yes. But Elza will get him, too, sooner or later." Why did I say that?

She smiled. "Probably. She'll be fucking Spy before we get to the planet."

"A milestone for *Homo sapiens*."

"What's hard, one thing that's hard, is not having a place for us to go back to. While he was shut away in his own box, I could handle that. But are we supposed to pretend that it's over now; he got it out of his system?"

"No, of course not. I think you have to get him to talk about it."

"Get him to talk about anything, first. Then I could work it around to 'say, are you still crazy?'"

"You can't . . . it's a pity you can't have Elza mediate."

She smiled, a tight line. "She's the only one with a degree. But it wouldn't be a good idea."

"He might hit her again."

"I might ask him to." She grinned. "Just as therapy. For both of us."

I was feeling hungry and instinctively checked my wrist. The tattoo had showed the wrong time since we passed the orbit of Jupiter, but habits die hard.

"It's eight," Meryl said. "Had dinner?"

We put on slippers and walked, like grown-ups, to the kitchen. Microwaved packets of empañadas and supposedly Mexican vegetables. I went back to the middle of the garden and picked a sweet red pepper and chopped it up, feeling like Namir. Master zero-gee chef, not losing a single piece of pepper or finger.

"I'd kill for a cup of coffee," she said. "Hot coffee." The drink bags and squeeze bottles all had DO NOT MICROWAVE on them. So far nobody had put that to the test. Better keep an eye on Moonboy.

"So all he's said is hello?"

"Some politenesses. He said he was better, and we could talk later. It *is* later, though, and he's . . ." She laughed a little snort. "He's graduated from village idiot to whirling dervish."

She opened the seam on her vegetables a bit and squirted in some hot sauce. She held it out to me, but I declined, knowing its potentiating effect. If I could hold off shitting until we had gravity, I would be a much happier space tourist, and I probably wasn't alone. You can get used to those things, but you also get *un*-used to them.

(I had a sudden flashback of the day we'd learned to go in, or into, a zero-gee toilet, with its helpful little eye-in-the-bowl. Not a part of myself I'd ever expected to observe in action.)

"Gravity might help him." Repeating myself.

"Or it might put him back in his cocoon." She was using chopsticks, and they worked better than my spoon, which tended to launch bits of food into my face or beyond. There would be some cleaning up when we restarted.

After we began eating, the object of our discussion headed our way, perhaps having heard the Pavlovian microwave bell. He bounced from the recycler wall to the bean trellis, off the side of the Martian quarters, and through both lounges, arriving at a reasonable speed surrounded by a nimbus of male sweat, not too unpleasant.

"Mexican!" He went to the fridge and started to rummage.

"In the pantry," Meryl said. "Under E, for empañadas."

"*Sí, sí; muchas gracias.*" He found the packet and put it in the microwave, and floated in front of it upside down. "I'm not interrupting?"

"Just getting a bite," she said, "but you can't eat with us unless your feet are in the right direction."

"*Comprendo.*" When the food was ready, he brought it over with a slow reverse roll. We were eating at the table, even though there was no reason to actually set the food down on it.

He sprayed hot sauce into the packet and speared the empañadas with a fork, more efficient than either of us. Without preamble, he said, "Have you thought about Spy not being what he claims to be?"

That was not a big stretch. "In what way?"

"Maybe he's not an alien at all, hmm? Maybe he's always been here, waiting for turnaround. To test us."

"Who?" Meryl said. "Who's testing us?"

"Earth. Testing our loyalty."

That sounded bizarre enough. "I don't get it. How could anybody be disloyal?"

"Be in the pay of the Others?" Meryl offered.

"Well, you know. Not pay."

"No, I don't know. What?"

He finished chewing, swallowed, and set his food packet floating just over the table. He folded his hands over his chest. "I'll spell it out."

"I'm all ears," she said.

"First, how possible is it that they could chase us eleven light-years, constantly accelerating, and wind up right here at the exact right time—with no evidence of having used any fuel? Without our detecting them?"

We did detect something, I thought; Paul had mentioned an anomaly in the proximity circuits. But I let it be.

"How much more likely is it that they've been here all along? That the supposed 'alien' was already installed before we got to the iceberg? Tell me it couldn't be done."

"Okay," she said. "It couldn't be done."

"Even if it could, why would they bother?"

"Like I say, to test our loyalty."

"That's . . ." She didn't say *crazy*. "That makes no sense."

"It seems awfully elaborate," I said. "They built this alien-looking spaceship, and Spy, and a convincing Other, and kept them hidden for years, to trot them out at turnaround, to see how we react?"

"You've got it. That's it exactly."

"Moonboy." Meryl's voice quavered.

"Where did they hide them for three years?" I persisted.

"Out in plain sight. No one's gone out to look till now."

"But Paul can look outside anytime he wants. Or anyone who goes into the control room."

"Oh, Carmen, don't be naive. It's not like looking out a window. Paul sees an electronic image that's supposed to match what's out there. They could fix it so he wouldn't see the ship until the time was right."

"And they'd do all that just to check our loyalty? Who is this 'they' anyhow?"

"Earth!" He was suddenly even more intense. "They never have trusted the four of us from Mars."

"They chose us for this," Meryl said.

"And sent along three spies!" He glared at Meryl, then at me. "Could it be more plain?"

I stared right back. "Something's pretty plain."

"Three spies. One seduces me and tries to play with my head, my memories of childhood. One attacks me physically, unprovoked. The third has worked himself into a position of authority, from which he can poison your minds against me. Is any of that not true?"

"Listen to me." I took his hand in both of mine. "Elza tries to seduce everybody; that's her nature. Dustin hit you because you fucked his wife, then broke her nose. Namir is a career diplomat and a natural leader, and I don't think he's ever tried to influence my opinion of you."

"Considering that you also fucked *his* wife," Meryl said, "and broke *her* nose, I'd say he's been a model of objectivity."

He jerked his hand away. "You've both bought it. Bought the whole thing. Or you're in on it, too." He kicked away from the table so hard he hit his head on the ceiling with a thump. He drifted back to the fridge and kicked off from it, to drift away over the crops.

After a bit, Meryl picked up his lunch. "Want some of this?"

"Too much hot sauce."

She nodded but reached into it with her chopsticks. "Guess you can get used to anything."

7

ABOUT TIME

Humans are always talking about heaven, even if they claim not to believe such a place exists. I have the feeling that it's not just metaphor or semantic shorthand, but rather an internal state that they are forever grasping for but never attain.

I have come close to heaven, for a Martian, these past few days—free of the ship's constant crushing acceleration. This morning it began again, and while I wait for the pool to fill up with water, I will distract myself with writing these notes.

Let go of the stylus and it falls to the floor. Depressing. But I will enjoy the water.

The next time we are weightless will be when we come to the planet of the Others. I wish there were some way we could just be there now. What good is science if it can't do a simple thing like that?

Of course, that day might be the last day of our lives. But if so, then let it be. Whatever death is, it won't include gravity. Or acceleration.

I could tell that the humans were disappointed, that I seemed to have learned so little about Spy and the Other-prime. Not everything I learned can be expressed in human terms, though. Can we trust them? Yes and no. Do they understand humans? Not as well as I do—but better than I do, in some large way.

Language is a hindrance. Having to write this down means leaving out much of what is important. There is nothing close to a one-to-one correspondence between my natural perceptions and this written thing, forced through the filter of human language. There are no human words, literally, for much of what Spy expressed while it was investigating *ad Astra*. Some basic assumptions about time and causality, for instance—I don't know whether they are "actual," from a human point of view, or just an alien (to them) way of expressing commonplace observations.

How could something as basic to reality as *time* be different for two different races? The dissimilarity must be just in the perception, or maybe expression, of reality. Time must *be*, independent of the creature experiencing it.

It was curious about details of your social and personal relationships. I complained that it should have been talking to Snowbird about such things; it said that it would, eventually, but it wanted to "triangulate," a human term it had to explain to me, between its observations and mine.

This is clear now: it knows more about humans, and human nature, than I do after living side by side with you for years. The Other-prime has been observing you remotely for tens of thousands of years, though like us has only been monitoring human communication since the invention of radio.

I didn't know this when I led Spy through the ship when it first contacted me, and if I were human I would feel embarrassed at the naive answers I gave to its calculated questions. I suppose it was satisfying its curiosity about Martians as well as humans.

Snowbird says the water is deep enough.

8

LOOSE CANNON

Am I the only creature aboard this boat that's glad to have gravity back? Maybe the Jew in me needs to suffer.

I suppose one reason I like it is the aging athlete's anxiety about keeping in shape, not slipping back. I can use the treadmill harness in zero gee and work up a sweat, pretending to run, but my legs tell me they haven't really worked. Which is probably unscientific nonsense.

Once we started decelerating, Moonboy settled into black depression again, no surprise, and again stopped communicating. Most of us are probably relieved. He was not a wellspring of light banter during zero gee. Unless you're amused by paranoia.

He hasn't taken any meals since we started decelerating, though I set a place for him. He may be raiding the pantry odd hours, but Elza thinks not. She's afraid for his mental state. Anorexia can precede suicide.

He sits plugged into his keyboard, and every now and then touches the silent keys. Carmen says she doesn't think he's actually composing;

she glanced at the screen while he was working, and the page number hasn't changed in two weeks.

I am not so much concerned for his well-being as I am afraid that he might fly off the handle and do some kind of irreversible damage. Paul has similar misgivings. When I broached the subject, he confided that the control room is kept locked now, and will not respond to Moonboy's thumbprint. I would be inclined to go further and keep him sequestered in his room. Drugs could keep him from becoming suicidally depressed, and might even give him a measure of happiness—which I think he will never attain otherwise.

If we put it to a vote—shall we lock Moonboy up?—it would be a tie, along gender lines. Elza would be against it because it would be admitting clinical defeat (and because she can't deny her role in precipitating his crisis); Carmen is by nature too humane, and Meryl, alone, loves him and wants to think he will grow, or snap, out of it. Dustin and Paul and I see him as a loose cannon that needs to be tied down, for everyone's protection. I think Fly-in-Amber would agree with us, though I'm not sure about Snowbird.

So I suppose nothing will be done until Moonboy himself forces the issue. I'm not quite Machiavellian enough to set him up, but if he strays too close to the edge I might give him a nudge.

When I was in school, the consensus among medical people seemed to be that all mental illness would eventually be treatable by drugs, that psychiatry would be reduced to a systematic analysis of symptoms—identify the syndrome and prescribe its nostrum. In a way, I'm glad that the species has turned out to be more complex than that. Though I would not mind having a pill that could take Moonboy's stepfather out of his life. And whatever else it is that's turned him into such a liability. (I remember at first thinking that he was the one of the four that I would like, since he was unpredictable and amusing.)

Although we are in actuality going slower each day, it feels emotionally like we're rolling downhill. Committed now, in a way we weren't before turnaround. Wolf 25 or bust.

What do we mean by "now," really? It's odd to be compelled to think in relativistic terms. At this moment, the creatures on Wolf 25 (the planet circling its dark companion, technically) are unaware of our existence. We're twelve light-years away, so in twelve years they will be able to observe the raging matter/antimatter beacon of our braking engine.

If things have gone according to plan—you could also say "if things are going to be going according to plan"—our prerecorded explanation of what we are attempting to do will have preceded the beacon by exactly one hundred days.

Their response to our pacifistic message might be to blow us out of their sky as soon as the beacon appears. If they did that, when would it happen? How long do we have before we know they haven't killed us?

If we take the worst possible case, that they attack the instant they see us, their response can't come faster than the speed of light. So, if my notebook is right, we will meet our doom no sooner than three years and some weeks.

Unless they figure out a way around the speed of light. Then we could be doomed any old time. As we could, supposedly, any time Other-prime decides the universe would be better off without us.

So it's eat, drink, and be merry, for tomorrow we die. I can do something about the eat and drink part. Tonight it will be meat loaf without meat, served with wine that's not wine, all washed down with water distilled from our various body wastes. Be merry.

9

RELATIVITY IS RELATIVE?

On Spy's fourth trip into *ad Astra*, it dropped a bombshell. For some reason it chose me to tell it to, not exactly the most technically sophisticated woman aboard.

Spy had said it wanted to talk to us one at a time, so we were sitting on the floor in "the onion field," the part of the garden where we cultivated scallions and garlic.

We'd been talking about human history and customs, and as always, I was trying to extract information about the Others in return. I asked it about the voyage out here with Other-prime. Did they have anything like a social relationship? What did they do to pass the time?

"Carmen, there was no actual 'time' to pass. We knew in what part of space-time you would be turning around, and we just went there. Went here, approximately."

"Wait. You just went here? Without traveling the twelve light-years in between?"

"Of course we traveled the distance. We got here. But there was no reason for the journey to have any duration, so it didn't."

"You were on Triton one instant, and here the next?"

"That's what it feels like, but of course *time* isn't shut down; there's no way around relativity. But time is not the same thing as duration. This universe is twelve years closer to its end. But we didn't have to experience the passage of the years."

"You mean . . . your spaceship is some kind of time machine as well?"

"No, not really." He seemed cross, exasperated. "This is like trying to explain to a bird how an elevator works. *This is the way we go to the top of a building. We don't have to flap our wings.*

"Your own spaceship is a time machine; you compressed twelve years into less than four. What we do is no more magical than that. We just have better control over it; we're more economical and efficient."

I was completely out of my depth here. "Let me get Paul. I don't understand—"

"Paul wouldn't understand better. Like you, like any other human, he misunderstands the nature of time. His mathematics just compounds the error, because it's already wrong before 'one plus one equals two.'

"It's time I had a talk with all of you, or perhaps all except Moonboy. Can you arrange that in about one hour?"

"Sure. It wouldn't take an hour."

"I want to spend an hour looking at your library, the paper printed books. This may be my last chance."

"What? What's going to happen?"

"I said 'may,' not 'will.' Shall we say 15:21 in the compromise lounge? I want to talk to the Martians, as well."

"Okay . . . what should I say you want to talk about? Our ignorant mathematics?"

"Partly. Partly your survival." He turned, and walked toward the lounge, presumably the "library" corner.

I sat for a minute, collecting my thoughts. Then I pinged Paul and told him what was going on. He said he'd make a general announcement and asked what I thought Spy was up to. "That's as close as they've come to an actual threat."

"I know." My voice cracked. I wiped cold sweat from my palms. "See you there."

I made a cup of tea and took it back to our room. I'd just begun a letter to my mother but couldn't think of anything to say. Dear Mom, my survival was just threatened by a robot from another planet. What have you done when that happens?

I wondered what Spy meant by "our" survival. The people on this ship or humanity in general? Dear Mom, you may have only twelve years to live. Unfortunately, I wrote this twelve years ago.

Jacket and scarf and knitted socks. Might as well be nice and toasty for the occasion. I went over at precisely 15:20 and sat on the couch next to Paul.

Everybody but Moonboy was there, including both Martians. Rare to see them together outside of their tub. I guess if you bathed with someone twenty hours a day, you might avoid him the rest of the time.

Spy came in exactly on time and stood in the door. He was wearing his space suit, holding the helmet. "Other-prime has decided that we should precede you to Wolf 25. We have learned enough about you to help the Others there deal with the problem. So we will leave this iceberg and speed on to our mutual destination. We should arrive about eight months before you."

I didn't know whether to feel relieved. We wouldn't have them looking over our shoulders, but then we wouldn't learn anything more about them, either.

"We are going to impose something upon you that may be unpleasant, but Other-prime feels it is necessary. Your group is unstable in various ways, and there is a real possibility that not all of you, or perhaps none of you, will survive the rest of your trip.

"To keep this from happening, we will cause you to travel the way we do. The time it takes you to go the twelve light-years will not be affected, but the duration of the trip will be negligible. I just explained this to Carmen."

"You did, but it made no sense."

"Do you remember about the elevator and the bird?"

I looked around at everybody and shook my head. "You said that describing it would be like telling a bird how an elevator works."

"Yes. How you can get to the top of a building without flapping wings. It would never understand. But that would not affect reality."

"Of course not."

"What would happen if you put the bird into the elevator and took it to the roof?"

"It wouldn't like it," Paul said.

"No," Spy said, still looking at me. "But it would get to the rooftop."

It turned to Paul. "It will happen tomorrow morning. I will call you a half hour ahead of time. People should be strapped in, including Moonboy."

"Will I be shutting the engine down?"

"Not for another twelve years. Objective time. That would be about three years and three months in your decelerating frame of reference. Seconds, in your new one. It will all be clear."

Clear to whom, I wondered. To Paul? "Spy, I don't understand. You and I were sitting down in the garden, talking about, I don't know, marriage . . ."

"Social connections. Friendships."

"And now suddenly we're going to be the birds in your elevator, flapping around and going crazy, I assume. What happened?"

"The Other-prime contacted me and said it was ready."

"What if *we* aren't ready?" Paul said, tense. "This is a pretty big deal."

"Just have them strapped in, Paul. You will find it an interesting ride."

"Wait," Namir said, and it was like a command. "Suppose we don't want to take your shortcut? Maybe we'd rather continue as planned and have those years to prepare for meeting your people."

"They aren't mine, and they aren't people," Spy said. "If all of you would prefer the old slow way, tell me now. I will ask the Other-prime."

Meryl spoke up first. "Not me. The sooner the better."

Dustin nodded slowly. "Me, too."

"Paul?" I said.

He tugged on his ear, a sign that he was conflicted. "Spy . . . we know our technology has worked this far. I can understand Namir's reluctance to try something new and untested. Just on your say-so."

"I won't argue with you." It was looking at Namir. "But technology is not involved at all. It's just that the way you experience time is connected to the way you think about time, and that is flawed."

"And you can change that?" I said. "The way we think about time?"

"No, no, no. The bird does not have to build the elevator to ride in it."

He moved his gaze to Paul. "What it is . . . Let me put this as simply as possible. We are—or you and the Other-prime are—here together in a definite place in space and time. In a simple Einsteinian way. Twelve years from now, you will again share a place in the space-time continuum. Share a point. So what connects those two points?"

I remembered that from school. "A geodesic," I said, simultaneously with Paul and Namir.

"Exactly," it said, and looked at the two Martians. "A geodesic in space-time is something like a line drawn between two points on a map."

Fly-in-Amber sketched a line with his finger. "The shortest natural distance."

Spy nodded. "True and not true. There's only one shortest *line* between the two points, but there are many geodesics. It gets complicated if you have gravity and acceleration."

"But there's no magic wand," Paul said. "You're talking about going from here to there, a really long distance, with no time elapsing. That's not possible, no matter how fast you go."

I think that was the only time I ever saw Spy laugh. "Tell that to a photon. Or tell it to me tomorrow. Which will be twelve years from now, after a trip of no duration."

"Unless we refuse your offer," Namir said.

"Like the bird refusing to enter the elevator? I'm afraid you're already in the net. As I said, I could ask the Other-prime to set you free, but at least two of you do want to take the shortcut. How about you, Carmen?"

"Wait. What if something goes wrong en route? The hydroponics spring a leak or the ship's guidance system lets a pebble through? We won't be able to deal with it."

"Nothing will happen—literally nothing, because with no duration there are no events. If there were two independent events, there would be a measurable time between them."

My head was spinning. "There's no hurry, is there? I want to hear Paul's take on it, and Namir's."

"Paul's argument is based on ignorance and Namir's is just fear of losing control. But no, there is no hurry. Just let me know when you've made up your mind."

"Whereupon you will do whatever you want," Namir said. Spy smiled and turned to go. "Won't you?"

"Just let me know," Spy repeated. Paul followed him, to operate the air lock, and nobody spoke until he came back.

"Spy's wrong," Namir said. "It's not about control. It's just about understanding what's going on."

"Which is apparently impossible for mere humans," I said.

"What do you think, Paul?" Meryl said.

He sat down heavily and picked up his drink and stared into it. "I think we'd better get ready for an elevator ride."

✳

Ultimately, even Namir agreed that going along with Spy and the Other-prime would be the wisest course, not only to maximize our own chances for survival, but also to establish a record of cooperation before we met the Others. And abandoned ourselves to their mercy.

We went through the habitat getting things ready for zero gee; Spy had warned us that we would be in orbit, not accelerating, when the "elevator ride" was over.

Paul led us through the seldom-used corridor that connected the lander to the rest of *ad Astra*, basically two air locks with a silver corridor in between. A handy metaphor for any number of things—birth, rebirth, death. Perhaps robotic excretion, the life-support system that had sustained us for years expelling us with relief.

We got all strapped in and sat in a stew of collective anxiety, thick enough to walk on. Paul fussed with his controls and came back to crouch next to me, holding hands, for a couple of minutes. He was able to smile, but then he's an official hero figure, and has to.

He returned to his place and strapped in, and in a few minutes said over the intercom, "We should be about a minute away." Then, "Let's count down the last ten seconds together. Ten, nine, eight . . ."

We never got to seven. The ship was suddenly flooded with sunlight, from the right—and on the left, my porthole was filled with a nearby planet, resembling Mars but more gray.

I felt gray.

There was no physical sensation as such. Only what you had to describe as deep loss, or longing, or sorrow. Some people were weeping. I bit my lips and kept tears away, and tried to sort out what was happening.

I unbuckled the harness and looked back down the aisle. Familiar faces contorted with all-consuming grief.

Except for two. Moonboy's expression was blank, catatonia.

So was Namir's.

10

RAMPAGE

Elza's face kept swimming out of darkness, into focus, then I would fade back to Tel Aviv, reliving the worst time of my life in every dreadful detail. It seemed like weeks of nightmares, but it was less than a day.

I was in my room, surrounded by images from the Louvre. Watteau's *Jupiter and Antiope*, Regnault's *The Three Graces*, Corot's *Woman with a Pearl*, and Gericault's terrible *The Raft of the Medusa*. That one persisted, all the dead and dying.

Elza had just given me a shot, and she was cutting away a tape that bound my left wrist. My right one was sore.

"You'll be all right now?"

"What's . . . the wrists?"

"You were hurting yourself. Pulling out hair."

My hand went to my head. Almost bald, sore in places.

"All that loose hair in zero gravity. It was a mess; I used the vacuum razor. You're a little bit tranquilized. I didn't think you wanted to sleep anymore, though."

"No. Please." I felt my head. "The razor with the vacuum attachment?"

"It looks nice. Evened up."

"Was everybody . . . no. Other people can't have been affected as strongly as I was."

"Nobody. Well, you can't tell about Moonboy. But nobody else passed out. It could be your age." She caressed my head. "Spy supposedly didn't know what caused it, but it wasn't just a human thing. Both the Martians were uncomfortable."

I took a squeeze from her water bottle. "Memories. I felt trapped inside memories."

"You have some sad ones. Worse than the rest of us."

"Not sadness." I had to be honest with her, of all people. "It was guilt. Murder."

She was quiet for a moment. "You mustn't feel guilt for being a soldier. We've gone over that pretty well."

"Not that. Long after that. I . . . never told you." I hesitated, aware that the drugs were loosening my tongue. Then it came out in a rush.

"It was right after Gehenna; right after I found my mother dead. I raced back into Tel Aviv, putting a list together in my mind.

"My Working Group Seven had been formed in response to a persistent rumor that a large-scale act of terrorism was imminent, one that couldn't be traced to a single political or geographical entity because it was not centralized at all. We had a couple of chemically induced confessions that indicated the group was large but divided into small independent cells.

"Anti-Semitism doesn't have borders, and in fact some of the people we were looking at were Jews themselves, with strong opposition to the current power structure. Current at that time, liberal.

"I privately suspected that two or even three of the people in my office were moles, making sure that we were distracted by false leads.

The one woman in whom I had confided this was the first person I saw die, a few minutes after we heard the bombs that were the second phase of the poisoning.

"As I raced down alleys and bumped across playgrounds and parks—none of the regular roads were passable—I was making a list of people I had to talk to *that day*.

"Because anyone who was not stunned that day was guilty. Ipso facto. And . . . there were so many dead bodies lying around that a few more would not raise any suspicions."

She was behind me, rubbing my shoulders. "How many, Namir?"

"Eleven that day. I tracked them down one by one, along with seven or eight I looked at and spared."

"You just shot them in cold blood?"

"No. Bullets would look suspicious. I got them alone and strangled them. Then they looked pretty much like all the other corpses."

"There were more than those eleven? Other days?"

"Six had flown out that morning, including three from my office. To London, Cairo, and New York. In London and Cairo I used my hands. The ones in New York I did shoot, with a pickup gun I'd had for years. Then tossed it in the Hudson."

"Like the .357 in the shoe box at home?"

"Yeah, behind the drywall. You are such a snoop."

"It's in the job description." Holding on to my shoulder, she floated around in front of me. "Cold-blooded murder isn't."

"My blood was not cold that day. Those days."

"Do you still think they were guilty?"

"I think now that two, at least, were not. But since we have never been able to pin down the organization responsible, I can't ever know for sure."

I closed my eyes. "I shouldn't have told you, burdened you with it. I've never told anyone before."

"Not even Dustin?"

"No. He knows I've done some wet work that was not formally sanctioned. He doesn't know how many, or the fact that I was on a rampage."

"I won't tell him. Or anyone. They killed your mother. And four million others. Including the seventeen they killed using you as an intermediary."

"That's about the way I rationalize it. But it is a rationalization. Deep down, I know I've committed the one sin that can't be reversed. Or forgiven."

"God would forgive you. If there were a God."

I smiled at her. "Yeah. That's a problem."

She held me to her softness for a warm moment, her cheek against mine. "There's another problem," she whispered. "We seem to be at the wrong planet."

"Wrong what?"

"Show you." She pushed away from me gently and floated down to the bed, as I rose to the ceiling. She pushed a couple of buttons on the wall there, and the paintings faded, replaced by a huge dun circle, a planet that resembled Mars. Clear atmosphere, a wisp of cloud here and there. No obvious craters, though; I wasn't sure what that meant scientifically. Weathering, I supposed.

"We aren't at Wolf 25?"

"We are, apparently—just not at the planet of the Others. Another one in the same system. Much closer in."

"Why?"

"Spy said we're going down tomorrow. Until then, we're free to speculate."

II

DEAD WORLD

Some of the humans, like Paul and Namir, were disappointed or apprehensive when they learned that we were not going down to the planet's surface in our own lander, carried twenty-four light-years for that purpose, but instead were to go down in Spy's "starfish" spaceship. I was relieved. Going to and from a planetary surface in a rocket is unpleasant and dangerous, even if it is "the devil we know," as Carmen put it. We had no idea how the starfish worked, but the Others had probably been using them for a long time.

We had to cross over to their ship holding on to a cable, as before, and Snowbird did not enjoy the experience any more than I had the first time. This wasn't in cool starlight, either. We had the huge disc of the ashen planet looming beneath us and the brilliant glare of Wolf 25 moving overhead.

Moonboy was not able to cross by himself. Paul and Namir carried him over like a deadweight.

Spy had told us that we couldn't pronounce the name of the planet in any Martian or human languages, but that it translated to "Earth" pretty accurately. We might call it "Home" to reduce confusion.

"Whose home?" Carmen asked.

"Allow me to be mysterious," Spy said, though the answer was obvious, if the details were not.

The air inside the ship was oppressively hot and humid, probably comfortable for humans. When we took off, though, the gravity was light, about normal for Mars.

It was not acceleration-induced "gravity," either. It didn't change direction or strength when the ship took off.

A circle opened in the floor of the craft, like a large window. We got an interesting view of the engine side of the iceberg/asteroid, which seemed to have diminished by about a third, in regular concentric grooves where the automatic ice-mining machines had gnawed their way around.

The landing was as smooth as the humans say their space elevator is, no lurching or vibration. As we approached the ground, though, the gravity increased to about that of Earth. Spy apologized to the two of us but said there was no way around it.

We approached the ground very fast. Snowbird and a few others reacted, but I assumed the Others hadn't gone to all this trouble just to smash us into a planet. It was too fast, though, to get a good idea of what surrounded the landing site. Just a hint of regular architectural structure, and we were on the ground, and the floor window irised shut.

"The abrupt landing was necessary because of the physics involved," Spy said. "We will observe from low altitude later."

It had warned us that we would have to "suit up" before we left the ship, so Snowbird and I had not removed our footgear, and it was only a matter of donning four gloves and letting the protective cloaks form around our bodies. So we were the first two out the air lock, the human crew following by a few minutes.

Carmen would later say that it was "beautiful in a horrible tragic way," which juxtaposes three contradictory ideas in what I realize is a standard human ironic frame. About beauty I have no opinion, and horribleness and tragedy are just dramatic observations about the fact that the universe runs downhill.

This is what I saw: on a plain that extended to the horizon in every direction, there were regularly spaced objects that we were told had once been space vehicles. The outer shells had mostly been eroded or corroded away; a lacy framework of some more durable metal remained, a gleaming cage for more corrosion within.

I wondered whether everybody else was thinking what I was thinking: The fleet that humans were building to protect the Earth might as well be paper airplanes.

"This was an invasion fleet," Spy said. "It was poised to attack the planet of the Others."

"How long ago?" Paul asked.

"It was about thirty thousand of your years ago. The planet was more hospitable to you then, more like Earth than Mars. A world with plentiful liquid water and oxygen; you could have survived here without protection."

"We couldn't now?" Carmen said.

"That's correct. All the plant life died. Things oxidized and dried out."

"And how did that happen?" Namir asked.

"Things got very hot for a short time. When it cooled down, it left mostly ash and carbon dioxide."

"The Others fried the planet," Namir said.

"I think 'baked' would be more accurate. They raised the surface temperature, as I said. I think for only a few minutes."

"Enough to kill everybody," Namir said.

"Every thing, I think. There is nothing alive now."

"This is what they wanted to do to Earth," Carmen said.

"Not quite as extreme. Though few humans would have survived."

"The ones on Mars would have," I said.

"The Others knew that," Spy said. "And eventually they might have wound up coming here."

"And met the same fate," Namir said.

"Who can say? Let's return to the ship."

"Wait," Paul said. "Can't we look around for a while?"

"First I want you to see something else. Rather, the Others want you to. They suggested that before you meet with them, you have the proper context."

"If they want to convince us that they can destroy us all, here and on Earth, it isn't necessary," Paul said. "We knew that before the plans for *ad Astra* were drawn up."

"I'm not sure exactly what they want to do. Our communications are necessarily slow and indirect. I do know what they directed me to show you. You may have time for exploration later."

We filed back through the air lock into the starfish, and it rose slowly and hovered. The engine made noise, a barely audible rushing sound. It had been silent, dropping from orbit.

We rose high enough for the horizon to show a slight curve. The humans all gasped at the sight, though it was not surprising. Thousands of the ruined ships stood in precise ranks. It was an impressive display of destruction, though I was more impressed by the idea that they could raise the temperature of an entire planet enough to cause this to happen.

Before we sped away, I counted 4,983 of the relics, though presumably there were more over the horizon.

"These creatures were of course intelligent," Spy said, "and they knew that aggression against the Others might result in their extinction. So they left a record nearby." As it spoke, we descended toward a glittering golden dome.

"One index of their mastery over the physical universe is this hemisphere of absolutely pure gold, more than a meter thick and almost five hundred meters in diameter. Its roundness is mathematically perfect to within a millionth of a meter."

"I wonder why they would bother to do that," Paul said.

"To show that they could," Namir said.

"That's probably true," Spy said. "It also gives the structure some resistance to certain weapons. What's inside is more interesting, though."

The ship floated down to rest next to the dome, the window closing as we approached the ground. The humans had been told not to remove anything but their helmets, so they put them back on, and we were through the air lock in minutes. They left Moonboy resting behind.

We picked our way over an expanse of weathered rubble. Whatever else had been here was made of less durable stuff than gold.

The dome did not have an air lock; just a door. There were unambiguous symbols incised in the metal, lines of dark dots that pointed toward a dark square. When we approached it, the square opened.

I was second to enter, after Spy, so I knew that it had been dark inside, and lights glowed on as we entered. The light was bright and warm, the same spectrum as Wolf 25.

It was a display, like a museum. There were no words, written or spoken. It was obviously designed for any audience capable of getting here and standing at the door.

In the center was a large globe of a planet that resembled Earth—more water than land, with polar caps and clouds.

"This is what the planet used to look like?" I said unnecessarily. Spy nodded and led us to the first display case.

This must have been the race that built the fleet of spaceships. The exhibits showed what they looked like, inside and out, and demonstrated various aspects of their lives.

They looked very much like us, with four legs, but only two arms, which at first made them uncomfortable to look at. They also had tails, which made them morphologically similar to the Other-prime, and presumably all the Others.

The first display was kinetic, disassembling a model of the creature, then reassembling it one organ group at a time, which was also uncomfortable to watch but no doubt educational. Likewise, the next display showed mating and budding, processes almost exactly like ours, but strange to watch.

Then it moved from the strictly biological into social, showing a thing like a playground, or the humans' creche on Mars. Lots of immature ones living together under the supervision of two adults.

This was followed by six similar play scenes, with different details, like the background scenery or the level of technology in the rooms. In two of them the creatures were colored reddish or blue, rather than black.

Carmen figured it out. "They're different cultures," she said. "They're showing the different ways their young are handled, around the planet." That interpretation was reinforced by the next seven displays, which showed the same different cultures, or races, having meals. Then there were seven showing what appeared to be social gatherings, or perhaps religious meetings. Then seven that appeared to be athletic competitions. This brought us back around to the door.

"Seven different cultures," I said, "but one species. They're Martians, aren't they? Despite having only two arms."

There was no doubt in my mind that these creatures were our ancestors. And the Others killed them all.

Spy did not respond directly. "Be ready," he said. "One of you is about to learn a lot."

I was suddenly overwhelmed, overloaded with information. My legs buckled, and I collapsed, knowing that this was what I was here for, and not liking it.

12

NO SURVIVORS

I first met Fly-in-Amber back when I was "The Mars Girl," before we knew, or thought we knew, what the different colors of Martians did. I just observed that they wore different colors and seemed to group together by color.

Five years later, we thought it was all sorted out, and his yellow family seemed to be the one that had the most obvious and easy-to-understand function. Absolute memory freaks, who never forgot anything they saw or heard.

Then, in 2079, we found out they had another job—in fact, the primary job of the entire manufactured Martian race: to serve as intermediaries between the Others and Earth's human race. The Others couldn't predict with any certainty when, if ever, the humans would develop spaceflight, so they created the Martians and put them on the planet that came closest to the Earth. When a member of the yellow family was taken to Earth orbit, he went into a trance and recited a complex message in a language he couldn't understand; a language only comprehensible to the Martians' leader, whom we called Red. He had been studying the language since childhood, knowing, like all his predecessors, that it might be extremely important but not knowing why.

The Others' message to Red was ambiguous and disturbing. They had the ability to destroy life on Earth but might not do it. Depending on various factors.

Red was supposed to keep this threat to himself, but wound up passing it on to me, and I told Paul. We were overheard, and everything unraveled.

So here we were again, with Fly-in-Amber speaking in a mysterious tongue, but instead of Red, we had Spy to decipher it for us.

Fly-in-Amber had babbled on for about ten minutes, Spy paying close attention. Then the Martian shook himself all over and groggily got to his feet.

"Did I do it again?" he said. "Talk in the leader language?"

Spy confirmed that he had. It was all recorded, and he could hear it back in the relative comfort of the starfish, whenever Fly-in-Amber felt strong enough to move. "Two minutes," he said, and did some kind of breathing ritual or exercise routine. Then we made our way across the uneven ground, Snowbird shuffling alongside Fly-in-Amber, supporting him.

The interior of the starfish had been reconfigured. There were enough comfortable couches for all of us and, amazingly, a deep pool of water for the Martians. They stripped with comical haste and slid into it. We helped one another out of our suits, too.

There was a table with pitchers of water and plates of what looked like cubes of cheese. Namir picked one up and sniffed it.

"It is food," Spy said. "Rather bland, I suppose."

Namir bit into it and shrugged. "Won't kill us. How long?"

"That partly depends on the message, and your reaction to it." It sat on the couch nearest to the Martians. "Sit down if you want."

I ate a couple of the cubes. They had the texture of tofu but less flavor. I wished for salt. And wine. Maybe a whole bottle of wine, and a big steak.

Spy waited until everyone was seated. "As you may have deduced, this planet is where the Others came from, and the people, or creatures, you saw in the displays are their ancestors, in a manner of speaking."

"The Others didn't evolve from them," I said. You didn't have to be a xenobiologist to see that.

"Not in any biological sense. About thirty thousand years ago there was a profound disagreement, what you might call a philosophical schism. It was about the fundamental nature of life, and the necessity for, or desirability of . . . its ending. Whether thinking creatures should die."

"They had a way around it?" Namir said. "Not just longevity, but immortality?"

Spy nodded, but said, "No. Not exactly.

"It's difficult to put this into terms that have universal meaning. That would mean the same thing, for instance, to humans and Martians."

"But we can agree about what life is," I said, "and that death is the cessation of life."

"I don't think so," Snowbird said. "That has always been a problem."

"Don't get all spiritual," Elza said. "As a doctor, I can assure you that dead people are much less responsive than living ones. They also start to smell."

Snowbird held her head with both large hands, a laughter expression. "But the individual was alive in the genetic material of its ancestors, and also will be alive in the ones that follow after the organism dies."

"Not me. I don't have any children and don't expect any."

"But it's not limited to that," Snowbird said. "Before the individual was born, it was alive in the teachings that would eventually form it. Everyone you meet changes you, at least a little, and so becomes a kind of parent. As you yourself become a parent to anybody's life you touch. It's the only way, for instance, that humans and Martians can be related. Many of us feel closely related to some of you. Fly-in-Amber and I are closer to you humans here than we are to many Martians." And I had been closer to Red, I realized, than I'd ever been to my own father.

"I'll grant that's true in a certain sense," Elza said, "but it's not as physically real as a genetic connection."

"You claim your brain is not physically changed by accepting new information? I think that it is."

"This is good," Spy said. "It's one aspect of the disagreement between the Others and you people. But only one aspect.

"Over the centuries, the ones who would become the Others physically isolated themselves, first on an island, then in an orbiting settlement, which grew by accretion. The separation became more complete as the ones on the planet encouraged belief systems that were inward-looking, antagonistic to space travel.

"The Others also pursued research into longevity, which most of the ones on the planet came to consider blasphemous."

"Let me guess," Namir said. "There was a war."

"Several, in fact. Or you could see it as one ongoing war with phases that were decades apart. Centuries.

"The Others moved farther and farther out, for their own protection. Meanwhile, their individual life spans increased, up to what seemed to be a natural limit. They couldn't push it far beyond about eight hundred years, with half of that life span in reduced circumstances . . . basically, alive and alert, but maintained by machines. You see where this would lead?"

It was asking the question of me. "They would . . . devalue what we would call 'normal' life? In favor of life partnered with machines? There's something like that going on on Earth, even now."

"Really? The Others might want to get in touch with them."

"That would be fun," Elza said. "Some of them are halfway aliens already."

Spy looked at her with an unreadable expression. "Most of this I knew from Other-prime. But Fly-in-Amber added a turning point, a missing link.

"The final separation between the two groups came about when the Others discovered free power, the ability to bleed energy from an adjacent universe."

"The same as our source of power," Fly-in-Amber said.

"That's right. You got it from them, though I take it that neither Martians nor humans really understand how it works."

"Only how to use it," Paul said.

Spy nodded. "This discovery allowed the Others to put a safe distance between themselves and the enemy, to move out to Wolf 25's dark companion.

"They thought that this would make their physical separation complete. At almost the same time, they took total control of their life processes and abandoned their carbon-based form in favor of the virtually immortal bodies they have now."

"So they downloaded their minds," Paul said, "into artificial creatures with low-temperature body chemistry." The Others had told us that their version of organic chemistry was cryogenic, based on silicon and liquid nitrogen.

"It wasn't as simple as transferring information. Each individual had to die, and hope to be literally reborn in its new body."

"They had no choice?" I said.

"Apparently they did. But the ones who didn't change died out long ago."

"Probably helped along by their successors," Namir said.

"That could be. I don't know.

"What I do know is that the ones left behind on *this* planet grew fearful. So they began building this huge invasion fleet."

"Why on the ground, I wonder," Paul said. "If they'd put them together in orbit, the ships wouldn't have to be streamlined. And the net energy saving would be huge."

Namir laughed. "They wouldn't have to worry about that. They couldn't have done this if they didn't also have the free-energy thing."

"And that was really what doomed them," Spy said. "Even without the huge fleet, their discovery of the power source put them essentially next door to the Others."

Unlike us, I hoped to think.

"Maybe if they'd remained in friendly contact, there might have been some accommodation. But there was no commerce or even communication between the races. So the Others hit them with one overwhelming blow."

"As they attempted to do with us," Paul said.

"No, not at all." Spy shook its head slowly back and forth. "You have to stop thinking that way. The Others posed a problem for you, and you successfully solved it. This Home planet was too close for them to risk that."

"If there were no survivors." Fly-in-Amber said, "where did we come from?"

"There's no direct line of succession. You were modeled after these Home creatures but independently manufactured. There are various anatomical differences."

"I'm glad we have the extra hands," Snowbird said, wiggling fingers.

"And you're organized differently," Spy said. "Each one of you is born into a specialty, born with its appropriate language and vocabulary. These Home ones were born dumb, like humans, and had to learn language."

"But they had freedom to do whatever they wanted?" I asked.

"That isn't known," Spy said. "The Others left Home before you humans parted company with the Neanderthals." There was a barely audible scraping sound. "We're back."

"Back where?" There hadn't been any sensation of movement.

"In orbit, on your iceberg." I moved to where I could see the ports by the air-lock lips. They showed our lander with the transfer cable.

Namir stepped over and looked out. "So. We go on now? To meet the Others?"

The expression on its face was close to embarrassment. "Actually, not all of you. We discussed this, Other-prime and I, with the Others. All of them."

"Just now?" Meryl said.

"No, we had time to talk with the Others for about a month before we left to meet you here. They discussed various possible courses of action.

"This one is best. Of course, they can't have a conversation with you in any sense. So they worked out every probable combination of relevant factors and allowed me, with Other-prime, to make the final evaluation and speak for them. Other-prime gave me a final piece of input a few minutes ago."

"Telepathy?" Dustin said.

It tapped its ear. "More like radio. We won't kill you all, which was an option much discussed, and still favored by a minority."

"But you will kill some of us," Namir said, almost a whisper.

"No, not killing, not like murder. We must take two of you, a human and a Martian, back to the planet of the Others."

"For how long?" I asked.

It paused, I think not for drama. "It would be forever. You would be joining the Others, physically."

"Frozen *solid*?" Elza said.

"You would have nitrogen, a liquid, in your veins."

"The Martian would have to be me," Fly-in-Amber said.

"That's right," Spy said. "The human . . ."

There was a lengthy silence. Paul half raised his hand. "I—"

"You're the pilot," Namir said, "and not expendable. I'm the oldest"—he looked at his spouses—"and, among the military people, I have the highest rank. The honor will be mine."

"No!" I said. "Namir, be practical."

"It can't be Moonboy," he said. "He's not competent. Did you want to volunteer?" He was smiling, rueful rather than mocking.

"With all respect," Dustin said, "this is not a job for an espionage specialist. You want a philosopher."

"A doctor," Elza said. "I know more about human beings than both of you combined."

"We should do it by lot," I said. "Excluding Paul and Moonboy." When I said it, my stomach dropped. I looked at Meryl, and she nodded, looking grim.

"This is fascinating," Spy said, "and I'm tempted to let you keep fighting it out. But what makes you think the choice is yours to make?"

"The fact that Moonboy has been unconscious since arriving here makes him the most attractive of you, to the Others."

"What?" Namir said. "He's mentally incompetent."

"Your mental competence is not an issue. The most intelligent of you, which would be Dustin, is still only human. What's more interesting about Moonboy is that he's immune to any consensus the rest of you might have arrived at since coming here. He is a tabula rasa with regard to the Others, and therefore will be easier to work with."

"What makes you think you can wake him up?" Elza said.

"He won't be awake when he joins the Others. He won't even be alive, technically."

"So the human race is going to be represented by a somewhat dead lunatic," Namir said.

Spy paused, as if deciding whether to make a joke of that. "His individual characteristics and experiences are not particularly important. His recent experiences are, though; the less he knows about the Others, the better."

"I think I understand," Fly-in-Amber said. "Like positive feedback in a circuit. Interfering with the signal because of its similarity."

That was the most science I'd ever heard from Fly-in-Amber. "You aren't upset about this, yourself? Being kidnapped and killed and stored in a deep freeze?"

He clasped his head in appreciation of humor, a gesture he rarely used. "Another way of saying it is that it's a chance at literal immortality, representing my race among the Others. How many foreign races would I be joining, Spy?"

"Two hundred forty-eight. Though more than half of them would be so different from you that communication would be unlikely."

"You see, Carmen? As Namir said, it's an honor."

"I was not being literal, Fly-in-Amber. My feelings are more like Carmen's."

"I think Moonboy's would be, too," Meryl said, her voice thick and shaking. "We should try to revive him."

"Shock him out of it?" Elza said. "And tell him 'Prepare to die'?"

"That is what it would be," Spy said. "If his comfort or happiness is at issue, I think your course is clear."

Meryl crossed her arms over her chest, holding herself. "My course is not clear. It's euthanasia to treat mental illness. For my husband of twenty-three years."

"One of you is headed there." Spy stepped toward her, and his voice lowered. "An objective observer would see that he is giving up the least. You can't say that's not true."

"You're not going to be able to care for him. He needs constant medical attention."

Not if he's going to die, I thought.

"In terms of duration," Spy said, "he will spend less time going there than you will spend returning to *ad Astra* from here. Minutes."

"It might be a kindness," Dustin said. It was clear that Meryl was struggling with it—it would be a kindness to her, as well, of course.

"Take me, too?" she said.

"No. We don't have two of any race. Not possible."

She sat down and stared at nothing.

"I wonder if it would be possible for me to kill you," Namir said quietly.

"It's an interesting thought," Spy said. "How would you propose to do it?"

"Physical force. I've done it to bigger and stronger creatures."

"It wouldn't be smart," Paul said.

"We're running out of smart." Only his lips moved, and his eyes. But the quality of his poise changed. He was gathering himself, ready.

"Don't," I said. "They can kill you with a thought."

"We could," Spy said, "but might not. Go ahead and try."

After the longest second in my life, Namir said, "It was a hypothetical question. You've answered it," and relaxed, turning his back. Spy looked at each of us in turn, perhaps recording our reactions.

"So. We just go back to Earth?" Paul said. "How will that work?"

"You set up the flight as you normally would. You will begin to accelerate, then, after a period of no duration, stop. That will be at the turnaround point. You spend thirty hours or so there, turning around again, then you complete the journey, also with no duration. Almost twenty-five years will pass, of course, while you travel the twenty-four light-years."

"Will we be seeing you again?" I asked.

"I don't know. Perhaps you'd better hope not."

13

END OF A WORLD

So we left Moonboy and Fly-in-Amber to the tender mercies of the Others and made our weightless way along the cable back to *ad Astra*. Before we got to the air lock, the starfish rose and sped away. Namir stood still and watched it depart. I wished I could have seen his face.

Once inside, I stayed close to Meryl, but she didn't want to talk about it. We all raided the pantry for human food, however uninspiring.

"I'll need a day or two to consolidate the data we have about the planet; make sure all of it's mapped," Paul said. "Though we could spend years mapping and measuring, and scientists on Earth would still want more. The first detailed observation of an Earth-like exoplanet."

"It probably won't be the first," Dustin noted. "They'll have had fifty years to explore nearer Earth."

Paul laughed. "I hope you're right. There ought to be robot probes all over the place."

I pulled gecko slippers out of the rack by the air lock and followed Snowbird into the Martian quarters. Not too cold for a short visit.

She was inspecting the racks of mushroomlike plants. "Hello, Carmen."

"Hello, Snowbird." I didn't know what to say. "You will be lonely?"

"Only for a short while, if what Spy said is true. I may be on Mars soon."

"That will be a comfort."

"Neither Fly-in-Amber nor I ever expected to see it again."

"I will miss him," I said. "Though there hasn't been time for it to sink in, him or Moonboy."

"Don't feel sorry for Fly-in-Amber. This is the best possible outcome for him. He was extremely happy when we left." She turned slightly, to face me. "We will never know about Moonboy, I suppose. He may never know what's happened to him but just die."

"Probably." Though what his chill reincarnation might be like, we could only guess. No worse than dying, we could hope.

I shivered. "You're cold," she said. "I'll see you later, in the compromise lounge. I'm sure there will be a meeting."

"There always is," I said.

I went back to our room and changed clothes. Funny to think that the old ones would sit there for a quarter century before being cleaned. My mother would just shake her head and say "typical."

Would she be alive still? She was born in 2035 (three years older than Namir) and we would be back in 2138. She has good heredity for long life, but did I really expect to see her at 103? Did I want to?

Well, who knows. With a half century of progress in cosmetic science, she might look my age. Younger. That would be too creepy.

Paul came in over the intercom and asked for a meeting in a half hour, in the compromise lounge. Snowbird would smile, if she had a human mouth.

I got there a bit early, which was fortunate. Namir had found a jar of Iranian caviar, which we cautiously slurped with two spoons, and some dexterity in midair retrieval.

Paul joined us in time to help scrape the bottom of the jar. He'd also had the foresight to put some alcohol in the freezer, half and half with water, so we could wash the fish eggs down with ersatz vodka.

Meryl came out, dressed in a pretty plaid shift with a peasant blouse, mincing along gecko style. "Is that booze?"

Namir tossed it slowly. "Cheap vodka. Pretty cold."

I'd never seen her drink anything stronger than wine, and not much of that. She squirted a big blast of the vodka into her mouth, and on her face, and immediately had a coughing fit. She started to laugh, then sneezed, with enough force to free her slippers and start her in a slow pinwheel. The skirt billowing around was quite pretty, in an abstract way, though the performance might have been more dignified with underwear. She wound up laughing and crying, not a bad combination under the circumstances.

After we were settled down, Paul said, "I just wanted to make sure everybody has everything sorted out. I'm planning to go into the lander tomorrow at noon. Push the button and see what happens."

"Do you want us up there, too?" Namir said.

Paul paused, probably remembering Namir's reaction last time. "Strapping in wouldn't be necessary. But maybe we should all be in the same place."

The diffuse feeling of grief, of loss. Elza took Namir's hand. "We should," she said.

"I would like that, too," Snowbird said. "Even with the heat."

"We don't know anything about the process," Dustin said. "The emotional impact may be less, now that we're expecting it. Or it may be of a different nature. Joy, perhaps."

"Or anger," Namir said. "Perhaps we should all be restrained. All but one, who has the key."

"Sometimes you scare me," I said, smiling, but meaning it.

"Then you should hold the key." He shook his head. "Actually, it was only Moonboy and I who had severe reactions last time. Maybe in lieu of a straitjacket, I should have Elza give me a sedative."

"And anyone else who wants one," she said. "Except the pilot. Snowbird, I wouldn't know what to give you."

"There is a food that prepares one for the unexpected. It worked well enough last time."

"Wish they made it for humans." Paul said. "I'm going to assume that with no time elapsed, or no *duration*, we don't have to do anything special with the plants. Just everybody complete the maintenance roster before noon tomorrow." He shrugged. "I know you would anyway. Guess I'm just at a loss for anything constructive to say or do." He passed around a handwritten note:

Don't say anything of a sensitive nature to anyone until we know we're at turnaround. The walls have ears etc.

"Can't play badminton in zero gee," I said.

"Namir," Meryl said, "could you get your balalaika and do me a song or two?"

"Yes," Dustin said, with no sarcasm in his voice: "I would like that, too."

"The end of the world is at hand," said Elza.

14

PREDICTIONS

I woke up slowly from the sedation Elza had given me. I remembered having had dreams. They hadn't been as intense or persistent as the first time, but they left behind the same malaise, guilt and self-loathing.

If the process had driven Moonboy back into that childhood closet, bound and gagged and strangling in the darkness, I could only hope for his sake that he was truly dead now. Memory is a prison from which there is no other escape.

But there are distractions. I found my slippers and went out into the hall, and rip-ripped my way along the tomato vines toward the exercise machines, which I could hear ticking along.

A tomato was floating free, so I ate it like an apple. Not quite ripe, a little sour. My stomach gave a warning growl, so I saved most of it to finish with some bread.

No need for parsimony anymore, of course. We probably had two hundred times the amount of food we could consume between here and Earth.

Carmen and Paul were working out on the walking and bicycling machines, their VR helmets in tandem. I could hear her soft voice, not quite understandable over the noise of the machines, as they chatted.

She was wearing a white skinsuit, translucent with sweat. Perhaps I was studying her too intently.

"Nice view," Dustin said in a whisper, behind me. "How are you doing?"

"Not quite awake yet." I held up the tomato. "Eating in my sleep."

"Dreams?"

"Not as bad this time. Seen Elza?"

"In the library with Meryl. Looked kind of deep. Get some chow?"

"Sure." We took the long way around to the kitchen, avoiding the library. I settled for cheese and crackers to go with my tomato; Dustin zapped a steak sandwich. I got a squeeze bag of cold tea out of the fridge; he opted for wine.

"Paul verified that we're where we're supposed to be and got the rotation started." He checked his watch. "It's 1340 now. We've got, um, twenty hours, twenty minutes, till we point 'er toward Earth and go. Away from Earth."

I set my watch. "I slept late."

"Last one up."

"Let me guess: Paul wants a meeting."

He smiled. "Good guess. He said 1500 if you were up."

Couple of hours to kill. Normally, this time of day, I'd ping Fly-in-Amber and see whether he wanted to practice some Japanese. Not that he ever needed to practice old vocabulary, since he never forgot.

My only Martian friend, dead now six years.

"New game?" Dustin said.

It took me a second to sort that out. "Sure. I believe you're white?"

"Pawn to K-4."

"God, you sneaky bastard."

*

We bundled up and met in the compromise lounge.

"So what are we going to find on Earth, fifty years in the future?" Paul said. "Worst case, Namir?"

I guess someone had to articulate it. "In the worst case, there will be nothing there except a messenger from the Others, which will detect and destroy us with no hesitation or explanation." No one looked surprised.

"The main assumption is that one or both, Moonboy and Fly-in-Amber, survives the transformation process with memory intact. That memory will include the construction of the fleet, and once that's revealed, Earth will go the way of the Others' Home. They can make the flight to Earth a little faster than we, with more acceleration, so the destruction may be a fait accompli by the time we arrive."

"Always the starry-eyed optimist," Paul said.

"You asked for the worst case. Anybody want to try for the best case?"

"It was all a bad dream," Dustin said. "We wake up in 2088."

And discover we've been fed a psychotropic drug," Elza said, "which gave us all the same dream. Or we could hope it is all real, but the Others will take a long long time to respond, like thousands of years."

"Or they may not care," Dustin said. "The fleet's just there to protect the Earth. It's not capable of interstellar travel, not by several orders of magnitude."

"Not yet," Elza said.

"It would take too much fuel," Paul said. "How many icebergs like this one are there? And the logistics and expense of launching just one were like a major world war."

That seemed kind of simplistic to me. The only reason we need the iceberg is that we haven't completely figured out how the "free" energy works. We use the free energy to initiate fusion, which makes the antimatter which makes . . . energy.

"None of you are considering a middle course," Snowbird said, "between being destroyed by the Others and being ignored. But I think this is the most likely: they long ago predicted this situation—creation of the fleet—as a possible outcome of their actions and yours. Their response to this outcome was decided before we even left the solar system. And the machinery to implement that response was also in place before we left."

I had to agree. "That does sound like them, Snowbird. What do you think that machinery might be?"

"Doomsday," Elza said. "Like last time, but bigger."

Snowbird made an odd gesture, two fingers on her small hands pointing out and counterrotating. "I think not. That would be inelegant."

"Too direct?" I said. "They do seem to prefer doing things in complicated ways." Like the roundabout way they first contacted us, a code within a code, even though they understood human languages and had no apparent reason to be obscure.

"It's stranger than that," she said. "Complicated becomes simple, and simple becomes complicated.

"This is something that Fly-in-Amber and I disagreed on. He felt we understood the Others better than humans do. I think we just misunderstand them in different ways."

"You're products of their intelligence."

She nodded, bobbing. "It's like a human play, or novel. *Oedipus Rex* or *King Lear*—the children can misunderstand their parents in ways that nobody else can."

"Good examples," Dustin said. "Happy endings."

15

CHANGES

Paul and I twice tried to make love during turnaround, but we were too nervous and distracted. Doom-ridden, perhaps.

A couple of hours before we filed into the shuttle, we all together made a long transmission to Earth, explaining everything as well as we could and hoping for the best for all of us. If Spy's description of the process was accurate, they would get the message less than a year before we arrived.

It might come just after the Others had blown humanity into elementary particles. There was no need to say anything about that.

We weren't sure exactly where we would arrive. When we went from turnaround to Wolf 25, we were deposited in orbit around the wrong planet, technically, since we'd planned to go to the moon of the gas giant where the Others lived.

So now, we presumably would go wherever in the solar system the Others wanted us to stop. If it was back where the iceberg started, past Mars orbit, we'd have a longish trip back to Earth.

Or maybe Mars, if Earth wasn't there anymore.

Paul followed the rest of us into the shuttle and helped Snowbird with her harness. Then he floated up the aisle and strapped himself in. He swiveled around partway and looked down at us.

"Does anybody pray?"

After a long silence, Namir whispered, *"Shalom."*

"Yeah." Paul's finger hovered over a red switch. "Good luck to all of us."

We were all ready for the transition's emotional blow, but most of us cried out, anyhow. And then a gasp of relief.

The blue ball of Earth was below us, the Pacific hemisphere. To my left, the Space Elevator, with the Hilton and Little Mars, Little Earth, and several new structures, including three smaller elevators.

I could faintly hear a burst of radio chatter from Paul's direction.

"One at a time!" he shouted. "This is Paul Collins, pilot of *ad Astra*. We are safe." He looked back at us with a grin. "I should have thought up something historic to say."

"One long trip for a man," Elza intoned; "one ambiguous stumble for mankind."

❖

We were quickly surrounded by identical small spaceships that were obviously warcraft. No streamlining, just a jumble of weaponry on top of a drive system, with a little house in between. Probably called a "life-support module," or something equally homey.

Earth was in a panic because we had inexorably approached, decelerating full blast, without answering any queries or attempting to communicate.

"The explanation is both simple and complicated," Paul said, echoing what Snowbird had said a couple of days, or six years, ago. "I think it's reasonable that I start with the highest possible authority."

The battalion commander identified herself and demanded an explanation. "Of course we know what you are. But we've been alongside you for weeks and have gotten no cooperation."

"I am not under your command," he pointed out. "This is not anybody's military expedition. Is there still a United Nations?"

"Not as such, captain. But all nations are united."

"Well, let me talk to whoever's in charge. With some science types listening in."

"This is completely against protocol. You—"

"I don't think you have a protocol covering how to deal with a half-century-old spaceship returning from a mission to save the planet from destruction. Or does it happen all the time?"

"We have been expecting you, sir, since your message arrived last month. But when the ship did not respond as it approached Earth, we had to expect the worst."

"The worst did not happen. Now I'm going to break contact and will talk only when I can talk to someone who outranks everyone who outranks you. Out for now." He cut off the battalion commander in midbluster and spun half around. "Drink?"

I tossed him the squeeze bag of ersatz Bordeaux. "Holding out for champagne, myself. In gravity."

He took a long drink, two swallows, and passed it to Namir, who had been sitting silent.

"Suit yourself," Namir said to me, his voice husky. "It might be a long wait."

I unstrapped and swam up front to visit with Paul and watch the monitor. The wait was less than a minute.

An elderly man with a seamed dark face and white full beard came into the monitor as it pinged. A voice said, "Mervyn Gold, president of the United Americas."

"Paul?" the old man said. "'Crash' Collins?"

Paul stabbed a finger at the camera button. "Professor Gold!"

He smiled broadly. "We've both come up in the world, Paul."

Paul laughed, and said to me, "He was my history prof at Boulder. You met him."

Subtract fifty years and the beard. He'd come to Little Earth with some government agency and talked with Paul for hours through the quarantine window.

"Amazing," Gold said. "You don't look a day older. You'll be hearing that a lot, I suppose."

And from really old people, I thought.

"The Others did some trick with time."

The old man nodded. "I saw your transmission from turnaround. Some people thought it was *all* a trick, you know. If they'd prevailed, you wouldn't have made it to Earth."

I hadn't thought of that possibility. Just as well.

"I'm glad you didn't listen to them."

"Oh, I listen to everyone; comes with the job. But I don't have to *obey* anyone." He shuffled some papers, an everyday gesture that we hadn't seen in some time. "First, let me tell you that you will come to Earth, not New Mars. The quarantine was lifted, oh, about twelve years ago."

"That'll be great."

How many years since I'd actually been on Earth? I was not quite nineteen when I stepped aboard the Space Elevator. Thirty-four when *ad Astra* left. Fifteen years plus about four, subjective, that we spent going to the Others' Home and back.

Exactly half my life—thirty-eight actual years. Whatever "actual" means.

The president and Paul were chatting about our return. "We could take you down on the Space Elevator, which would be more comfortable than using the lander. But the lander, an actual landing, would be really good for public morale."

"Propaganda." Paul said.

"I wouldn't deny it. Do you think it would be safe?"

"Well, it's never been used, so it's brand-new in a way. It's been sitting around for years, which isn't good for any machine. But that is what it was designed to do."

I wished telepathy would work. *Space Elevator Space Elevator Space Elevator*. I'd had my fill of atmospheric braking.

"If you're uncertain," the president said, "we have two qualified pilots waiting at the Hilton."

I guess you don't get to be president without a knack for psychology. "Oh, there's no question I can do it. No question at all. I've done seven Mars landings and a hundred on Earth, in flight training."

"And one on the Moon, I recall." The one that saved the Earth. Paul smiled. Score one for the prez.

"So when do you want me to bring her down? Where?"

"They still have the landing strip in the Mojave Desert. Um . . ." He looked to his right. "They say they have the old software to guide you in, but want to test it out with a duplicate. Anytime tomorrow would be fine. Daylight, California time?"

"No problem. We came on board with one suitcase apiece. Won't take us long to pack."

"Good, good. Will you accept our hospitality at the White House?" Another glance to the right. "Once the medics let you loose, that is."

"An honor, sir. Professor."

"See you tomorrow in California." He looked at his watch. "Would you mind debriefing with my science and policy advisors, say, an hour from now?"

"No problem, sir." He let out a big breath after the cube went dark. "Let's move this circus back downstairs. Get Snowbird out of the heat."

"Paul," Namir said, "be careful what you say to them."

"Sure. Careful."

"If they don't like what they hear . . . if they don't want the public to hear what we say . . . this is their last and best chance to silence us." He looked around at everybody. "There could be a tragic accident."

"That's pretty melodramatic," I said.

He nodded, smiling. "You know us spies. We come by it naturally."

※

The cabinet members who talked with us were urbane and friendly, not at all threatening. If they were planning to have us all murdered, they hid it pretty well. They mostly worked from a transcript of our long transmission from turnaround, asking us to clarify and broaden various things.

I actually knew one of them, Media Minister Davie Lewitt, now a dignified white-haired lady. She had been the brassy cube commentator who gave me the name "The Mars Girl." She remembered and apologized to me for that.

After the cabinet people thanked us and signed off, they were replaced by a couple who introduced themselves as Dor and Sam, both pretty old and probably female. Dor was muscular and outdoorsy and had about a half inch of trim white hair. Sam was feminine and had beautiful long hair dyed lavender.

"We wanted to help you prepare for returning to Earth," Dor said. "We were both in our early thirties when you left, so we were born about the same time as most of you."

"Twenty years after me," Namir said. "I suppose the first thing most of us would like to know is whether we have living family. I doubt that I do; my father would be over 140."

"Rare, but possible," Sam said. She unrolled what looked like a featureless sheet of metal, obviously a notebook, and ran her fingers over it. "No, I'm afraid he died a few years after you left." She stroked her neck, an odd gesture. "I think it would be best if we mailed this information to each of you privately?"

I nodded, curious but patient. I looked around and nobody objected.

"Which brings up a big thing," Dor said. "This is kind of like the Others, or like your poor friend Moonboy. We do have people, many thousands, whose legal status is ambiguous, because it is not clear whether they are dead or alive."

"You're getting ahead of yourself, Dor," Sam said. "This was just starting back when you were alive—shit! I mean before you left, sorry."

"No offense taken," Dustin said. "We really are like ghosts from the dead past."

"*Cranach versus the State of California, 2112,*" Dor said. "Cranach was a lawyer. He was dying, and needed more and more profound life-support equipment, which in his case—he was very wealthy—eventually included a complete computer backup for his brain and associated nervous system.

"Because of the way California defined 'brain death,' Cranach deliberately let his body die, but first essentially willed everything to himself—the computer image of his brain, which was technically indistinguishable from the original organic one."

"When his body died," Sam said, "nobody noticed for weeks, because the computer image had long been in complete charge of his complex business affairs and investments. And it was a person; it had a corporate identity independent of Cranach himself.

"What you're saying," Paul said, "is that this guy Cranach, dead as a doornail, could be legally immortal, at least in California, as long as his brain is not brain-dead. Even though it's a machine."

"Exactly," Dor said. "And people like him, like *it*, are only the most extreme examples of, well, they call themselves 'realists' in North America."

"As opposed to 'humanists,'" Sam said. "It had started when we, and you, were young, in the mid-twenty-first. People who spent most of their waking hours in virtual reality."

"Robonerds," Meryl said. "Some of them even worked there, jobs piped in from the outside world."

"We didn't have much of that on Mars," I said. "Except for school."

"There still isn't," Sam said. "Mars is a hotbed of humanists."

"But even on Earth," Dor said, "most people are somewhere in the middle, using VR sometimes at play or work or study. Depends on where you live, too—lots of realists in Japan and China; lots of humanists in Latin America and Africa."

Paul scratched his head. "They give the name 'realist' to people who escape normal life in VR?"

"Well, it is a higher reality," Dor said. "The VR you have on your ship is antique. It's a lot more . . . convincing now."

Sam smiled broadly. "Yeah. You can tell when you're unplugged because everything's boring."

"Guess who's the realist here." Dor patted her on the knee.

"Not really. I don't spend even half my time plugged."

"I'm curious about politics," Paul said. "Mervyn Gold is president of what? What is this United Americas?"

"Let me see." Sam moved her hands over the notebook. "It's most of your old United States, except Florida and Cuba, which now are part of Caribbea, and South Texas (which is its own country) and Hawaii, which is the capital of Pacifica. The United Americas otherwise runs from Alaska down through English Canada, the old U.S., most of Mexico, and most of Spanish-speaking Central and South America down to the tip of Argentina. Not Costa Rica; not Baja California."

"Thank God for that," Dor said. "Baja's such another world."

"The United Americas are really not that united." Sam continued. "It's an economic coalition, like Common Europe and Cercle Socialisme.

"The smallest country in the world is the one we're citizens of, Elevator."

"The smallest country but the longest," Dor said. "The Space Elevator Corporation declared sovereignty back when there was still a United Nations."

"And now?" Namir said. "Instead of the UN?"

"All nations are united," Sam said, echoing the commander. Her expression was a tight-lipped blandness.

United against the Others, I realized, through the fleet, which they couldn't mention in public. Everyone else was probably thinking the same thing.

"I wonder who will pay my UN pension," Namir muttered.

Sam overheard him. "You have all been well taken care of. The world is wealthy and grateful."

For what, I didn't want to say. We took a long trip to talk with the enemy, and they sent us back without even saying a word. But at least the Earth wasn't destroyed. Something to be grateful for.

So we were each given fifty million dollars to spend, in a world where Namir's New York City penthouse could be bought for ten million.

The only thing I really wanted was a hamburger.

My mother and father were dead, no surprise, though she had made it to 101, waiting for me, and left behind a brave, wistful note that made me cry.

My children were still on Mars as well, but were not speaking to each other, the girl a total humanist and the boy a total nerd realist. I spent over an hour in difficult conversation with both of them, difficult for the twelve-minute delay as well as emotional factors. I signed off promising to visit both of them as soon as I could get to Mars. Though with the realist I'd have to communicate electronically, no matter what planet I was on. He'd sold his organic body for parts.

That gave me a flash of irrational anger, but it passed. He actually only had half of one cell of mine.

My brother, Card, was also a realist, but he had not yet become bodiless. He lived on Earth now, in Los Angeles, and promised he'd put on his formal body (he had three) and come see me when we landed. I waited while he made a few calls, then called back and said he'd gotten all the vouchers and permissions to make the trip.

I wondered how free the Land of the Free was nowadays. But I guessed I could always go back to Mars.

16

MOONBOY SPEAKS

I put the two balalaikas in the padded boxes I'd made for them, and set the Vermeer book, and the Shakespeare and Amachai and cummings poems, into the titanium suitcase. I'd done a laundry in the middle of the night, unable to sleep, and padded the books with clean folded clothes I would never want to wear again.

What were the actual odds that we were about to become dead heroes rather than inconvenient witnesses? Small but finite, as a mathematician would say. We really knew nothing about current politics. When President Gold had been Professor Gold, Paul said he taught medieval history—Machiavelli and the Medici. The Borgias. He could make them seem like current events, Paul said. Maybe current events, then and now, were not so far removed from those good old days.

We hadn't been publicly interviewed yet. That was disturbing. But they had let us talk to relatives. So they couldn't be claiming that we didn't make it back.

(Assuming people did talk to their relatives, and not to VR constructions. Cesare Borgia would have liked that little tool.)

Well, they couldn't really claim the *ad Astra* hadn't returned. What's left of our iceberg is still bigger than the Hilton, and you can see that in the sky all over the Pacific, brighter than the Pole Star.

Of course, when we got off the lander, we'd go straight into biological isolation. No telling what kind of bug we might be bringing back from the Others. Though a bug that thrived in liquid nitrogen might find human body temperature a little too warm. And there had been nothing alive on the planet Home to infect us. If Spy had told the truth.

We might have been infected with something accidentally or on purpose. Spy was an artificial organism designed to interface with humans. But then so were the Martians, and they had carried the pathogen for the juvenile pulmonary cysts that gave the colonists such trouble.

I should have asked about Israel—find out whether the country I worked for all my life still exists. My notebook didn't pull any new information about anything, which was not necessarily suspicious. Fifty-year-old hardware and software. But it would be nice to find out some information about the world that hadn't been handed to us by handlers.

I should be grateful for a few more hours of blissful ignorance and obscurity. The idea of celebrity is not compatible with my choice of career, and thus with my personality. Not that I will ever be a spy again, whatever Israel is or is not today.

Maybe I'll take up music seriously. Practice several hours a day. That would keep Dustin out of the house.

My notebook pinged in my personal tone. Funny, the only people with that number were close enough to come knock.

I thumbed it, though—and an image of Moonboy appeared!

"I trust I have your attention."

"Moonboy?"

"Yes and no." There was a short transmission delay. "This signal is coming from the Moon, but Moonboy is not there. This is a sentient cartoon. The signal is an encrypted and filtered tightbeam that only you, Namir, can receive and decode."

"Okay. What's up?"

"This cartoon has detected that you are not on Earth."

"That's right. We're in orbit, near—"

"You must land on Earth as soon as possible. Leave space by midnight, Greenwich time, April 23. Tell no one that I talked to you."

"Not even other—"

"Midnight, April 23."

The screen went blank. I asked it for the source, and it said LUNA NEAR CLAVIUS.

Midnight on the 23 would be 7 P.M. April 22 in New York; 4 P.M. in the Mojave Desert. We'd be landing that morning, if things went according to plan.

Best make sure things do go according to plan. There was no way to interpret that message other than ominously.

I could use a drink, maybe something stronger than wine. I opened the door, pulled myself up the trellis, and floated over the arbor toward the warehouse.

Paul and Carmen were already there. They turned and looked at me without saying anything.

"Let me guess," I said. "You just got a message that you're not supposed to share."

"From a person who died twenty-five years ago." Paul tossed me a squeeze bottle with brown liquid. "I think we better do as he says."

Scotch flavor, pretty harsh. "Yeah." I coughed. "Almost a day to spare."

"If the lander works, and Earth doesn't screw things up."

I wished there were some way to pour a drink over ice in zero gee. "What if they say they can't be ready by that time?"

"Hm. I've landed these things on gravel beds on Mars and the lunar regolith, with no ground support. If it's working, I can find someplace flat. But then we'd have to explain why we left early."

"Life-support emergency," Carmen said, "or a medical emergency. Hard to fake."

Snowbird drifted over. "A Martian medical emergency. There is probably no one on Earth who could say I wasn't sick." Upside down, she bumped against the couch and righted herself. "In fact, I probably will be, with all the gravity and oxygen. California heat."

At turnaround we'd suggested leaving her on Little Mars, and it was the closest we'd ever seen her come to losing her temper. She was going to be the first Martian to swim in an ocean, or die trying!

Dustin and Elza joined us, then Meryl.

"Maybe we should tell people," Meryl said. "They're obviously planning something dramatically destructive, in space."

Carmen disagreed vigorously. "The last time we broke a promise of secrecy, the Others almost destroyed the planet in retribution. And we've seen what they did to their own Home, because it posed a threat."

"Putting two and two together," I said, "or one and one . . . I assume they've learned about the fleet, and are going to destroy it. Within Moonboy's time frame."

"We could save some of them," Meryl said.

Paul pointed out that we had no idea of how many they were. "If they actually did build the fleet up to the planned thousand strong, and they're in a defensive array between the Earth and the Moon . . ."

"If they all suddenly withdraw," I said, "the Others will know we betrayed them. And strike immediately." If the fleet are warriors, I did not say, warriors have to be ready to die.

Paul shook his head slowly. "The logistical problem. Landing a thousand ships would be impossible if you had a week. Twenty hours?"

"And I wonder how many people are in orbit who aren't in fleet ships," Carmen said. "Little Mars, Little Earth, the Hilton, all those new structures. Surely hundreds, at least."

"Maybe they wouldn't be in danger," Meryl said. "Not being part of the fleet."

"He didn't say anything about that," Paul said. "'Leave space' and 'go to Earth'—that doesn't leave much room for interpretation. And even if you warned the people here, in Little Mars and so forth, what could they do? You might be able to cram a hundred into all the Space Elevators, but in twenty hours they wouldn't be anywhere close to Earth. They'd still be in space."

I wondered where Spy would draw the line between space and not-space. Never in all my unpleasant space experiences had I so fervently wanted to have my feet on solid ground.

17

CLOCK-WATCHING

We put on our gecko slippers and lined up at the air lock. I turned around for one last look at the cave in the ice that had been our home for almost four years.

It would have been twelve without the Others' gift of time compression. Hard to imagine eight more years' confinement here. We'd all be crazy as Moonboy.

I knew every square centimeter of it better than anyplace I'd ever lived before, but there was no sadness in parting. I hoped never to see it again.

A robot crew was coming aboard to maintain it as a historical artifact. It would become a museum, eventually. But first it could see service for other starflights, to places nearer than Wolf 25, before its fuel ran out.

If it survived whatever was happening tomorrow.

"Here you go, girl." Elza smoothed a patch on the back of my hand. I immediately felt calmer. She gave them to everybody else but Paul and Namir. And Snowbird had her own resources.

We secured our luggage in the back, the stern I suppose, and came forward to strap in. I was right behind Paul, and so had the dubious privilege of being able to watch us land, if my eyes weren't squeezed shut.

Namir was in the copilot chair, though he'd only flown light planes. More than the rest of us, though I didn't know how much good that experience would be. Paul cheerfully told me it was like landing a slightly streamlined brick.

He had been talking quietly over the radio, I assumed to the control people on Earth. He switched on the intercom, and said, "Brace yourselves. We're gonna kiss this rock good-bye."

The steering jets made a low rumble and a sharp hiss. In the forward viewscreen, the rock-strewn ice fell away. Then a gentle acceleration pressed me back into the soft seat.

I half dozed for an hour or so as we approached the atmosphere. Then the ship started to vibrate and shake. Then buck alarmingly, with serious-sounding creaks and pops.

It had been more than six years since I last went through atmospheric braking, landing on Mars. Earth is more violent, but shorter. And when the red glow faded away, I was looking down at blue ocean!

We banked around and started falling toward the desert, which was not at all like home. Too much vegetation and high mountains everywhere. Maybe hills, technically. Mountains to me.

I knew the approach angle was going to be steep. But it felt way too much like a vertical drop. I shut my eyes so hard I saw stars, and didn't open them until the huge thump and then jittery scraping as Paul executed a somewhat controlled slide toward some buildings on the horizon.

We stopped in a cloud of dust, which rapidly blew away. A vehicle almost large enough to be called a building lurched toward us on tracks.

Paul swiveled half around. "There's a decontamination unit coming toward us. They say it will only take an hour or so, with, quote, 'a minimum of discomfort.' At least for the humans. Snowbird, they have to take you to another place."

"I'm on Earth, Paul. It's all another place."

We all unstrapped and did some stretches. I felt a little weak and had twinges in both knees, but the gravity wasn't too oppressive. It was good to be on solid ground.

My wrist tattoo was working again, and it had set itself to the right time zone, 10:32 A.M. So we had about five and a half hours before something impressive happened.

"Should we say anything?" Meryl said. "About—"

"No," Paul said. "What would we say? What would be safe?"

Namir nodded. "Some of the pilots and crew might be able to take measures to protect themselves. From whatever it is. But then our Others get pissed and fry the Earth. Or bake it, as Spy suggested. Or cover it with sulfuric acid. Too big a gamble."

The decontamination team hooked their vehicle onto the lander with a crinkled metal tube like the one we used in space. They came on the viewscreen and asked for me and the other women first.

I went through two air locks into a white room, where three female techs were waiting, clad in heavy protective suits. Meryl and Elza went into other rooms.

They asked me to disrobe and filed all my clothing into individually sealed plastic bags. Then they *vacuumed* me, an experience that could be full of erotic possibilities, depending on who was doing it to you.

Then the internal part: they gave me a glass of what they called a "super-nano-laxative," and warned me not to drink it until I was seated on a toilet. It had a pleasant lime flavor and a less pleasant explosive effect. A businesslike enema completed the charming sequence. All of this internal fortune duly cataloged and sealed away.

I was ready for a shower then, and got the most thorough one of my life, three strong women scrubbing away where angels fear to tread.

When I was finally able to dress, they had some fancy and futuristic clothes waiting. Formfitting but also form-altering, with smart fabrics that applied light pressure here and there. Very flattering. Hundreds of tiny bright strings hung from the fabric, revealing and concealing. Men who never gave me a second look back then . . . well, they'd be too old to *do* anything but look now.

They gave me a bowl of vanilla ice cream and put me in a darkened room with a couch and suggested I might want to rest for an hour or so. I got a light turned on but couldn't find anything to read. No flatscreen or cube obvious; no controls. But I said "space news" out loud and a cube appeared, no projection frame, with a picture of us landing, with this big crawler in the foreground.

Then it showed the president, beaming over his beard, congratulating us and saying that he would be out in California for the landing and the debriefing.

The station noted that live coverage would begin at 7:00, Eastern time. They might have a bigger story than they bargained for.

⁂

I did doze for a little while. It was after three when a big blond tech (whose name I didn't know but who knew parts of me better than Paul did) woke me with the news that I'd been pronounced clean and was wanted at the Green Room.

She stopped me just before I got to the door. "Oh, you wouldn't know this. The president's from Kentucky, and he'll offer you his favorite bourbon. It's a hundred proof; you shouldn't refuse, but you might not want too much of it." Doubly true since all I'd had to eat on this planet was a bowl of ice cream. But hell . . . I could knock back a couple of shots and ask Professor Gold if he'd like to play some Texas Hold-'em.

A lot of famous people do seem larger than life when you meet them. I knew Gold had been a large man from his visit with Paul a half century ago. But now he was an old shaggy bear, moving with slow sureness, glowing with charisma, a man obviously happy with the world he'd helped to make. The world that had twenty-five minutes to go.

His hand was warm and dry, a measured fraction of large strength. "Paul tells me you don't care for spirits," he said. "So instead of a tot of Blanton's, perhaps you'd like a glass of champagne? A big glass?"

An assistant came up with the biggest champagne flute I'd ever seen, and I took my place at a round table. There was only one other empty place—no space for Martians?—and Namir came in, accepted a glass of bourbon, and sat down. He spooned an ice cube from his water glass and put it in the whiskey.

"Should I address you as 'General'?" the president said.

"We have no rank together, sir. Only Namir."

He nodded and leaned back in a chair that was slightly larger than ours, slightly higher. "I exercised my right as Grand Inquisitor of this honky-tonk, and asked the scientists whether I might talk with you first. They acted like a bunch of folks who *do* have a sense of rank, Namir, not to mention tenure. So they agreed."

I think our response was appropriate, for six people who were trying to behave like a proper audience while actually wanting to scream. Twenty minutes.

"What I'd like to do, before we go on camera and do all the cube-ops, is ask each of you, if it's possible, to sum up your feelings in a line or two." He smiled a wry curve. "Something I can misquote in an off-the-cuff speech. Namir, you're oldest."

"May we speak without fear of *being* exactly quoted? Let alone misquoted. No one will like what I have to say, and I would as soon have it not be 'on the record.'"

"There are no recording instruments in this room. You have my word on that."

Namir took a sip and his brow furrowed. "It's not complicated. Never trust them, not one iota; not on the most trivial thing. But never forget that we have to live with them." He set the glass down and smiled. "The lone Israeli speaks. I got that with my mother's matzo."

Meryl was next. "I think we should find a way to disconnect from them. Even if it means giving up free energy; even if it means giving up space. They're too powerful and too unpredictable."

Gold chuckled. "Watch out, Meryl. That attitude could get you elected in thirty states. Elza?"

"I think we're in a position like a child with a toxic, abusive parent . . . who is also extremely rich. So our problem is twofold: Can we live without the wealth? And can we leave it somehow without the parent exacting revenge."

"I disagree with you both," Dustin said.

"Your turn."

"We can't maneuver our way out of this, Mr. President. They're too powerful, and they've said outright that they're testing us. We have to pass the tests. Channel all our energy right there. Maybe they'll give us an A and leave us alone."

"And if we fail the tests?"

The air shimmered and a holo of Snowbird appeared between the two men. "I have been listening; sorry for not appearing.

"If you fail the tests, then you cease to be. If you were Martians, then that would be of little consequence."

"So if we were Martians," Gold said, "the problem would disappear. Along with us."

Her image pressed her head. "You are a humorist, Mr. Gold."

"That's a nonanswer," Dustin said.

"Wait," the president said, and touched his ear. "Oh my God."

I looked at my wrist. It was 1600:22.

"Pipe it in here." He shook his head angrily. "Jesus Christ! They don't need clearance to see the fucking *moon*!"

An auditorium-sized cube suddenly filled a third of the room. It was London, the Thames at midnight, ancient Ferris wheel lighting up the darkness, the full moon's reflection a rippling ladder up the river.

The moon suddenly changed. It became much brighter, and the markings on its face faded to an even glow. It grew to double its size, triple . . . and then it faded into a fuzzy round cloud, glowing dimmer as it grew.

"Was that the Others?" the president said, unnecessarily. "They actually blew up the moon?"

It could be a lot worse, I thought. Still could be.

"They sent a message. Just before it happened." The weird night landscape faded, to be replaced by a huge face, all too familiar: Spy.

"You lied to us," it said. "You sent emissaries, machine and man, to say that you were pacifistic. In return for our aggressiveness, you said, you sent a plea for peace and understanding.

"All the while, for fifty years, you were building a gigantic fleet of warships. Hidden from us."

"Not for invasion!" the president cried, as if the image could hear. "Just to protect Earth!"

"Those thousand ships are about to be destroyed," it said. "We are going to disassemble your Moon and use it for ammunition, from gravel-sized pebbles up to huge boulders.

"High-speed projectiles will target every warship, and all their support. Other rocks will destroy every smallest satellite structure. Your Space Elevators will have fallen by dawn.

"All of the space between the Earth and what is now the Moon's orbit will be filled with gravel. Any spaceship you attempt to launch will be a sieve before it leaves cislunar space.

"We do this with a spirit of charity and generosity. You must realize that we could easily drop mountains on the Earth, and humans would go the way of the dinosaurs. But we do want to give you another chance and see what you do with it. This is your last test.

"I am speaking to you from the crater Clavius. In a few moments, it will cease to exist."

The face disappeared. The Thames was dark except for the blinking lights of emergency hovercraft. A brilliant meteor lanced through the sky, then two more, then another pair.

We sat in stunned silence.

I would never see Mars again?

18

RESPONSES

The president had delayed flying for a day. All civilian flights were canceled as well, until the danger from the constant meteor shower could be assessed.

At night they fell like brilliant snowflakes, with occasional bright crawling fireballs. But those were mostly grains of sand, or dust. Every now and then one would be large enough to make it to the ground, but most of those were man-made, the debris of thousands of satellites. (*Ad Astra* no doubt was pelted, but the iceberg had so much mass it stayed put in orbit.)

There were no casualties on Earth that first day, though seven thousand did die in space, mostly in the first few minutes. Worldwide havoc had been expected, especially from the Space Elevators, unraveling and lashing the surface of the Earth like huge bullwhips fifty thousand miles long—but they had been engineered with the possibility of disaster in mind, and the cables disintegrated into harmless dust as they fell. Two passenger carriers flamed into the land and sea, their human cargos ash.

So there was no danger to atmospheric craft, but the peril to spacecraft was real. Every cubic centimeter of space between Earth and where the Moon had been held a piece of gravel.

Eventually, in tens or hundreds or thousands of centuries, all that cloud of rock and gravel would settle into rings, like Saturn's, very pretty and easy for a spaceship to avoid.

That was longer than Paul wanted to wait. And with us on Air Force One was a man who thought he wouldn't have to: U.S. Air Force General Gil Ballard, the president's defense secretary.

Namir coldly excused himself and went back to the press side of the huge plane. He later told me he had read the man's remarks about our mission and left before he could make a scene in what looked like a ceremonial meeting.

I wished he had stayed. It might not have changed things, but it would have been good theater.

The meeting room in the middle of Air Force One was extravagantly massive, a projection of masculine power—heavy woods, fragrant leather, deep carpeting. General Ballard, a large, intense man, maybe sixty, blazing eyes and shaved bullet head, fit the room perfectly. He sat next to the president, facing us across the table.

"It's just a different scale from what you did with *ad Astra*," the general argued. We had used powerful lasers to vaporize things the size of grains of sand, and maneuvered out of the way of larger obstacles. "Same principle. Just going slower and dealing with more interference."

I had mixed feelings. I wanted Paul to be happy, and he'd always said he could never be happy without space. But having space hardly seemed possible anymore. Or smart.

And after mourning for Mars, I started to feel a kind of long-repressed relief. I've spent half my life off Earth and was ready to try living here again. Imagine, oxygen and water and food that you didn't have to recycle endlessly through yourself. Just let the planet do the recycling for you.

We might even try raising actual children, maybe even making them the old-fashioned way. I was ready to start ovulating and being difficult once a month.

Paul's reaction pulled me out of my reverie. "No way it's the *same*, General. Much more seat-of-the-pants." They both smiled, jet jocks imagining a situation that would have a normal person quivering in fear.

"And you'd want a lot of physical shielding," Ballard said, "which wouldn't help the handling characteristics."

"It would be a job and a half," Paul said.

The general laced his fingers together on the table and looked Paul straight in the eye. "You'd need the best pilot in the world."

The president hadn't said a word. He looked at Paul expectantly.

Paul's expression was blank, but I could read him pretty well. He was choosing his words.

"If the best pilot in the world . . . were also a lunatic, he might say yes. But no."

"We could do any number of practice runs in VR," the general said. "You wouldn't have to go up physically until you were sure."

"We wouldn't want to lose you," the president said.

"But what else might we lose?" Paul shook his head. "It's not the danger, the physical danger. It's what the Others might do in reaction."

"They said it was a test," the general said. "This is the most direct response." What?

"I respectfully disagree, sir. They're not testing our ability to solve a tactical problem."

"It was a warning!" I blurted out. "I thought that was pretty clear."

The general looked at me. He tried without much success to keep condescension out of his voice: "He did use the word 'test,' Dr. Dula." My father's name. "It might be a warning at the same time, but against aggression, not simple space travel."

Dustin came to my defense. "General, that's like saying someone who puts a high fence around his property doesn't care whether people break in."

Elza added, "Nothing we learned at Wolf 25 indicated that they have anything like subtlety or patience. That was a punishment and a warning."

The president stood up. "Thank you all. This is all very valuable. We'll talk more later . . . I have to go get camera-ready for the landing. General?"

The general also stood and thanked us, and followed the president into the inner sanctum.

"I sure feel valuable," Elza said. "How do you feel?"

"Doomed," Dustin said. Paul nodded agreement.

19

INFALL

All sorts of festivities had been planned for us hearty heroes, but their execution was somewhat muted by doom and gloom and the regular infall of meteors. A lot of expensive liquor was spilled at a congressional reception when a boulder the size of a grand piano redesigned a shopping mall in nearby Maryland, a town improbably named Rockville.

By the time the sound reached us, it had attenuated to where it was only as loud as a land mine going off in the next room. I dove under a table and found two younger people had beaten me there; so much for combat reflexes. A good place to be when the chandeliers are raining glass, though, and the girl I had landed on was agreeably soft.

Of course all the congratulatory speeches had to be rewritten with appropriate funereality, and I came to dread the cognitive dissonance that united them all in clumsiness. As if good things and bad things couldn't happen at the same time. I suppose that if one is to stay sane as a soldier, that incongruent congruence always has to be there in some part of your mind: no matter how terrible are the things you have seen and done, in another country there is room for happiness and friendship, beauty and love.

American soldiers in their war against Vietnam had a bleak catchphrase for when the worst happened: "Don't mean nothin'." I heard about that when I was a teenaged soldier generations later, and knew exactly what it meant. Nihilism is the soldier's ultimate armor.

Soldiering and the memory of Gehenna might have made it easier for me to accept the huge cataclysm of the Others' revenge, easier not to surrender to anger. Don't mean nothin'.

There was a huge amount of anger in the air, understandably, and frustration—a profoundly powerful enemy who is absolutely beyond reach, now and for any foreseeable future.

If the moon's destruction had only deprived us of spaceflight, most people wouldn't see it as a tragedy. For many people, space is just an expensive playground for scientists and the military. Keep that money and brainpower at home.

But modern civilization needs satellites. Most communication and entertainment goes by optical fiber, with the satellites a backup except in primitive countries. But GPS devices are in the heart of every car and plane. Big-city traffic, dependent on computer control, froze solid. Nonessential flights were grounded. Computers died.

Of course, we get some fallout from that. Even among the sophisticated government and news workers who are our daily companions, there is the undercurrent of blame, and it's not undeserved, if someone does have to be blamed. We were the only people who could have done something, out where the Others live, and all we did was deliver the message, the lie, that precipitated this disaster.

The plain fact that we could have been the aggressors—the kamikaze option—is generally known and widely discussed. From one very understandable point of view, we should not have considered any other course of action.

It's interesting that among our crew, only the Martians thought the kamikaze option was a reasonable idea, but to them death is an unremarkable event. It's not as if we humans couldn't do the math and apply the logic. What if we had all been Shinto or fundamentalist Moslem or Christian extremists? We might have just as universally discarded the idea of negotiation and blasted full speed ahead toward the enemy planet.

That might be alien to our culture, but it's not alien to human nature. In the twentieth and twenty-first centuries, suicide attacks have often been used as a practical response to an imbalance in technology. There were uneven results—the handful of suicide pilots in America's 9/11 had a stupendous kill ratio, but the five thousand Japanese kamikazes only sank thirty-six ships. In both cases, though, it was an understandable military sacrifice, when the enemy's technological base made them unbeatable by conventional methods.

And their situations were nothing compared to the technological imbalance between the human race and the Others. Should we feel guilty for not making the ultimate sacrifice? Do we deserve to be condemned as cowards? Having been there at the time, I'd say no. Those with the benefit of hindsight may feel differently.

There have been threats on our lives. Our public appearances have two cadres of bodyguards, I found out—armed soldiers in uniform surrounding us, but twice as many in civilian clothes circulating in the audience.

So I was relieved when the celebrations were abruptly canceled after two days. We didn't get to return on Air Force One—would never see the president again—but took a spartan private jet back to California, where we'd left Snowbird.

She was more or less hidden for the time being. As unpopular as the six of us were with the angry populace, we could only imagine how they would react to a Martian. Alien tools of the Others.

She would eventually be moved to a sanctuary in Siberia, where conditions were more Mars-like. A foundation had been set up there when the quarantine was lifted, and now it would support as well as study the five or six Martians marooned on Earth. She would find edible Martian food growing there, and the company of her own kind. But she wanted to say good-bye to us first, and take a swim in the ocean.

She would get that, but not much more.

20

THE LONGEST JOURNEY
BEGINS WITH A SINGLE STEP

The last person I talked to on Mars was my good old mentor Oz, who said he was not quite 64 years old now—that's in Martian years, though, which comes to about 120 on Earth. He didn't look a day over a hundred, though. Wizened and wrinkled, but still with a wry intelligent look and a sparkle in his eye.

We were in the space communications room at Armstrong Space Force Base, where we'd landed from orbit. It was a bright clean room that felt old, too many coats of paint. Paul exchanged pleasantries with Oz, then left after the twelve-minute lag.

"How bad is it, Oz? Can the colony survive without support from Earth?"

Following the same protocol as we'd used fifty years before, Oz's image froze on the screen when he hit the SEND button. I'd brought the *Washington Post* to read while the signals crawled back and forth.

The only story about us was on page 14, and it wasn't complimentary.

Oz came back smiling. "We're completely self-sufficient, Carmen; have been for more than twenty years. Human population's over three thousand, a third of them native-born. Our living and farming space is probably twenty times what it was when you left.

"The big debate over here is whether we should stay out of space; whether the Others meant to include us in their warning. There were no Martian ships in the fleet.

"A majority says stay home. We have a Space Elevator, and they didn't blow it down, but its only real function was as a terminal for the shuttle to and from Earth.

"Personally, I think that Earth can go to hell in its own way. My big regret is that now you and Paul can't come home. You could have a natural baby or two now; they solved the lung problem and recycled the mother machine for scrap.

"And you're still young enough. In-fucking-credible.

"Look, I have to go off to the old folks' dinner. Can you call me again tomorrow"—he looked offscreen—"about 1600 your time?"

"Definitely at 1600," I said. "If you have new art, bring some to show me."

It wasn't going to happen.

I heard Paul in the next room, one loud bad word. Went through the door and found him staring at a flatscreen monitor.

"Shit," he said. "Would you look at this?" It was a picture of a human newsie, male and handsome, standing in front of a familiar background: here. The Armstrong Space Force Base.

"We on the news?"

"Not really." He picked up the chaser and ran it back a minute or two. There was an obviously simulated picture of a lander like ours taking off tail first, the way they did spaceflight before the Elevator.

"Back to old-fashioned ways," the newsie said. "Our Space Force is sending a rocket up into the cloud of rocks that now surrounds our planet, to get some close-up observations—and perhaps work its way through. Blasting the little obstacles with the powerful laser in its nose and maneuvering around the larger ones.

"The Space Force confirms that they don't believe this first try will actually penetrate the millions of miles of debris, but it will be a good start. And no human pilot will be endangered; all the flight controlled by virtual-reality interfacing. Rumor has it that the VR pilot will be none other than Paul 'Crash' Collins, back on Earth, still young through the magic of general relativity!"

"Rumor has its head up its ass," Paul said. "Nobody's said anything to me."

"Could you do it? Would you?"

"No, and no way in hell. I never trained for that kind of launch off Earth; only from Mars, where it's a lot simpler. But more, it's . . . it's thumbing our nose at the Others. Are they insane?"

Maybe they all are, I thought; the culture. "Maybe they have a more complicated plan. Looks like propaganda, doesn't it?"

He calmed down a little. "Might be. Shoot up an empty rocket that they know won't make it through. Just to show that they're doing something. But I won't be in on it with them."

"Best we all stay out of it. Those crowds in Washington." I leaned on a bookshelf and looked out the window at the dry brown hills. "Let's get away, Paul. Just disappear from the public eye for a while. We have plenty of money."

He nodded. "The government would be glad to see us go. Let's talk it over with everybody tonight. Have to arrange for Snowbird to get to that Siberia place safely."

"The swim first. That's important to her."

✳

We talked it over with the Space Force press people and came up with a workable plan. There was a beach to the north of the base, closed to the public, which would afford a good view of the launch. Snowbird could get her swim, and they would get publicity shots of us watching the launch. (With Paul "regrettably" declining the VR pilot's seat; too tired and out of practice.) Then we could fade out of sight, to the relief of all concerned.

Namir and Elza and Dustin wanted to go back to New York City. That didn't sound smart to me. Elza thought with hair dye and a dab of makeup, they'd regain their former anonymity, lost in the crowd. I thought Namir was too handsome for that, and Dustin too weird-looking, his hair in spikes, but I kept it to myself.

We had a last family dinner in the mess hall, Namir ecstatic at having actual steaks to grill. Real potatoes and fresh asparagus. Bottles of good California wine.

I didn't sleep well, and neither did Paul. Crazy days.

Just at dawn, we all piled into Space Force vans and went down a bumpy gravel road to the beach. There was a hard beauty in the dusty, persistent plants.

The ocean a churning, eternal miracle. Snowbird was awestruck, speechless.

Paul and I rolled up our pant legs and waded into the frigid surf with her, hand in hand. "So warm," she said. "Feel the sand."

We gave her a line to hold, just a clothesline that was in the back of the van, and she floated out past the breakers for a few minutes, Space Force divers watching her anxiously. They didn't want to preside over the first Martian to die of drowning. She might have enjoyed the irony.

The time for the launch approached. The camera crew had written our names in the sand (Dustin remarked on the metaphor) where we were supposed to stand. We took our positions and watched the countdown on the off-camera monitor.

I had visions of the old twentieth-century launches, a roaring fury of fire and smoke. But they didn't have free power. In our case it was kind of a hiss and a screech, a nuclear-powered steam engine. A blue-white star sizzling in its tail.

It rose slowly. At first it looked like *ad Astra*, but of course it was one of the replicas they'd used for practice. The nose had some white stuff painted thickly on, which Paul called an "ablative layer." I had to think of the thick white sunscreen he'd been wearing the day we met, in the Galápagos, the day before I left Earth.

It was pretty high when the light in its tail went out. The monitor went out, too, then flickered back on as the sound of the rocket stopped abruptly.

Spy again, on the monitor. Shaking its head.

"You don't listen, do you?"

The rocket started falling in a tailspin, then rolled to point down.

"I suppose we have to be less subtle."

The rocket nosed into the ocean, about a mile away, raising a high white spume.

"All this energy that you call 'free' comes to you at the expense of a donor world in a nearby universe. You are donors now." The monitor went dead.

A tracking airplane pancaked into the sea and sank. Another plummeted to crash on the beach to the south.

The camera crew were shouting into their phones.

A jet plane that had been high screamed to its death in the sea.

I went to my purse. The phone was blank. Namir slid into the driver's seat of a van and punched the START button over and over.

Snowbird stopped toweling herself and looked in some direction. "So this is the end," she said, as if you had asked her for the time.

"Idiots," Paul said.

"Surprise," Dustin said.

Even Elza was almost speechless. "So what do we do now?"

For some reason they looked at me. I was standing at the gate. I tried it and it swung open, its electronic lock dead.

"I think we better start walking."